PRAISE FOR *BEING MARY RO*

"A charming book."
THE SUDBURY STAR

"*Being Mary Ro* is a story about independence. . . .
Find out for yourself. Read *Being Mary Ro*."
THE BEACON

"I cannot imagine anyone not enjoying *Being Mary Ro*. The material is suitable for mature young readers, contains small sketches (by Melissa Ashley Cromarty), and is an excellent first novel for Ms. Linehan Young."
THE MIRAMICHI READER

"We're only halfway through the novel when Mary pulls the trigger. The strength and courage required to shoot the pistol is the same strength and courage that afterwards allows Mary to travel to . . . and pursue an independent career as a . . . I'm not telling. Find out for yourself. Read *Being Mary Ro*. It's first-rate entertainment."
THE TELEGRAM

The Promise

~ A NOVEL ~

Ida Linehan Young

FLANKER PRESS LIMITED
ST. JOHN'S

Library and Archives Canada Cataloguing in Publication

Title: The promise : a novel / Ida Linehan Young.
Names: Linehan Young, Ida, 1964- author.
Identifiers: Canadiana (print) 20190045981 | Canadiana (ebook) 2019004599X | ISBN 9781771177191
  (softcover) | ISBN 9781771177207 (EPUB) | ISBN 9781771177214 (Kindle) | ISBN 9781771177221 (PDF)
Classification: LCC PS8623.I54 P76 2019 | DDC C813/.6—dc23

© 2019 by Ida Linehan Young

PRINTED IN CANADA

MIX
Paper from
responsible sources
FSC
www.fsc.org   FSC® C016245

This paper has been certified to meet the environmental and social standards of the Forest Stewardship Council® (FSC®) and comes from responsibly managed forests, and verified recycled sources.

Cover Design by Graham Blair

FLANKER PRESS LTD.
PO BOX 2522, STATION C
ST. JOHN'S, NL
CANADA

TELEPHONE: (709) 739-4477   FAX: (709) 739-4420   TOLL-FREE: 1-866-739-4420

WWW.FLANKERPRESS.COM

9 8 7 6 5 4 3 2 1

Canada   Canada Council   Conseil des Arts   Newfoundland
          for the Arts   du Canada   Labrador

We acknowledge the financial support of the Government of Canada through the Canada Book Fund (CBF) and the Government of Newfoundland and Labrador, Department of Tourism, Culture, Industry and Innovation for our publishing activities. We acknowledge the support of the Canada Council for the Arts, which last year invested $157 million to bring the arts to Canadians throughout the country. *Nous remercions le Conseil des arts du Canada de son soutien. L'an dernier, le Conseil a investi 157 millions de dollars pour mettre de l'art dans la vie des Canadiennes et des Canadiens de tout le pays.*

Dedication

To my dearest loves, Samuel and Parker. I am truly blessed that you were born. I hope to share the most wondrous adventures as you grow (and maybe even be the cause of some of them). To your mommy, Shawna, and my other two daughters, Sharon and Stacey, you are my life's blood. To Thomas, a simple thank you for holding my heart through the ups and downs. You make the good times so much better and the hard times more tolerable.

To my book collaborators—Mona, Bea, Brenda, and Georgette—thanks for being there for me.

To the "real" Erith, thanks for coming into my life. Thank you to Carla and Brian for introducing us and to the Clarkes for "loaning you out." Your name is the inspiration behind this story, and you will forever be woven into the fabric of our family.

To my family and the people of North Harbour, your influence is always there.

For Marg: From my earliest childhood recollections through to adulthood, Marg was part of my life as my aunt, my godmother, my friend, and my mom's best friend. I, as well as countless others, were drawn to her as if she were the moon and we the tides. There was always a happy, welcoming cloud surrounding her and in her home. My physical as well as my spiritual self were nourished by her. She was a teacher, social worker, psychologist, psychiatrist, counsellor, lawyer, doctor, nurse, tax auditor, an advocate, community leader, priest (and bishop), banker, and she was even a mortician. Marg was all those things, with a summer school teaching education when she was in her late teens, paired with an altruistic thirst for life. Most important to her, she was a wife, mother, and foster mother. Family, including her extended offspring, always felt valued, no matter our age or circumstance.

She was a woman ahead of her time, and she had the stuff that kept our small community of North Harbour alive and vibrant. Marg was happiest in what others might call noise and chaos. She shared, welcomed, argued, told stories, laughed, cried. She was real. She shaped me. Rest easy, Margaret Power née Collins (November 26, 1933 – July 28, 2018). Immense is our loss, for so deep was our love. I'm so fortunate and so grateful to have been in your life's dash. You will never be forgotten.

Prologue

In the late nineteenth century, Newfoundland was a large island colony off the east coast of Canada in the northwest Atlantic Ocean. Though a Dominion of the British Empire (along with Canada, New Zealand, the Irish Free State, and Australia), the island was self-governed and had its own monetary system until it joined Canada as a province in 1949.

In 1890, the population of the capital of St. John's was approximately 25,000, but the island's huge coastline (6,000 miles) had another 50,000 people attracted by the rich cod fishery and scattered throughout thousands of tiny communities in coves and bays. Typical settlements had between forty and 200 residents—by design the numbers could sustain a reasonable inshore trap fishery.

Labrador, the continental part of the Newfoundland Dominion, had another 4,900 miles of coastline which, with the exception of the small numbers of indigenous peoples, was migratorily settled in the summers and early fall for the Labrador fishery.

Newfoundland merchants gave material credit to local

fishermen consisting of goods and gear necessary for their prosecution of the fishery and winter survival. At the end of the fishing season, the merchants' ships collected dried salt cod as repayment. The cod was sent to Britain, Canada, and the United States through Boston and New York.

After the first snow, most of the settlements were isolated into clusters and cut off from civilization until the spring thaw. Residents lived on salt cod, summer-grown vegetables stored in root cellars, farm animals, merchant provisions (tea, flour, molasses, beans, etc.), as well as wild game, seals, and seabirds that were hunted during the winter and early spring.

Poverty in Newfoundland was more prominent and constant than in any other colony under British rule in North America. Most impacted and vulnerable were the children. Childhood mortality rate was high. Fatherless or parentless children were housed in orphanages paid for by the Commission, by the churches, or through fundraising efforts in their support. The Church of England Widows and Orphans Aid Society of St. John's, the Methodist Orphanage of St. John's, Immaculate Conception Orphanage, Belvedere Orphanage, and the Villa Nova Orphanage all relieved, in part, the societal dilemma of the plight of the orphan in the Dominion of Newfoundland.

1

So tightly knitted joy and woe . . .
Newfoundland, early March, 1894

"Sorry for your loss."

Mrs. Power, her prominent hump shrouded by a yellowed knitted shawl, took Erith Lock's hands between her warm, twisted fingers and patted them in a gesture of comfort and condolence. Erith cast her eyes downward. Her thick, untethered mane of wiry strawberry blonde hair hid her face from the old woman. Her preoccupation could have been mistaken as some kind of sorrow. There was none. She chose to remain distant. Besides, she couldn't settle her mind on anything except the persistent, maddening words that were like a briny liquid on her open sore.

Without making eye contact, Erith mumbled and nodded her way through several of the remaining mourners who were making their way out from the sitting room. She glanced farther into the room, at the plain pine box where her stepmother's powdered face was propped on a pillow. A face that should have been relaxed in death still wore the grimace of an unhappy woman, a scowl etched forever in her granite features. For her entire fifty-seven years of life, Erith was sure, the woman didn't smile. At least she hadn't in Erith's twenty-four years on earth.

She was sure that the neighbours, who were often the target of the woman's bitter tongue, were being kind for her sake. Her stepmother obviously hadn't revealed what Erith had done, or things might have been different. For as long as she could remember, she'd listened to her complain to anyone and everyone about the burden Ben left her when he died. That burden was Erith—the only child of Ben Lock. She vaguely remembered, or perhaps dreamed, his smile and his singing to her when he put her to bed at night. It was the last time that Erith was happy. At least, she believed herself to have been happy.

Tomorrow, when her stepmother was buried, she'd be free from the obligation she had inherited only out of respect for her father. For his sake, she'd endure the appropriate mourning period of the Roman Catholic community.

Now Erith had a big, empty, two-storey house, a dry goods store, and the mail service at her disposal. That realization should have thrilled her. It was exactly what she needed. But for now, she was supposed to be . . . what? Grieving? Did anyone really expect that? Besides, she couldn't spare time to be excited about the new opportunity. She had another pressing need to deal with. Damn Kathleen Lock.

"Erith, do you hear me?" Startled, she almost thought her stepmother was admonishing her. "You should go to bed, dear. Get some sleep."

"I'm all right, Mrs. Patsy. I'll stay up."

"There's no need, child. Me and Jim will stay and sit with Kathleen, God rest her. It's our Christian duty."

Erith nodded her acceptance, knowing the tradition

well—the dead weren't left alone before they were buried. Although, foolishly, she was half afraid to go to sleep in case she woke up to it all being a dream. She even wondered if the consecrated ground would spew Kathleen Lock's earthly remains back out after closing over her.

Mrs. Patsy and her sister had stayed up the night her stepmother died, after which they'd washed her, dressed her, and laid her out for the wake. Neither one had mentioned the horrible oaths and curses that her stepmother had shouted at Erith in the last moments of life. Both had patted Kathleen Lock's hands and tried to soothe the ravings before the woman had succumbed to the cancer.

The doctor from Colinet had been through four weeks prior and left a bottle of laudanum to help ease her pain, but her stepmother had long since used that up. There was a doctor closer in the summer, in John's Pond, but he was in Boston during the winter with his wife, who was studying medicine. They weren't due back for another month or more. Local remedies couldn't ease the pain, and her stepmother went out in a flurry of obscenities directed at Erith, cursing the day she'd come into her world.

When Erith told her what she knew, Kathleen had become extremely agitated and crueller than ever. Mrs. Patsy and Mrs. Helen had reminded Erith that her stepmother was out of her mind in pain, but Erith knew that wasn't entirely true. Everyone in North Harbour knew her stepmother was a horrible woman, and no one was sad that she was dead—although those words wouldn't be spoken aloud—and anyone who thought them would surely follow it with the sign of the Cross and a whispered, "God rest her."

Erith gave a cursory nod around the room at the few remaining people before going upstairs for the night. Tomorrow her stepmother would be gone. Foremost in Erith's mind were the words she'd said during her final moments of coherency—at least Erith desperately needed them to be lucid.

The words *She's alive, you know* were spoken into her ear in a hushed whisper. Erith wasn't sure she had heard it correctly, but her stepmother's slight nod, her glassy, wide-eyed stare, and raised eyebrows told her she had. Was this true, or was it the woman's last attempt to drive Erith out of her mind?

2

Danol Cooper was intrigued more than he should have been. His black felt hat covered his dark hair and hid his piercing blue eyes—eyes that didn't miss much. He couldn't help but feel there was something not right in the graveyard. His years as a detective with the Boston Police taught him to go with his gut, and it was rarely, if ever, wrong. The advantage of a tall frame allowed him to survey the mourners before him. Nothing stood out, yet something was bothering him.

He had come to the area a few years before to capture the criminal who had murdered his father, a New York City policeman. The killer had robbed a bank, slaughtered several policemen and his own accomplice, and attempted to flee to Europe with his new, ill-gotten wealth. Danol took a leave of absence in Boston, laid chase, and ended up near death on the shores of John's Pond, two miles over the ridge from where he decided to put down new roots.

He'd had the good fortune of being concealed by a reclusive young woman, Mary Rourke. Mary had been trained by her mother in the art of nursing and surely saved his life, not once, but twice in just a few days. Danol grew very fond of the woman and wanted to repay her. He successfully convinced her to go to Boston and study to become a doctor. At first he thought it was because he had feelings for her, but he wasn't one to yield to such nonsense, and soon he realized it was his own struggle with where his life was headed that confused him.

Once Mary settled in Boston, he used the reward money from the New York robbery to put a substantial down payment on a boat. Well, he guessed it was more than a boat, since it was outfitted as a medical ship. Each summer he brought Mary and her new husband, a doctor as well, to the little coves and inlets peppering the bays of Newfoundland, to care for those who would otherwise do without. They had saved many lives over the past few years. He was fiercely protective of Mary and her new family. Her husband, Peter, had become a good friend. Danol liked him, though it had taken some time. Mary was like the sister he hadn't had. He was alone in the world except for Mary, but he was comfortable being alone. Danol guessed it was what he was used to growing up. His mother died when he was very young, and his father was a career policeman who spent very little time at home.

That was the reason he chose to settle in North Harbour, as opposed to John's Pond. It gave him room. He needed room, though he didn't really question why.

The first year that he'd wintered his boat, *Angel Endeavours*, in the harbour, many of the local men came to help him tow her up on the beach. He was going to rent, or even buy, a horse to do the chore, as would be expected back in Boston, but he wasn't long learning that what was customary there did not belong here.

First, ten men showed up from both the north and south sides of the harbour. There were three horses and two hauling sleds loaded with sticks—wood to shore up the boat and to make a slipway to get her out of the water. As the tide was lowering, the men built the slip. They went home to eat and were back in greater numbers to pull up the boat when the tide was high.

Danol worked beside the men, not too proud to leave it to the more skilled to show him how it was done. When the boat was secure, he offered to pay, but the men wouldn't hear of it. He opened a bottle of rum, and they all had a drink before heading for home. When he got back home, a plate of fried fish had been set on the table. He later learned that his neighbour, Mrs. Whalen, had dropped it off because she figured he'd be hungry after working all day.

Danol was a stranger but was welcomed. And he had learned rather quickly that, despite not being a God-fearing man, there were social obligations he would have to uphold if he wanted to survive in the community. That included attending funerals.

Mrs. Kathleen Lock was being laid to rest. He stood in the graveyard listening to the recited prayers, which were muffled by his thoughts of something being out of place. He had delivered goods to Lock's on the north side several times over the past two years—his boat was used for making supply runs when not otherwise occupied with the medical trips. Mrs. Lock was one mean woman. She always accused him of having cheated her in some way, or of not bringing the right things, or of being late, or of being dim-witted. Always something. She didn't smile. He learned to ignore her rants and get on with the business transaction. Trying to be friendly, as he was with the other shopkeepers on his route, was out of the question at Lock's Dry Goods. He concluded business and left. That was satisfactory to Mrs. Lock and cut down on the aggravation for him.

Danol hadn't realized she'd been married, let alone had a

child. He looked toward the daughter standing near the grave. There it was again. She was looking at him. Just glancing from beneath her hood, but definitely toward him. He moved a few feet, and her eyes followed him. He tripped on a white marble headstone and quickly righted himself. He was having difficulty focusing on the prayers, and a couple of the mourners cast him a look when he moved a second time.

She wasn't crying. Maybe she was glad the shopkeeper was dead. He'd seen that before—relatives happy to inherit what others had worked so hard to attain. Sometimes, he surmised, helping the sick along to access the money more quickly than God intended. However, she was well-dressed, and his first impression was that she had an air of somebody who was well-to-do.

The *Angel Endeavours* was dry docked on the beach near his house waiting to be recorked. Except for that, he might have been on the mail run that had brought the daughter here. He had overheard one of the women say she hadn't seen the young woman since she was fifteen or sixteen. It was common in coastal communities for young girls to leave, marry, and not return. With the temperament of her mother, he figured she was probably happy to have left.

However, she wasn't crying, not even in pretense. While others had their heads bowed in prayer, she was taking quick glimpses at him. Surely he wasn't the only new person here since she had left years ago, and even if that were the case, it seemed odd that she'd be noticing that now. Then again, he was looking around, too, so he shouldn't fault her for that, he supposed. But his mother wasn't being buried, either.

When prayers ended, he stayed behind to fill in the grave. He didn't get a chance to speak to her because Mrs. Power ushered her home, out of the cold. The men covered Mrs. Lock, and they dispersed in silence. He walked the muddied path toward the crossing with Gene Burton, one of the only other men in the community as tall as Danol. Gene talked about the weather and asked when he was putting the boat in the water. After a bit of chit-chat, Gene tipped his hat and veered off toward home.

Danol crossed the ice, being careful to follow the markers. He was bothered by the woman in black. Erith was her name. He hadn't heard that name before. There were many things about this Erith woman intruding on his thoughts, and he didn't like it. She was pretty enough, although it was hard to get a good look with the hair flying around her face. She seemed a bit distant, or maybe she just wanted to get the whole thing over with. Who was he to judge? He was itching to get back on the water. The boat was ready now. He'd be heading for Boston before too long.

He took his hammer and decided to work on the room upstairs. He liked building things. The house was coming along nicely, and the loud echo of hammer hitting nail would keep his mind occupied for the afternoon. The second time the hammer tapped off his finger in a glancing blow, he knew it was time to give it up. He made his way downstairs to fill the woodbox. With the last armload neatly stacked, he turned to look out the window while deciding what to do next.

Danol thought his mind was playing tricks on him when he saw her. He stared, transfixed, when reality gave him a knock. What was she doing? He bolted from the house toward the beach.

"Don't let me be too late," he whispered into the arctic wind as he raced along the ice-littered beach.

3

Eight years earlier . . .

Erith had the sudden and unfamiliar urge to hug her step-mother. Barely sixteen years old, she was leaving the woman who had raised her.

Erith's parents moved from England and settled in North Harbour shortly after she was born. They opened a post office and dry goods store in a house her father had built for his first wife. They had planned to fill it with children, a dream not realized.

His wife—Erith's mother, Beatrice—had died in child-birth when Erith was almost five. Kathleen, the attending midwife, married her father, Ben Lock, within the year to help raise his daughter while he was away at sea. Kathleen had not been inclined to nurture, and Erith was sure that the woman was grateful not to have given birth herself. She often said she bore the wants of her husband because it was a wifely obligation. Erith's father was supposed to take care of his new wife and not leave her with a young child and a business to run.

Now she'd get her wish to be rid of Erith. Although unspoken, Erith knew her stepmother wasn't sad that she was leaving. She had, in fact, made the arrangements. A step-uncle, Dinn Ryan, whom she hardly knew beyond the two or three times he had come into the store over the years, needed a housekeeper in Dog Cove. His wife had died with complications from pleurisy during the winter, leaving him with three children to raise. Now that fishing was under way, he had sent word to North Harbour that he needed a housekeeper, and her stepmother had volunteered Erith.

"Mind yourself, now." Her attempt at some sort of familiarity was lost in her pinched face and harsh tone as she stood, arms folded, on the bottom step of the stairs and looked down her nose at Erith. The grey hair that was pinned back in a tight bun seemed to be trained not to go out of place, a style she had forced on Erith after her father died, sometimes pinning it so tight Erith's head would ache for days. "Make sure you have all your clothes." She turned and went upstairs to perform a cursory check of Erith's room.

Mr. Hand, a balding man in his early forties, with one side of his dark, greying hair flattened across a balding skull, poked his head in through the door. "Are you ready, miss?"

Erith nodded. "I'll be there shortly."

She heard her stepmother at the top of the stairs. "Looks like you've got everything."

Kathleen saw Mr. Hand. "She'll be right along." She dismissed him with a wave. He grabbed Erith's bag, glanced up the stairs, and nodded.

The older woman ran the post office and the store, and she had added a boarding house to the business. In the winter she usually boarded the teacher, but this past year was different. Two men from Trinity Bay had been icebound off North

Harbour Point in January after taking shelter in St. Mary's Bay during a storm. They stayed with the Locks and fixed the ice-damaged boat as soon as the weather broke. With little money to speak of, they had made a bargain with her stepmother to get wood over the winter and codfish in the spring to pay their debt. An agreement was struck, and Mr. Hand and Mr. Noftle took up temporary residence in their large house.

Today they were heading out to the fishing grounds and, along the way, landing Erith in Dog Cove. It would be cold on the water. Erith buttoned her long, grey woollen coat around her plaid cotton dress. She tied the blue and white bonnet close around her pinned hair and took one last look around the kitchen. This was probably the last time she would see this place. She couldn't imagine coming back here.

Many girls her age had a beau, but her stepmother had strongly discouraged any possibility of a love interest coming around. Her closest friend, May, had gone to St. Joseph's to keep house for a Daley family last November and hadn't returned. Erith wasn't sad about leaving, but she suddenly yearned for what could have been had her father still been alive.

Her father was well-respected in the community. He had been a good provider, so her neighbours said. In January 1875, he hired on as an engineer with Captain Isaac Bartlett on the steamer *Tigress* to go to the seal fishery. Her father and twenty-one others were killed when a boiler exploded while they were icebound hundreds of miles from shore. Her father, badly burned, lived for almost a day before dying in what must have been horrific pain. Captain Bartlett had dictated a note that Erith's stepmother threw in the stove shortly after getting the news of Ben's death. Erith could barely remember being on her father's knee, right here in the kitchen, while he sang songs to her. It seemed warmer then, too. That time was a distant memory now.

She didn't look back at her stepmother as she closed the porch door. The wharf, built by her father, was just a few feet from the house. Erith trod along the worn path leading down to the edge of the sod. She refused to feel scared of what was to become of her in Dog Cove with her step-uncle and his family. She was sure she would treat the children lovingly and help them with the loss of their mother. Erith believed herself to have a caring nature. She held her head high and stepped from the grassy embankment. The old, worn sticks creaked and bent beneath her weight, but she was sure-footed and confident that they would hold her small frame.

Mr. Hand helped her down the ladder into the ribbed cage of the boat. Erith caught a faint whiff of pine tar from the new oakum her stepmother had supplied to seal the joints between the frost-warped planks. Despite her efforts to hold it at bay, fear washed over her, taking her breath. She swallowed hard to recover. She was going to a new and different world, even though all she knew was the one she tolerated and was leaving behind.

Mr. Noftle, a portly man in his early thirties with a crop of light brown, stringy, greasy hair, shoved the boat off from the dock. The two men grinned at each other. "Thank the Lord we're on our way," chortled Mr. Noftle.

"Good riddance to this place," Mr. Hand said under his breath. Both men eyed one another. Erith missed the smile on Mr. Noftle's lips as he winked at his companion.

Erith sat upright on the weather-worn forward thwart between the fish pounds. The boat was remarkably clean, with no sign to be seen of fish ever having been gutted or split.

"How long to Dog Cove?"

"We'll be there for morning tea if we catch some wind," Hand said.

Erith looked over her shoulder toward the houses on the south side of the harbour. "Might as well be the moon," she mumbled. The south side was a short row by dory from her house, but Erith had not been there since she was a child. She barely remembered her father taking her to a garden party in the lower meadows one sunny Sunday. She acknowledged that she might have even imagined that, after seeing the celebrations there the last number of years. Erith's scope had since been limited to the fifteen houses that dusted the north side of the harbour and the families who lived in them. Every three months or so, when the Roman Catholic priest came through, the residents on the south side flocked to the little church that was coming into view through the trees. "Bye Mama, bye Papa," she whispered and blessed herself when they passed the church and graveyard.

Erith looked forward, to where she was headed. All the scenery was new to her as they passed the last house. They hugged the shoreline close on her right. When North Harbour Point disappeared into the sea on the left, the vast ocean opened before her. Erith marvelled at the distant shore but had no idea what communities were there. Maybe that was the one where her friend May had gone. She couldn't be sure.

Mr. Hand's voice startled her. "I've been meaning to ask you where you got that name, miss."

"My parents gave it to me. My father said I was named after a little town in England where my mother was born."

"Your mother doesn't sound English."

Erith didn't answer. The thought of the mother she hadn't known was suddenly raw on her palate. She couldn't speak as her mind flooded with a beehive of images and sounds of her father and a happier time. Instead, she gazed toward the shore, where towering cliffs rose from the ocean floor and then suddenly dropped off to show rocky beaches fold into tree-lined fields. They passed between the beach and two fishing boats from North Harbour. Mr. Walter Power and Mr. Gene Burton were busy hauling traps and hardly noticed their passing.

A small cove came into view a short time later, and Mr. Hand dropped the sail while Mr. Noftle took up the oars. Erith looked back at the two men from her perch on the pound board. "Is this Dog Cove? Where are the houses?"

"We're not going to Dog Cove," Mr. Noftle said.

"We're not?"

"We're not," said Mr. Hand.

Erith was confused. She quickly looked back to the shore to see if she had missed the houses. They could be trying to play a trick on her, although she couldn't imagine why. There was nothing ahead of her that showed any sign of life. Some trees in the sheltered cove, a small stream splitting the land, a green patch where the grass and clover were just getting a taste of the warmth of the sun—but no houses.

She looked back at the two men again. "So . . . we'll be stopping here and then going on to Dog Cove?"

They didn't answer.

"Mr. Hand?"

"I'm not Hand."

"And I'm not Noftle."

Erith slowly shook her head from side to side. "I don't understand."

"You'll understand soon enough," the man she knew as Mr. Noftle said.

Something didn't feel right, but Erith didn't know if she should be afraid. "You're dropping me off here?"

"Something like that," Hand said under his breath.

The boat was going too fast, and it lurched when it struck the beach. Erith lost her seating and fell hard into the pound, hitting her head on the gunwale. She was sure she saw stars and felt the sting of a bump rising near her temple when she caught a glimpse of Noftle jumping over the side of the boat. What was happening? Erith tried to make sense of the situation.

"What are you doing?" asked Noftle, his eyes fixed on the man behind her.

Hand spoke behind her. "It's a hanging offence either way."

As she scrambled to get to a sitting position, she turned, following his voice. She caught a glimpse of movement and ducked, but not in time. Hand struck her a glancing blow to the head with the blade of the oar. Erith cried out. Her arms flailed as she tried to right herself, but she tumbled over the thwart into the pound. Blackness awaited.

4

Erith was dazed. She felt a cold dampness around her bare legs. Mortified, she opened her eyes. Pain stabbed through her head from the movement. Her skirt covered her face. She winced as she gingerly patted her cheek through the thick cotton. A tentative tug on the material caused a pain in her temple. Taking a deep breath, she gently pulled until it gave way and then threw it to cover herself.

She shivered as she swept her fingertips along the skin on her brow. Her hand felt sticky. Erith flinched when she grazed the swollen cheek. Her left eye wouldn't open, and her jaw hurt.

Shame of her nakedness pressed her to move. She was lying in the low tuckamore. She forced herself to roll toward the sound of a nearby creek and felt the sting of the craggy branches clawing at her legs as they bent beneath her weight. The effort was excruciating. Erith instinctively pulled her coat around her and tried to sit up. The effort brought waves of pain to her head, and it was difficult to breathe.

She tried to get up, but her legs betrayed her, and she

tumbled on the grass. Her mouth was dry, and her lips were cracked. She wormed her way along the dampened turf to the little stream. Lifting the frayed hem of her dress, she dipped it into the cold water and carefully wiped her temple and eye. The coolness soothed her as she cleaned.

She carefully cupped water in her shaking palms and splashed it on her face. The shock helped clear her fogbound mind. Erith quickly patted herself dry with the sleeve of her coat and tried to stand again. By moving slowly, she managed to get herself upright. She hobbled to her shoes and stockings strewn on the tangled grass. The movement ignited a burning pain.

Where was she? How did she get there? How would she get out of there? Then a flash of memory stole through the pain. She froze in place. Her heart thumped in horror, and she uttered a wild cry. The meadow seemed to echo her misery with tears of its own as dew shimmered on the new clover. Her stepmother was going to kill her for this. She crumpled to her knees, sobbing until she fell into an exhausted state that was somewhere between sleep and death.

Cool dampness penetrated her clothes and drew her back to the reality of her circumstance. Something called to her from deep in her belly. A primal urge kicked in that wouldn't allow her to give up. Erith slowly got to her feet and faced the ocean. Her head spun for a minute, and then the horizon settled and came into focus.

The sun was almost directly overhead now. She had left the wharf in North Harbour just after daylight. At least half the day had passed. Nobody was going to miss her. Her stepmother thought her gone, and her step-uncle wasn't sure when she would be showing up and might think she had changed her mind. She willed the panic to settle. Erith was on her own, but she wouldn't wallow in pity. She had to act. Clear thinking escaped her, but to stay here was sure to be her end.

It was less than half a day's walk between Dog Cove and North Harbour in the winter. She knew this because people came for the mail or supplies every now and again after the boats were pulled up. She wished she had paid more attention. As near as she could figure, she guessed she might be halfway between both settlements.

What of Hand and Noftle? Panic flared as she scanned the sea and the shore to make sure they were gone. What would she do if they came back? Frantically, she limped to the edge of the woods to hide in case they steamed around the headland. She would spend the rest of her life in the woods before facing them again.

A million thoughts, from sensible to ridiculous, raced through her aching head. Surviving trumped them all. She had to get somewhere while it was still daylight. Erith realized that was vague and didn't make sense, so she decided she would go back to what she knew. Her stepmother was cruel, but Erith was sure she would help her.

There was a trail somewhere inland that joined the two communities, but Erith didn't know how far back in the country it was. She believed it wouldn't follow the coastline. However, the coastline offered the chance that she would see someone tending their traps. But then, what of the cliffs?

Despite the questions, she had to get going, so she carefully crossed at the narrowest part of the brook. The movement was enough to make her vomit. She retched on her hands and knees on the silty embankment before getting her bearings again. Her head throbbed, her throat hurt, and she was dizzy.

She picked up a long, thin piece of driftwood from the beach to help steady herself and, using it as a crutch, continued out of the cove toward the home she knew. The tide was falling. The beach rock skittered away under each footfall. She stumbled twice on the landwash, which forced her to solid ground.

Erith had to think. She carefully lowered herself onto the moss at the edge of the woods to ponder her predicament. She would have to find the winter trail. If she didn't, then she would come back to the shore and wait until morning.

A few marshberries, which had survived the winter in the wet moss, assuaged her hunger. She pushed off with her makeshift crutch into the thick woods, following the river. Tangled tree limbs pulled at her hair and struck at her eyes, sometimes causing the blood to flow from her temple again. The terrain was rough. A scourge of blackflies and mosquitoes tormented her. Her stockings were ripped to shreds, and her legs, scratched and bleeding, were itching. She forced herself to ignore those particular pains and fixed her mind on home.

Erith was near exhaustion when she emerged onto the bleak barrens. The wind whistled and wailed through the yellowed grasses, cooling her. The mournful sound from the moor was like a death knell. Erith suddenly shivered when she thought of how alone she was. She would not be found.

The velvet touch of the scant, tall grass brushing on her fingers sought to calm her misery. The cry of an eagle in the distance urged her on. This couldn't be the end of her.

The blackflies rallied against the breeze as if to test her will. She grabbed handfuls of black bog and coated her exposed areas to keep them from their feast. Erith couldn't escape the wretched pests in her eyes, nose, mouth, and hair, but they wouldn't bite through the rapidly drying cover.

A half-mile or more into the marsh, she spotted an impression on the land. Could it be the trail she sought? Or perhaps an animal path? Erith followed it to the embankment and along to where the river narrowed. Someone had thrown sticks across the watery divide as a makeshift bridge. This was what she had been looking for. She quickly crossed the weathered wood. With renewed energy born from hope and desperation, she headed along the trail toward the trees.

After entering the mantle of the treeline, she had a few minutes' rest on a windfall. She stumbled on and almost fell more times than she could count and rested frequently, though sitting was as much a chore as standing. Each time she felt the trickle of blood down her cheek and onto her neck, she took a break. She tore a strip from the tattered hem of her dress and tied it around her head, wincing as the cloth tightened.

Erith had almost given up the notion that she was going in the right direction, when she climbed a small rise and let out a deep sigh of relief.

Looking out at the expanse of the harbour, she saw that the north side, her destination, was tucked in somewhere beneath her vantage point. The sun would soon be veiled by the horizon behind her, but she figured she could make it before being swallowed by the night since it was all downhill.

She could clearly see the houses on the south side and North Harbour River, which split the community in half. There were two sandy points of land that almost touched to form the harbour, and then the land hourglassed out beyond to the brackish pond at the mouth of the river. From here the pond looked comparable in size to the harbour, but there were no houses on the near-landlocked body, and the sandy points often shifted with the tides and river currents.

People with business to conduct on either side of the harbour usually crossed at the points. The Ryans, Singletons, and Daltons kept dories there, and residents used them whenever they needed. Erith knew it wasn't a great distance, because people would joke how it took them a few minutes to row and many times longer to walk to the store for the mail.

The trail went over the rise on the distant shore. John's Pond was a few miles farther. Erith hadn't ever seen the path as clearly as she did from this height. She knew Colinet would be the next community, a few miles farther on. It was out of her view, mixed somewhere in the trees.

After catching her breath, Erith faced the trail. The hill was steep and rocky from water runoff, and she felt a downward pull. As daylight waned, she abandoned her cautious step for a faster, wilder, almost frantic gait. She tripped and stumbled on exposed roots and loose rocks, sometimes spearing herself with the piece of driftwood she continued using as a crutch. Suddenly, she broke out of the trees and almost ran into a fenced potato garden. The house below, near the shore, was Mr. Art Power's place. The last remnants of a will to survive outweighed her exhaustion by just a fraction as she scaled the five rungs of the fence. The weathered wood buckled despite her small size.

Erith nearly cried out with relief as she reeled down the steep hill toward the house. One more fence and she would make it. Unable and unwilling to stop, she hit the barrier hard and toppled over the top rail without her feet having touched the bottom rail. She collapsed in a pile on the grass and rolled down the lesser incline, folding around the rocks at the base of the aging clothesline pole. Her eyes closed. When they opened, a moonless night had taken hold of the land.

Erith was unable to get up. This couldn't be it. She was so close. Mr. and Mrs. Power would surely be home and their three young children in bed. She tried to shout, but no sound came out. Gasping for breath, she tried again. A hoarse whisper frustrated her efforts. She untangled herself from around the cribbing and tried in vain to get up. Her muscles wouldn't co-operate, and her ribs ached—a new pain. Mr. Power would find her dead in the morning.

The cold ground awakened her once more. No. There was a sound. Somebody was on the step. Mrs. Power was throwing out the dishwater.

Erith weakly flailed her arms in the blackness. She thought she screamed, but Mrs. Power didn't answer. Erith slapped the ground hard with her open palm. Mrs. Power, a dark figure outlined in the dim light from the lamp, turned over the pan, and water splashed near the step. She paused for a second. Erith slapped the ground two more times.

"Who's out there?"

Erith repeated the motion. Mrs. Power went back inside. Erith put her head down, and with every ounce of strength she could muster, she dragged herself toward the door. If she could get to the step . . . just a few feet.

She heard the hinges creak as the door opened again, and Mr. Power stood shirtless with a shotgun across his arm. "Art, dear. I heard the noise from over there." Mrs. Power held the lamp out ahead of her. "It could be caribou in the garden."

Erith slapped the ground again to draw their attention downward. The Powers came slowly off the stoop and moved toward her.

"Who's there? Show yourself!" Mr. Power demanded. The halo of light reached her outstretched hands. "What the devil?"

Mrs. Power screamed. "Jesus, Mary, and St. Joseph! Who or what is that?" She quickly moved behind her husband and blessed herself.

"Shine the light, woman!"

Mrs. Power pushed the lamp forward. Erith started to cry. Mr. Power reached out and touched her hair. Like a rabbit in the throes of death, sounds like that of a wounded animal echoed in the still night air as Erith folded into a fetal position.

"My Jesus, Ellen. It's a girl. Get a blanket."

Art scooped her up. Erith shuddered in relief as Mr. Power laid her on the daybed in the kitchen. She allowed herself to feel the heat from the wood stove. In the light of the kitchen, Mrs. Power gently pushed back the tangled bush of hair matted in blood, turpentine, and bog. She gasped.

"My God, that's young Erith. Child, what happened to you? Art, you've got to get her home to Kathleen and fetch the nurse."

Mrs. Power made a cup of tea and added some cool water. "Here, try this." Erith couldn't hold onto the porcelain offering. Mrs. Power laid the cup on her lips to see if Erith could take a sip. "It's no use, Art. You'll have to bring her home. Go fetch Walter next door while I try to cover the poor child."

Erith had forgotten the state of her clothing. She was naked below her tattered skirts. She became frantic, and Mrs. Power tried to settle her as she wrapped a large blanket around her scratched and bruised legs. Erith calmed a little. She heard a baby cry upstairs.

"Oh, for the love of God. Now the children are up. I'll be down in a bit," she said before disappearing through the door at the bottom of the stairs.

Erith was losing time, fading in and out. She heard foot-
falls pounding as Art and Walter Power burst in through the
door. She tried to melt into the wall, but it was impossible.
Mrs. Power had cocooned her in a blanket. Erith hadn't realized she had come back. She passed out once again.

When she woke, darkness surrounded her and she could
feel her body moving. She was being carried. Noftle and Hand.
She tried to scream and release her arms to lash out at them.

"Hush now, child. You're safe. You're safe." Erith recognized the voice and felt herself being handed off to another
man. "Walter got you now. You're all right." Art Power practically cooed the words to try and bring her some comfort. She
drifted off again. . . .

Suddenly, she heard a fist pummelling a wooden frame.
"Kathleen Lock, open this door!"

Erith recognized the sound of the bolt being pulled back.

"What's the meaning of this?" her stepmother demanded.

"Young Erith's in a bad way."

"Erith's gone. She left this morning for Dog Cove."

Mr. Power didn't wait for an explanation and pushed past
her. "We have her here. Where's her room?"

"What do you mean? How can you have her?"

"We don't know what happened, and she hasn't been able
to talk. She needs the nurse."

As quick as a wink, her stepmother responded, "She'll be
all right. No need to trouble yourself. Go on home. I'll see to
the girl."

"You'll not dismiss this, Kathleen," said Art Power. "She
needs the nurse. Me and Walter will go to John's Pond for Mrs.
Rourke."

"You'll do no such a thing. I said I'll see to her."

"You haven't seen her. We're going to fetch the nurse. I'll hear no more about it."

"Fine. Waste your time, but I'll not be paying her."

"For God's sake, Kathleen. The child's hurt bad," Walter said. His tone and the grumblings of his brother indicated that both men were more than irritated. They turned to navigate the stairs with their precious cargo. They laid her down, then left, intent on getting medical help no matter what the woman of the house said.

"Erith, what in the name of God have you done now?" her stepmother muttered as she unwrapped the quilt. She didn't flinch as she looked at the battered, bloodied, bruised girl before her. Erith shivered. Her stepmother left her exposed on the bed, and a few moments later Erith heard the damper on the stove below and the scrape of the kettle.

"That young one will be the death of me yet. If it's not one thing, it's another." Erith had heard her stepmother complain so often about her lot in life that it usually didn't affect her. However, tonight was different. Erith felt abandoned and lost and somehow empty. Her heart felt hollow, and all emotion left her. She couldn't allow herself to feel. Her stepmother would show her no kindness nor compassion. The woman had none in her. Erith pulled the blanket around her and fell into a troubled sleep. Oblivion!

5

Erith felt hands on her. She screamed and flailed her arms and legs. She would fight harder this time.

"Erith, settle down. It's Dorothy Rourke."

Erith couldn't calm herself. She felt Hand and Noftle closing in. She became frantic and pushed on the quilts. They were heavy and drowning her.

"It's all right, Erith. I won't hurt you. I'll tend to your head, that's all." The woman continued to speak in a calm and low tone. Erith opened her eyes.

A dark-haired woman in her mid-fifties held a cloth in front of her. Though she had a kind face, her brows were furrowed, and her eyes betrayed her forced smile.

"There, now. That's it. I'm just going to wash the wound on your head." Erith hadn't seen Mrs. Rourke in over two years. She had heard that the woman had been a nurse at the Riverhead Hospital in St. John's, where she had met David Rourke. He had been injured in a boating accident and was recuperating there. They married and moved to John's Pond.

"I'll need to stitch your cut, and it's going to hurt."

Erith whimpered.

"Can I touch your head?"

Erith gave a slight nod, and Mrs. Rourke leaned closer to size up the wound. She asked for another cloth.

It was only then Erith realized they weren't alone. A red-haired girl sat on a chair at the foot of the bed. She had laid her hand on Erith's leg in a gesture of comfort. Her green eyes were kind when her gaze met Erith's. She smiled as if to reassure Erith that everything was going to be fine.

Erith didn't think it would ever be all right again. A moment in time had irrevocably changed the course of her life—an unthinkable intrusion of such magnitude as to scar her and leave her tattooed with shame and disgrace. She was ruined. The fight went out of her—what anyone did with her now would not matter.

Mrs. Rourke stitched the gash on the side of her head while her daughter, Mary, helped wash Erith's legs and arms. Erith was in and out of consciousness for most of the night as they both worked to clean her up. She saw her stepmother look in, once. The pinched grimace was enough to say that Kathleen Lock was not at all pleased with the situation.

Erith felt a warm weight as she struggled to open her eyes. She was trapped beneath something. It wasn't restrictive, but she suddenly felt scared. A hand gently touched hers.

"It's going to be all right. I'm Mary Rourke. I'll stay with you." The voice was soft and reassuring. Erith eyed the girl who was seated on a chair near her head. She couldn't be but a few years older than Erith. She smiled.

"Don't worry. You're safe. I'll stay with you."

Erith was confused. Where was she? It looked like her room, but why was she here? Who was Mary, and why was

Mary here? Then she heard muffled voices from below. One of them was Kathleen's.

"There's no need of all this to-do about nothing," Kathleen said. "Leave it to Erith to bring this situation home to me."

"Mrs. Lock, that girl is going to need lots of attention over the next couple of days. I'm leaving Mary here to tend to her."

That must be Mrs. Rourke. Mrs. Rourke. . . . Erith bolted upright in the bed and screamed. Images flooded over her as she tried to push back the covers, which had been weighted down with warm stones. Mary grabbed her shoulders and, gently yet firmly, eased her back in the bed. The girl made soft cooing sounds and then began to hum. Erith's heartbeat slowed, and her breathing calmed.

Mrs. Rourke returned and sat in the chair that Mary had vacated. She held a glass of warm, sweetened rum to Erith's lips and helped her drink. Erith felt as if her face was flushing as heat flooded through her veins. She instantly relaxed and closed her eyes before Mrs. Rourke left the room and Mary returned to the wooden chair next to her.

"Good day to you, Mrs. Lock," said Mrs. Rourke. "I'll be going for some salve and ointments and will be back around midday. Mary will keep an eye on your daughter."

Erith heard chairs scrape across the floor and doors slam. Somebody must have come for mail or an item from the store, because she could hear her stepmother's high-pitched *What do you want?* penetrate the walls. Kathleen wasn't having anyone nosing around. Erith knew her stepmother believed that she had brought the ultimate scandal upon the house.

Silent tears ran down her cheeks as she fell into a fitful slumber. Mrs. Rourke returned sometime later and put lanolin cream mixed with gentian violet on her hands and legs. She used honey and lanolin for her face to avoid the deep purple tint of the first salve. What was left for her after this? What was going to become of her? Her fate had been decided in the wilderness somewhere between North Harbour and Dog Cove.

She overheard a conversation downstairs about the two men being "nowhere to be found." She hadn't realized that the menfolk in North Harbour and John's Pond had gone searching for Noftle and Hand. Apparently the two had disappeared, which wasn't surprising to Erith. They had at least a day's head start. She felt glad, in a way—she wanted to forget about the whole ordeal. Forgetting was best for everyone.

Erith didn't remember much about the next few days and nights. In her delirium, she believed her father was with her and holding her in a tight embrace. She was sure she saw whom she thought to be her real mother. The blonde-haired woman was like she remembered from her dreams. She cried out for them to take her with them.

Her dreams were broken by soft whispers. "Hush now, Erith, I'm here. It's Mary. You're delirious with fever." Erith felt a cool cloth on her forehead.

"You have to fight this, Erith. I'm here. It's Mary. I'm with you, Erith. I'm here."

She remembered someone fervently praying over her. Mrs. Rourke and her daughter said the rosary—Erith remembered hearing the rhythmic Hail Marys more than once. Sometimes she heard Mary Rourke humming songs.

Although she knew it to be a sin, she prayed for death. How could she live with the shame? Alas, it was not to be. Four days after being brought home, her fever broke. She would live.

Erith refused to speak. Mary Rourke read her books for

the next few days while Erith faced the wall and stared out the window. Mary seemed kind enough, but Erith couldn't bear the pity that she knew lay beneath the girl's smile.

Mrs. Rourke came around each day and got her out of bed. She walked back and forth across the hall upstairs before returning to her room to lie down. The teacher had once again moved out to a neighbour's house, and Erith was sure that her stepmother would blame her for that lost income. She heard people come for their mail or to the store and ask about her, but her stepmother, in no uncertain terms, told them to mind their own business.

Feeling sun on her face through the curtains didn't warm her. Mary encouraged her to get out of bed and come downstairs, but Erith refused. She knew her stepmother wouldn't want it. By the seventh day, Mrs. Rourke told her she had to attempt the stairs. There was no reason for Erith to remain in bed. She was kind in her request, but there was no refusing it.

Mrs. Rourke and her daughter accompanied Erith to the bottom of the stairs. Her stepmother heard the creaking wood and came from the kitchen. "You'll not be shaming this house, Erith Lock," she said. "You go back upstairs."

"Mrs. Lock, she'll do no such thing," Mrs. Rourke said in a defiant tone. "Mary and I are bringing her outside in the sun. There's healing in that."

"Well, make sure you're on the back of the house and not out front where the crowd comes in."

As the Rourkes took their coats from the rack, Erith remembered hers was in tatters and would need cleaning and patching. An unfamiliar scarlet red coat hung on the hook where hers had been. To Erith's surprise, Mary took it down and moved behind her.

"My sisters sent this from Boston. I think it should fit you just fine." Erith turned in confusion, and before she could argue, Mary said, "This is the third one they've sent. I've only need for one." Mary dressed her and fixed the coat around her shoulders. "There, now. It fits." Erith had been so caught up in her misery and was unfamiliar with such kindness that all she could manage was a simple whispered *thank you* for the exquisite gift.

The trio walked to the garden behind the house, and Erith sat in the sun on the sawhorse. It was too early for bees, but the blackflies began to gather. As the sun shone on her face, Erith looked up to the heavens, and silent tears escaped. Mrs. Rourke gathered her to her bosom and patted her head.

"Let it out, child, let it out." She cooed and sang and rocked her until she was spent.

Erith pulled away from the woman and hung her head when she looked into Mary's eyes. Mary reached for her hand and gave it a gentle squeeze. That made Erith feel a little better, but she was not familiar with this intimacy. She couldn't remember the last time anybody had comforted her and believed it would have been her father. Erith remembered standing by his grave and reaching for her stepmother's hand, only to have it denied. She never reached for it again.

"I want to go in now," she said. "I'm tired."

Mrs. Rourke motioned for Mary to link into her arm for support. Erith refused.

"I can do it on my own," she said, a little more curtly than she meant. Mary moved away from her.

Erith realized she sounded like her stepmother and quickly apologized, but both the Rourkes dismissed it as nothing. Inside the house, Erith took off her coat and headed upstairs. She could hear Mrs. Rourke speaking to her stepmother and telling her they would be leaving.

HE PROMISE

Hearing someone on the stairs, Mary peeked around the door. "I'll be going now. I've come to get my books," she said. Mary hesitated. "I can leave them for you, if you want."

"No. Thank you, though. I expect I'll be sent to Dog Cove before too long."

Mary nodded and collected her books. She stood near the bed and looked at Erith. She paused for a few moments before kneeling beside her. "Erith, I don't know how you feel, and I can't imagine what you've been through, but if you ever need anything, please send for me."

She said it with such sincerity that Erith felt the urge to hug her. "I will," she replied. "Thank you for everything."

Mary reached for Erith's hand one more time. "I was happy to be here with you. I'm truly sorry for what happened."

Although she didn't see pity, Erith looked away. She didn't want to cry again.

"Remember. Anything," said Mary, and she left with her books under one arm.

Erith heard the creak of the steps, some murmurs at the foot of the stairs, and a short time later the door closed, and the air moved in her room. She was alone in the house with her stepmother for the first time since the attack. She braced herself for what was coming next as she heard Mrs. Lock's footfall.

"By the God who rules over me, Erith, I'll be your butcher." The venomous statement was the beginning of a tirade that Erith had to listen to before her stepmother finally finished. "If the weather is good, the nurse and her husband will be back for you in four days. They'll bring you to Dog Cove. Not soon enough for me, but make sure you're ready." She turned on her heel and retreated to the kitchen.

Erith lay on her bed, put her head in the pillow, and cried

until her eyes hurt. Was it just a week ago she was looking forward to that trip?

Sometime later, she awoke to the smell of food. Her stepmother met her before she could enter the kitchen. "I'll bring up food when it's done," she said. "I don't want people coming in and gawking at you." She dismissed Erith to the confines of the upper floor.

Mrs. Lock soon brought her a stew of fresh meat. Erith had eaten very little in more than a week, and though she wasn't hungry, she made herself eat. She had to be ready to leave.

One of the fishermen from the harbour had picked up her bag in the cove where she had been assaulted. She stared at it for a moment, then noticed there were a few different cotton frocks in the room. They weren't new but were new to her. Erith didn't know where they had come from, but she knew they didn't belong to her stepmother.

With her belly full, she thought about her situation. She couldn't take it back, no matter what, so she had to deal with it on her own. Clearly she had always been a disappointment to her stepmother, and her current state had no bearing on that. Dog Cove was the best place for her. *It can't be any worse than here,* she thought. But then she remembered the saying, "It's better the devil you know than the devil you don't," and that struck fear in her heart.

Erith knew she was strong. She had made it back despite being thrown in the woods and left for dead. That was worth something. She was ruined, but she was still Erith. Erith mattered. Deep down inside, she knew that, and she wouldn't be scared. She just couldn't.

6

Four days later, as an outcast from her own home, Erith stood on her father's wharf. If she could take back the last number of days, this one would be happy. But she couldn't, and Erith felt more alone in the world than she guessed anyone had a right.

Mr. and Mrs. Rourke helped her into the skiff. Erith thought Mary might have come, but she had to stay and monitor a birth in her mother's absence. She sat in the bow of the boat and watched the familiar scenery pass by. As the graveyard came into view, she said goodbye to her father and mother once again and asked that they protect her and help her to be strong.

She was startled when Mrs. Rourke spoke behind her. "Do you mind company?" Erith shook her head as the woman moved to sit on the forward pound board next to her. Erith sat closest to the land.

Mrs. Rourke was silent. With the exception of the warmth from her body, Erith almost forgot she was there. She watched the headland, her belly clenching more and more the farther out the bay they went. She wasn't sure if she would know when they reached the new shoreline. But she did. She hung her head as they rounded on the cove where her life had been changed forever. Mrs. Rourke motioned for her husband to drop the sail, and the skiff began to drift slowly toward the beach. Erith panicked. Her pulse raced, and she tensed, clenching her jaw till it hurt.

Mrs. Rourke put her arm around her and said, "We're not going to land." She hugged Erith and reassured her that everything was going to be all right.

A comforting touch was foreign to her, and Erith cried inconsolably. Mrs. Rourke held her in a fierce embrace until Erith raised her head. She screamed to the heavens and wiped her eyes with the sleeve of her coat and suddenly became ashamed of her outburst. Mrs. Rourke produced a handkerchief, and Erith wiped her face. Mr. Rourke set the sail, and they continued toward Dog Cove.

"Erith, my child, if there was something I could do to take away the pain, I'd do it," Mrs. Rourke said. "I'm sorry this happened to you. You won't forget it, but you must learn to live with it. The wound will close over with time if you don't let it fester."

"I know," Erith said between sobs.

"Now, get yourself straightened away," Mrs. Rourke said. "Cape Dog Head is coming up, and we'll be in the harbour there shortly."

Erith took several deep breaths. Slowly, she managed to calm her breathing. She focused on the shoreline, looking for houses, but couldn't see anything. Mr. Rourke spoke from the stern as if he guessed her thoughts. "We have to go around Cape Dog Head and into the harbour. You can't see it until we pass the point."

Erith listened to the gulls scream overhead. They were anticipating a meal that wouldn't be forthcoming. She suddenly realized that Mr. Rourke was missing a day's fishing and said so.

His wife told her to pay it no mind, because she had to go see one of her friends, anyway. Erith didn't believe her but didn't mention it after.

They were so close to the face of Cape Dog Head that Erith was afraid they would crash. Mr. Rourke lowered the sail, took to the oars, and skirted the rocks before coasting into a sheltered port with ease and precision.

Erith looked in awe at the scene before her. The far side of the harbour was mostly low cliffs, similar to where they were entering. However, the bluffs levelled out to a beach ribboned from one side to the other. Mr. Rourke explained that the houses were all on the near side of the harbour because there were two rivers running into the bay that formed ponds hidden by the seashore. Erith saw several houses coming up on the right and two small wharves jutting out into the sea. Behind the houses on the hillside were several grassy, fenced meadows and gardens, a couple of barns, a henhouse—it was much like North Harbour in that respect. Woods and ocean framed the entire scene. The cove was sheltered from the North Atlantic, and Mr. Rourke said the water was very deep here.

They kept close to the rock face, then followed the length of beach to the wharf. The tide was low, and the knotty, weath-ered shores were almost completely exposed. Dark brown kelp and deep purple barnacles clung to the wood on the pilings below the high-water mark. Small waves from the wake of the oar gently set the kelp bladders to swaying on the clear blue water, which shimmered with a medley of greys, greens, and blues from the pebbles on the ocean floor. The smell of the salt sea was overpowering yet wholesome.

Between the two wharves, a wide slipway came into view. Rindless sticks lay horizontal and ladder-like from high on the beach to below the water's edge. Three boats were tied to the gump head of the farthest wharf, which was fully cribbed by chopped logs. One boat remained at the top of the slip, but fully beached and upside down—it was old and seemed unseaworthy.

Mr. Rourke guided his skiff onto the sticks and jumped out before grabbing the gunwale and pulling the bow out of the water. Erith marvelled at the size of the man, and at his strength and agility. He helped her and his wife out onto the slender wooden longers forming the slipway. "Watch your footing, they're slippery," he said as he held their arms and guided them—more sure-footed then they—over the damp kelp to the beach.

Mr. Rourke joined the fishermen on the far wharf near the lone stage that served as storage for all the men in the harbour. He immediately grabbed a knife from his rubber boot and helped them split the catch spread out on the table and in wooden tubs. It was as if he belonged right there. The men gave both women a cursory nod and a *good morning* without missing a beat with the fish. Mrs. Rourke walked ahead of Erith across a muddied path to the nearest house, a one-storey that had seen better days. They climbed the three steps to the porch. The gallery was weathered and hove a little sideways from the frost. The threads stretched and creaked under their weight.

"Hello," said Mrs. Rourke.

Maggie Ryan, a hefty woman in her mid- to late forties, with a thick crop of dark grey hair plaited and pinned behind her head, rushed outside and greeted the pair with a pleasant, one-toothed smile. She wiped her hands in her stained cotton apron and moved forward to hug Mrs. Rourke.

"Dot, it's been such a long time."

"Yes, it has. It's been a couple of years since I was out this way," Mrs. Rourke said. "How are you, Maggie?"

"Lots of work to keep us busy. We'll be glad for young Erith's help," Mrs. Ryan said. She looked Erith up and down and then grinned at her before turning back to Dorothy Rourke. "Hard going, watching the young ones and at the fish. Weather's been co-operating, too. The fog has stayed away."

"I heard the fishing's been good," Mrs. Rourke said. "I suppose the merchant will be around soon."

"Yes, we're expecting one next week. We've a lot of work to do before then and pray the sun will shine on us before he comes."

"I heard you might be pulling up your roots and moving out."

"We've been talking that way. Last year was bad, and the winter was long," said Maggie. She had a faraway look in her eye. "Then we lost Kitty. That was a big blow to us, and of course to Dinn." She cleared away the table as she talked. "It's been hard this spring with one less hand around, too. The days are longer, and we're not getting any younger."

Erith knew that the fishery was crucial to survival in the tiny outports. When the collector boats came around for the fish, they also brought staples like food, dry goods, and fishing gear. Her father had overseen the merchantry on one of those boats the first couple of years after he came over from England. She'd heard he had been fair to both the business owner and the fishermen and had a good name in the bays and coves along the Avalon Peninsula. If he had stayed with the Ayres, he might still be here, she guessed.

But he was an engineer by trade and wanted to have a good life for his children. He couldn't refuse the offer from Captain Isaac Bartlett, and that trip was the end of him. Any memory Erith had of him had since been overshadowed by the cruelty of her stepmother, who was forced to keep her due to provisions made by her father. She hadn't been entirely sure what that had meant when she overheard a neighbour say it one time. As she grew older, she figured it meant she was a burden—her stepmother had always told her as much.

But that was the past, and Erith had to make the most of the present. She would be the best housekeeper she could be, and she would look after the children for Dinn Ryan. She hadn't seen the children and didn't know their ages or even if they were girls or boys. All she knew was her step-uncle had three. She could make bread, if she tried. Her stepmother had made Erith work in the store to keep her out from underfoot, so she hadn't really had time to learn to prepare or cook a meal.

Erith was to stay with Maggie and her husband, John. Their son was married and lived across the meadow from his parents and closer to the ponds. He and his wife had three small children as well. Maggie had pulled double duty with Dinn's children and her grandchildren while the men fished. Erith wasn't sure why Maggie's daughter-in-law couldn't look after her own offspring, but she guessed she would find out before too long.

Maggie Ryan made tea. The kitchen was dull and dreary, but clean. There was a small table, the wood stove, and a few shelves on one wall where plates and cups were kept. By the time her eyes adjusted to the dim interior, Erith noticed a small child asleep on a daybed in the corner of the room. Maggie followed her gaze. "That's Dinn's boy, Tommy. He's two. The little one, Annie, is asleep on the bed. She's almost a year now. The other fellow, George, he's down by the wharf waiting for his father. He's four, soon be five."

Maggie pushed back the door of what must have been her own bedroom, and Erith saw two babies. "The light-haired one, that's Annie. The other child is Stephen. My son owns him." Erith couldn't tell which was which because both babies were swaddled in blankets with nothing showing but their faces.

The little boy, Tommy, also sporting a head of light hair, stirred and rubbed his eyes. He made an effort to cry, then turned in toward the wall and fell back to sleep.

"They're quiet young ones," Maggie said. "You won't have no trouble with them."

Suddenly, it was real to Erith. She would be responsible for these two little darlings, and she had no idea what to do. Mrs. Rourke, who saw her tense up, spoke behind her. "Don't worry, it'll come naturally to you."

Erith prayed she was right, because nothing was coming to her at the moment. She was here, and this was where she was supposed to be. She gulped twice to squelch the panic that was rising in her belly.

"Sit down," said Maggie. "I'll be here to help."

They heard a shout from the wharf. "Dot, are you ready?" asked Mr. Rourke. "The wind's picking up, and it's time to get on our way!"

They followed Mrs. Rourke outside, and Erith stood on the gallery beside Maggie Ryan and watched the Rourkes go. Her tiniest thread of connection to anyone around here would soon be going out the bay. Erith told herself that if she had gotten through the last few weeks, she could get through anything. This was her new home, and she would make the best of it.

7

Maggie went inside, leaving Erith on the stoop. Uncertain of what to do next, Erith leaned on the rail and looked out over the expanse of the polished seashore. With a better view from this height, she noticed some people off in the distance who had been hidden by the slope of the beach when Mr. Rourke was rowing in.

Two women and at least three children were moving about. She could see the children's heads bobbing up and down, and the women went out of sight when they squatted down.

The sun was warm on her face, yet the breeze held a spring chill. The fishermen pushed the Rourkes off from the slipway, expressing gratitude for their help. Erith could see two more boats loaded down with fish approaching the wharf.

She couldn't help but notice that everything that was made of wood had various shades of weathered grey. The houses hadn't seen a drop of lime in years—they matched the slipway, the stage, the wharves, the flakes, the sheds, the barns. Everything was the same.

The boats tied up to the first quay, and the fishermen, who had just finished splitting their fish, moved to the other wharf to give the new arrivals a hand. They made quick work of pronging the fish and throwing it from the pounds to the deck. Two men moved the splitting tables into place and sharpened their knives. Erith marvelled at how easy they made the task look.

The women who had been farther over on the beach came to the fish that had been split the longest. They each went to the water's edge with buckets and began the chore of washing the codfish.

Maggie joined her on the stoop again. "Would you watch the children while I go help Mamie and Agnes?" she asked. Agnes, a slim brunette in her early twenties, was Maggie's daughter-in-law. She came from the island, according to Maggie. Erith believed she meant Colinet Island but didn't ask. Maggie said Mamie was married to her brother. The woman looked to be in her early forties, with dark brown hair that appeared to be creased with splashes of grey. Agnes and Mamie both waved from the beach.

"What? Me watch the children?" Erith asked. "Won't they be afraid if they wake and you're not there?"

"They might, but the men need all the help they can get. I don't think you've ever washed and salted fish before."

"No, but I can learn."

"Well, it's too late in the day for learning," said Maggie. "Stay here with the young ones, and I'll send George up to quieten them down if they get upstrapless."

Without giving Erith the opportunity to say anything else, Maggie rushed down the steps, across the muddied footpath, and over the beach toward the wharves. Before going inside, Erith saw Maggie grab a small boy by the shoulder and point toward the house. He must have said he wasn't going, because she made a playful swat at him before he did as she said.

"You're Miss Lock, aren't you?" the boy asked when he entered the house.

"Yes, I am. You must be George."

"Yes, miss."

"Well, George, pleased to meet you," Erith said. He was a handsome little boy. His light brown hair was a little long with strands stuck everywhere because of static from his cap.

"Yes, miss."

They stared at each other, neither knowing what to say. Erith finally asked if he was hungry, not knowing what she would do if he said yes.

"No, miss."

She breathed a sigh of relief. Then, Tommy stirred on the faded flowery cushion on the daybed. Erith went wide-eyed in panic as he sat up and rubbed his eyes. He looked at her and let out a bawl. George quickly went to his brother and sat down beside him.

"It's okay, Tommy. It's our new mama." George looked at her with a sheepish grin.

Erith didn't know what to do. She would have to ask Maggie what was appropriate. She wasn't comfortable with the concept of being "Mama" to three children. She didn't even know what was involved with being a housekeeper. Her brow broke out in a sweat. She had some experience being around children at the schoolhouse, but the teacher had been in charge there. Her stepmother hadn't welcomed children in the store.

For God's sake, they're children. How hard can it be?

Maggie Ryan returned a short time later to find Erith entertaining the children in the middle of the kitchen floor. The two little ones were awake, sitting in loosely fitting diapers on each side of her, and Tommy and George were playing with the babies.

"They've taken a liking to you."

"Yes, it seems so," Erith said quietly. She hung her head as heat rushed to her cheeks. George had shown her where the diapers were when the two youngest started to cry. After four attempts with the pins, the slack cloths drooped on the two little ones.

"I forgot to tell you that I had bread in rise," said Maggie. "It's time for it to go in the pans. I was late making it this morning with so many around. I've gotten a bit rusty managing so many things."

Erith watched in awe as Maggie swiftly cut off fistfuls of dough, rolled them back and forth in her palms, and placed them side by side in metal pans on the table. She covered them with dishtowels before grabbing a couple of sticks from the woodbox and throwing them in the stove. "I have to keep the heat going to rise the bread." She closed the oven door to let it heat. "If I'm not back before the bread is ready, can you put it in the oven before it rises over the pans?"

Maggie got milk from the pantry for Annie and Stephen, pulled a thin rubber tube on two glass bottles, and gave one to Erith to feed Annie while she took the boy. Annie's blue eyes regarded her as she lay on Erith's lap and sucked the thin black nipple. Her light, wispy curls were soft on Erith's arm. The girl paused and smiled between attempts to drain the bottle. Erith felt a warmth that she hadn't known before. This little thing would depend on her, and Erith would not fail in that duty. Although she was scared, she felt what must have been happiness for the first time in a long time—at least, she supposed that's what happy felt like. A tic throbbed in her cheek as she smiled at the little face. Had it been so long since she smiled that her face would react so?

Erith nodded at Maggie as she left for the second time. The woman asked George to go with her to help with the fish, but he wasn't as eager to leave as Erith expected. She played with the three children and took turns bouncing them on her knee and singing silly songs like her father had done with her. Memories of him were coming back.

She remembered the bread before it was too late and placed the pans in the oven, then put wood in the firebox, hoping to God Maggie would be back before it was baked. Erith had no idea how long to leave it in the oven. She didn't have to worry, because Maggie sent George back to remind her of the bread, and then a second time to get her to take it out and move it around in the oven.

When Erith opened the oven door, she understood why. The loaves closest to the side where the fire was burning were a little browner. She moved them around, putting the lightest where the darkest had been, and closed the oven door one more time.

She rejoined the children on the floor as the smell of fresh bread filled the air. Erith smiled again at the excited squeals of the little ones as she sang and played with them.

Maggie and George returned a short time later, bringing some codfish to fry for supper. Maggie said that Dinn usually joined them. It was easier since Kitty had died.

Once the bread was out and the browned tops glowed from the slick of butter melting on the hot surface, Maggie asked her to come to the wharf and meet everyone. Erith opened her mouth, but no words came out.

"Come on," Maggie said as she picked up Stephen. "You take Annie with you, and of course little Tommy." She smiled as she tousled the little boy's hair, a smaller replica of his brother, and reached for his hand.

In an aside to Erith on her way out the door, Maggie said that Tommy didn't talk. He hadn't tried to speak since his mother died. Erith had noticed he was quiet when she was singing but attributed it to his being shy. The little boy was hurting, and she had known that feeling when her father died. She had been older than Tommy when her mother died, so she knew, sadly, that he would surely forget her, just like she had forgotten her own mother.

Erith picked up Annie, mimicking Maggie in how she carried Stephen, and followed her to the beach. There she met the full complement of citizens. There were six men and four women in Dog Cove, and Erith struggled to put faces to the names as Maggie introduced them. Aside from Maggie and her husband, John Ryan, there were John's two brothers, Tom and William, and William's wife, Mary Lucy. One of John and Maggie's five children, Patrick, his wife, Agnes, and their three little ones were there. Maggie's brother, Fergus Power, and his wife, Mamie, stayed in Dog Cove only for the fishery and returned to St. Joseph's in the fall. Then there was Dinn Ryan, who had been married to Kitty Power from Colinet Island, and his three children. Dinn was a distant cousin of John's family and was raised by John's mother and father in Dog Cove. Dinn's sister, Kathleen, who had married Erith's father and become her stepmother, had been raised by her mother's family in North Harbour.

John and Maggie's three daughters had married fishermen in St. Joseph's and Admiral's Beach, and her youngest, Mary, married a Young in Lear's Cove on the south side of Cape St. Mary's.

Dinn was a tall man in his late thirties. He had dark, almost black hair which was receding at the temples. His face was tanned and bore the weather-beaten lines of most of the fishermen who spent their lives in harsh conditions on the water and long days in the sun. His eyes were green like Erith's stepmother's, but his seemed kinder in some way. The three brothers—John, Tom, and William—were in their late forties or early fifties. They all bore similar features—long, slender faces, dark, sunken eyes, receding hair now gone mostly grey, and skin as close to leather as she suspected anyone could get. Mamie's hair was short, and the years had not been kind to her. She had a round face full of lines and skin as hard as any of the men's. Mary Lucy was the eldest of the women, well over fifty, and hunched over from years of back-breaking work. She, like Mamie, had been hardened to the conditions. However, a painful and crippling disfigurement in her hands had set in during the latter years, which made working quite difficult.

They all greeted Erith with a word or a nod and without missing a beat from their jobs while making the fish.

Erith was determined to be useful and took the children back to Maggie's house while the rest of the community worked on the fish. Tomorrow she would try to do her share. As she walked up from the beach, she noticed a barn in the meadow, a cow, and some hens, which must have been Maggie and John's stock. Perhaps there was something she could do with them. There were two other barns in the distance and a flock of sheep. The people here were truly isolated and had to depend on each other for survival.

Erith put aside her nervousness and tended to the three smallest until Maggie came to get supper. When she arrived, Maggie cut up two large cod, dipped the pieces in flour, and fried them in fatback pork. When the last of the fish was frying, she cut up three small potatoes and layered them on the pan.

Maggie told Erith the potatoes were scarce last year, so they were trying to spare what they had until new ones from the garden were big enough to eat. The ground was rocky, and they had to work hard to expand the field for planting. The men dug the furrows on blowy days that were too bad for fishing. Due to the declining crop, they figured the seed had run its course, so Maggie's brother, Fergus, had brought two sacks, one for eating and one for planting, from St. Joseph's when he and Mamie returned to Dog Cove.

Luckily, so far, the plentiful fish combined with the sunny weather had made for a prosperous spring. If the weather held and they could keep up to the washing, curing, salting, and drying, the little community would have a chance at having a good year.

That was all they needed. They worked during the summer to survive the winter, and the cycle began anew each spring. Erith realized she was lucky not to have been dependent on things so transitory, but she supposed she had been, in a way. If the fishery had failed, then her father's dry goods store would not have prospered, and she might have been left destitute and in an orphanage somewhere. But she was here now and would be part of the community's cycle of survival. She would learn, and she would work hard. Erith was fine with that.

When John and Dinn came for supper, Erith helped Maggie set the table and place the meal before them. She watched Maggie cut perfect slices from yesterday's loaf. The fresh bread had been too pliable for the knife. Agnes came for Stephen while Erith took care of Annie, and Maggie fed the rest.

"I'll have Erith up early tomorrow morning," Maggie said to Dinn.

"That'll be just fine," he said.

"Erith can make supper for you," Maggie continued. "You can make baked beans, can't you? You can take two loaves of bread for tomorrow." She gestured toward the bread.

Erith was sure it wouldn't be hard to bake beans. She would cook and keep the children at Dinn's house and ensure he had a meal when he got home, and she would keep the kids from underfoot and pitch in where she could with the rest of the women. It might take her a few days to get in a routine, but Erith was confident. She wanted to be useful, and she needed to be busy. That was important to her.

After supper, Maggie walked with her to Dinn's house and helped get George, Tommy, and Annie ready for bed. Dinn's house was much like the others. It was a small single-storey with two bedrooms. All the children slept in one room—Annie in a crudely made cot, and the two boys in a wooden bunk attached to the wall. There was a small pantry off the kitchen near the children's room, and Dinn's room was on the opposite side. The cast-iron stove was similar to the one at her house in North Harbour, with a firebox, four dampers, an oven, and a warmer at the top. The woodbox was full. Maggie said there was wood out back if she needed it. Dinn had started the fire before going to Maggie's for supper, so the place was cozy when they arrived.

Maggie brought some bread and fish with her. There was a small wooden pail on the table which she quickly wiped out before putting two pieces of fish in the bottom. Then she cut eight slices of bread off one loaf and buttered them. She layered partridgeberry jam on each slice from a crock on the table. Keeping the jam sides together, she placed them in the pail and threw a thin dishtowel over the lot. She showed Erith the water bucket and where the staples were in the pantry. Erith had a lot to remember, but was sure she could find things in the morning. George would be there if she had questions.

Erith helped Maggie get the children settled just as her step-uncle was coming in for the night. He had barely said two words to her at all that day. Maggie told him to go on to bed. As they were leaving, Erith saw him grab the kettle and a small enamel pan from above the woodbox as he bade them good night.

It was all surreal to Erith. She was among complete strangers, yet somehow she wasn't frightened.

The last remnants of daylight painted the sky various shades of red as they carefully picked their way along the path between the houses.

"Red sky at night, sailor's delight," Maggie said absently.

In a hushed tone, she told Erith that Dinn was a quiet man who worked very hard for his family. When his wife died, he could have put the children in an orphanage but decided against it. He wanted to keep them together. Erith thought how different he must be from his sister.

At Maggie's house there was no oil for the lamp, so they got ready for bed and an early rise. Maggie said there was no pack ice, so no seals to make oil, and they wouldn't have any until the supply boat came with kerosene. Erith didn't understand this—they had always had oil for the lamps at home. She remembered how they would run out of the bottles in the store, and now she knew why.

She was tired. It had been a long, eventful day. Erith dreaded the early night—it meant the demons would have more time to taunt her.

8

It seemed she had just closed her eyes when Maggie shook her. "It's time to get up."

Erith jumped out of bed and dressed quietly, surprised and grateful that she had slept soundly. She tentatively poked her head around the door, a little apprehensive about the day. Maggie urged her into the room and made her a cup of tea and two slices of toast on the hot damper. Erith sat with Maggie and John and enjoyed the fare in the dim morning light. Conversation was easy between the couple, unlike the stiffness she was used to at home. They were friendly to her, and she found herself smiling. She slowly released her clenched belly.

John grabbed what she assumed to be a lunch bucket and said he would take her up to Dinn's with him. Dawn hadn't quite breathed across the land, and the faded light surrounded her. She suddenly felt like she was choking at the mere thought of being alone with him and Dinn.

"I'll watch from the door to make sure you don't trip," Maggie said when she noticed her hesitation.

Erith grimaced at her own fear and smiled at the woman.

John carried on ahead of her on the path and went on inside the house. Dinn was putting on his coat when they entered. He nodded a good morning. The room was warm. There was an empty cup, some bread crumbs scattered on the table, and steam coming from the kettle on the stove.

"There's milk in the pantry for Annie. If you don't find what you need, ask Maggie," Dinn said quietly before leaving with John. And with that, Erith was left to her own devices.

She sat on the wooden chair near the table and noticed that this particular piece of furniture was worse for wear, with lots of knife marks criss-crossing the surface. Twiddling her thumbs, she wondered what to do first. She didn't want to wake the children, so she sat at the table until daylight filled the room. Pushing the chair back with great care to be quiet, she rooted around the pantry to see what food was in store and checked on the dishes and the pots and pans. She would count on George if she needed something.

Erith found a cast iron pot and lid and decided she would use that to bake the beans that Maggie had suggested. She found the remnants of a ten-pound burlap sack of beans, scooped out four mugfuls, and carefully poured them into the black pot. The thought occurred to her to lay it aside until the children got up, but she continued. The beans could bake while the stove was hot. She placed the cast-iron pot in the oven and closed the door and moved to cut several slices of bread. They weren't as even around the edges as Maggie's.

She sat in silence by the table until she heard Annie stir. Was she supposed to heat the milk? Where were the diapers? Were there any clean? Erith's pulse raced, her breath came fast and shallow, and her legs began to shake when she stood up. She pushed open the bedroom door. Little Annie stood with her hands on the smooth, worn handmade rail of the cot and grinned up at her. The child put her arms up to Erith and teetered back on the thin mattress. Erith grabbed her. Her heart swelled when Annie cuddled into her shoulder and cooed.

George stirred and rubbed his eyes. He saw her and beamed. Then he poked at Tommy until he woke. Erith saw some diapers folded on a little table near the window. She awkwardly placed Annie on her back at the foot of the boys' bunk. George immediately surged ahead and kept her from squirming off while Erith tried her best to change the little girl. Her diaper was soaked. Erith asked the boys to watch their sister while she grabbed a wet cloth.

With George's help, she made toast for the boys, fed Annie, fetched and filled the washtub, and washed the diapers and the wet sheet from the cot. As she ventured to the clothesline, she noticed that Agnes and Maggie had already strung a line and were over on the beach laying out fish. She could see other clotheslines off in the distance in the other direction. They, too, were full. Maybe she wasn't doing as well as she thought.

George and Tommy raced out of the house, eager to help with the fish, and Erith waved from the doorway when they looked back. She wondered where Agnes's baby was but guessed he must be sleeping. Erith could see the white heads of Agnes's two boys, James and John, who were a little older than Tommy. They were splashing rocks in the freshwater pond at the back of the beach.

She went back inside, pulled the cot out where she could keep an eye on it, and laid Annie in, then cleaned away the dishes and filled the stove. As she worked, she contemplated how she could help and keep Annie safe in the process. She didn't relish the thought of leaving a sleeping child alone for any amount of time.

"Let's see what we can rig up for you," Erith said to the smiling child. Annie chirruped and blew some bubbles from between her lips. Erith couldn't help but smile, her mouth twitching at the sides with the unfamiliar action.

She took two of the oversized flannel squares and tied the corners together, making enough room for her own head in the newly formed hole, then pulled it on and let both diapers hang from her shoulders. After making some adjustments to the knots to accommodate the child, she took Annie from the cot and gave her some milk. When she had her wrapped snugly like she had been at Maggie's, Erith knelt by the boys' bunk and put the baby on her chest. She pushed her belly against the bed to keep Annie from falling and quickly snagged the diaper ends from behind her back, then tied the corners at her waist and tried to stand.

Annie almost rolled to the floor between the edge of the diaper and her dress. Erith adjusted the diaper, making a sort of sack for Annie to sleep in. She stood again, fixed the baby within her cocoon, and walked around the kitchen. When she was sure that Annie was safe, she pulled on her own coat, determined as ever to be of use.

When she peeked, Annie's little face was turned up toward her, and she was dozing. Erith felt her heart swell. She hadn't ever felt this way before, and she liked it. Maybe it was because her head distracted her from the events of the past few weeks, but whatever it was, she relished these new feelings. She smiled as she left the house.

All the women had gathered on the beach. George's head popped up and down, and Erith caught flashes of Tommy's crown as she walked toward the group.

"Now, boys, be careful with the fish. Any bruise and the

price will go down," Maggie said as she bent once more to tend to her work.

As Erith reached the highest point, she stopped and looked in awe at the sight before her. There were four barrows full of split codfish on the massive rocky beach. Boughs had been laid, probably weeks ago, which kept the drying cod off the rocks and allowed air to move beneath. The women and the children were taking the fish from where they were stacked head to tail on the barrows and were laying them—again, head to tail—on the boughs. Erith guessed the men must have filled the barrows that morning and carried them here for the women. She watched for a moment as they laid out the catch with speed and efficiency learned from practice. She was here and would do her part, too.

"What do you have there?" Maggie asked, glancing up.

"I wanted to help but couldn't leave Annie."

"She'd have been fine," Agnes said. "Stephen will keep till I get back. We won't be long."

Heat rose in Erith's cheeks. She wouldn't have left the child alone.

George beckoned for her to come and see what he was doing.

"Don't just stand there," Maggie said with a smile. "Come help these young lads with the fish."

Erith fixed Annie within the sling and picked some of the salted fish from the barrow.

"Don't leave room between them or we'll run out of boughs and beach," Maggie said. She told Erith that they spread the fish behind the landwash to keep any ocean spray off and to take advantage of the sun and the breeze.

"We have to mind the sun, though. If the fish gets sunburnt, then it loses price. We have to turn them over after we eat, and twice more today, then pile them back on the barrows after the men get in with the next load."

"Where do you put it all?" Erith asked. She had seen raised flakes in North Harbour with fish drying but hadn't been part of the work.

Maggie explained that the fish took about three days to dry, depending on the weather. When the men came in, their fish would already be gutted. They would cut out the backbone so that it laid flat. The women would rinse it, the men would layer it with coarse salt in one of the stages where the fish would cure for a couple of days, and then the women would wash out the excess salt and lay it on the beach to dry. Maggie pointed to where the newest fish was drying on the landwash.

"This fish will be made after today," Maggie said. She pointed to another weather-worn stage and explained that it would be stored there with the fish that was already dried to perfection. They would pile it on the barrows and cover it with an old sheet until the men took it in. Sometimes, if the men were out all day or made a second trip, the women would take half-loads back to the stage and store it away.

Erith marvelled at how hard they worked, all the while taking care of the children and the household. Before too long, her back was aching, and the diaper which held Annie at her chest was cutting into her neck. She asked Maggie to tie the child tighter to her to get some relief, then checked to see that Annie was sleeping soundly. The boys gravitated toward her and helped her with her tasks. Maggie and Agnes worked swiftly, at least twenty to her one, while Agnes's two boys played on the rocks nearby.

With the fish done, Erith headed back to the house. Agnes

said she had bread rising and had to put it in pans, and Maggie had to do the same. Embarrassed, Erith asked if one of them would be willing to show her how to make bread, and Maggie said she planned to do just that on the next wet day.

Annie woke, and Erith changed the little one and fed her. George ran in and said Maggie had fish and invited her for the meal, so Erith filled the firebox, took Annie, and followed the boy. Agnes was there with Stephen. Just then, George glanced out the window and said the boats were coming in. Erith stayed back so the others could go out and tend to the fish.

She cleaned the dishes, played with the babies, and put them on Maggie's bed for a nap. From the gallery, she watched the community at work. Maggie's husband and son were first to land, and Dinn would be last, since he fished alone. The boats were full, but it was soon done with great efficiency, and the women headed to the beach to turn the drying cod.

"I'll look after Stephen. You go on," Erith said as Agnes came toward the house. The woman waved her thanks and trailed off behind Maggie. Tommy and George didn't follow, choosing instead to watch their father at work. They were eager to help but knew not to get in the way.

Erith put the dough in the bread pans. Her sticky hands made humps and hollows on the buns. They weren't as round and smooth as Maggie would have made them, but she got the job done. She called out to George to come back while she ran to Dinn's to check on the beans. She had almost forgotten them and was sure the fire had gone out.

When she opened the door, a curtain of smoke met her. It tumbled out around her and in her face. She coughed and gagged, stepped back, lost her footing, and toppled over the steps, trying to turn and catch herself on the wooden rail. Before she could blink, she was looking up at a pair of rubber boots rushing past her into the house.

Erith shoved her forearms under herself just as Maggie grabbed her shoulder.

"Are you all right, child?"

Before Erith could answer, Dinn came back out the door with the smoking pot of beans. John was behind him, flapping a dishtowel in the air to clear the smoke.

"What happened?" Maggie asked.

"The water must have boiled off the beans," Dinn said.

"Water!" Erith said awkwardly.

Maggie looked at her. "You never added pork and water?" She paused a moment when realization set in. "You've never cooked beans before? My God, dear, what did Kathleen teach you?"

"She wouldn't let me in the kitchen," Erith mumbled under her breath.

Maggie grabbed Erith's shoulders and stared at her. "Why did she send you here, Erith?"

"To be rid of me, as near as I can figure," Erith said matter-of-factly. Maggie's grip relaxed as the words sank in.

"That'll do, Maggie. No harm done," Dinn said simply. He pitched the burnt mass into the rushers alongside the house. Erith cringed as each bean hit like a cannonball. "I don't think the hens will eat these," he said in a lighter tone.

"Probably kill the lot of them," Maggie said jokingly. She pulled Erith into an awkward embrace. "You scared me. This old heart of mine can't take that, you know." She grinned this time as she released Erith and patted her ample bosom.

The men emerged from the house, clearing most of the smoke ahead of them.

"I'm sorry," Erith said. She hung her head and blushed as they silently paraded in front of her and back to the wharf. Dinn laid the steaming pot on the step and followed behind them.

"I'll have George bring a couple of salmon," he said to Maggie.

"Looks like you'll all be eating at our house," Maggie said. Then she burst out laughing.

"I'm useless, Maggie! I'm sorry." Erith was mortified at just how little value she brought to the place.

"Don't be a fool. Everyone must learn. The first time I made beans, we were eating them for a week." Maggie started up the steps and beckoned for her to follow. "Help me open the windows and let the wind blow through, or the youngsters won't sleep here tonight."

And there was no more to it than that. Her stepmother would surely have screamed at her and never let her forget her mistake.

9

The merchant boat came the next day, and the men spent the day unloading provisions—casks of molasses, barrels of pork, sacks of flour, potatoes, beans, fishing gear, kerosene, linseed oil, and a few other necessities. Once the goods were on the beach, they began to load the dried fish.

Erith helped the women turn fish, but mostly she kept the children out of the way of the men. The women weren't part of the men's business. Erith could hear raised voices on times but wasn't sure what was going on.

Mary Lucy hobbled across the beach toward them. "Looks like the merchant is trying to undercut the price of the fish. He says there's plenty, and he won't get a good price."

"John said he was afraid this would happen. Every year there's always something that brings it down," Maggie said.

Mary Lucy looked at Erith. "Last time we were treated fairly was when your father was doing the dealing."

Erith didn't know what to say. She hardly knew anything about what her father had done before he died.

"That's right," said Maggie. "Ask any of the men, and they'll tell you."

"I don't know much about my father," Erith said after a long pause.

"A fine man," Mary Lucy said. "A fine man, indeed."

Maggie pointed to an old boat that was rotting on the beach. "See that boat, Erith? Your father gave that to Dinn when he married Kathleen. Dinn was fishing with John. Patrick was going to join his father, which would leave little for Dinn, who was hoping to marry as well. Your father brought the boat and just gave it to him. Put Dinn well ahead, he did."

"Really?"

"Yes, and wouldn't take no pay for it, either," Maggie said with a faraway look in her eye. "The boat has since outlived its usefulness, but the men leave it there as a sign of better times and fair-minded men. The community would have been finished back then, but your father believed in what was reasonable and helped us all prosper. He traded well. He was a good man."

Erith felt a sudden pride that reinforced what she had always believed about her father.

"Now, for the most part, seems we almost always have just enough for supplies but not much more. No matter what the circumstance. Not many like your father," Maggie concluded as she bent over the fish.

They all went back to work in silence.

10

When the pantries were full in Dog Cove, the flakes and stages were empty. That was the cycle in every village on the coast. The boat would return in another month or so, and the men would get paid or trade for new gear. By the last run of the season, they would spend all their money and barter the last of the fish to buy provisions to last out the winter. Then came the hungry month of March, before spring renewed her covenant with the earth, and it started all over again.

There was no fish to tend that evening, and the women made pies to go along with supper. Maggie showed Erith how to mix the pastry. Erith rolled and decorated the pies in the pans with the last of the previous year's blueberry jam, and they smelled delicious.

Tommy and George spent the afternoon in the garden with their father, and Erith kept Annie with her. At suppertime they had a stew of fresh meat simmering in the black iron pot, and Erith made the pastry for the top with the new can of baking powder and some direction from Maggie. The mood was light at the table that evening. John told Maggie about the merchant's claim that he had too much fish. He and Dinn talked about the gardens and the weather while the children waited in anticipation for the pies and the fresh cream.

"Fine supper, Maggie," Dinn said as he took the last bite.

"Erith made the pastry," she answered.

"And a fine one it was," John said.

Erith blushed at the praise which was so foreign to her. She smiled.

"Can we have pie now?" asked George.

Erith cut the pie in pieces and handed slices around the table while Maggie retrieved the bowl of cream from the pantry. George had his pie gone before she got back.

"Can I have some more?"

Dinn ruffled his hair and grinned. "You have to ask Erith."

George looked at her and smiled. "Can I, please?"

Dinn nodded when she glanced his way.

"Of course, you can."

Erith cut off another slice and laid it on his plate.

"Erith made these pies, too," said Maggie.

"It's the best pie I've ever had," said George, rather eagerly.

They all laughed. Dinn picked up a forkful and nodded at her once more. "It is good pie."

Erith blushed again. "Maggie gets the credit. She showed me how to do it."

Maggie laughed. "You're well able to do it, my dear. You have a knack for baking."

"I like it," said Erith. Her face reddened from the attention.

After supper, the men went out and sat on the step. Dinn took Annie with him, and the boys played around their feet. Erith helped Maggie with the dishes. Maggie said she would show her how to milk the cow in the morning. There were so many things to learn, and Erith realized just how sheltered she had been from real life. She didn't know if that was a blessing or a curse.

The next day, Sunday, was a day of rest. The sun brazenly fought the morning fog back to the mists of the bay while Erith watched from the gallery at Maggie and John's. The door was still barred at Dinn's house, and there was no smoke in the chimney. Maggie spoke behind her. "They won't be up around for another spell. Come in and eat some toast."

Erith wasn't feeling the best. Hunger pangs were making her stomach feel unsettled. She turned and followed Maggie back into the house. The older lady buttered some toast for Erith, and they enjoyed a cup of tea together. Soon after, George and Tommy burst in, followed by Dinn, who was carrying Annie. Maggie set them up with toast and tea.

"Next week I'll have bread for you," Erith said.

"No rush," Maggie and Dinn said simultaneously.

"Where's John?" Dinn asked.

"He's gone with Patrick, looking to see where they can clear some more ground for gardens," Maggie replied. "Mind you, they won't put a shovel in the ground today but will be ready for the next blowy day."

Dinn left to find them, George and Tommy close on his heels. Agnes came in with Stephen.

"Thought we might take the children on a picnic after dinner, if you want to come," said Agnes.

"Where are we going?" Erith asked.

"Just on the other side of the pond. It's a good day for swimming."

"Swimming?" Erith hadn't done that before.

"We go every Sunday when we can," Agnes said. "I'll show you how."

"Don't worry, the men don't go," Maggie said. "I'll watch the little ones while you're in the water with the boys."

"It's great fun," said Agnes. "The men usually have a nap, and we get out of their way."

After dinner, they marched off across the beach and circled around to a grassy clearing on the back of the pond. The sun was hot, and the water was shallow. The four boys undressed to their underclothes and jumped in the water. Agnes unbuttoned her dress and joined them. Her frock and stockings were wet within seconds. Erith was apprehensive but finally gave in after Maggie and Agnes pestered her. The children kept calling for her to join them.

When her toes touched the water, she shouted, "It's cold!"

"No, it's not," Agnes said. She ducked down so that only her head was above water. "Just get wet."

Erith went as far as her knees and stood there with her arms folded around herself. That was as brave as she got the first week. The boys giggled and splashed but were careful not to get her wet. She spent the rest of the day on the bank, talking with Maggie and watching Agnes play in the water with the little ones. They ate pieces of pie, then returned home when the sun was getting low. Maggie hashed together the couldn's—what couldn't be eaten at dinner—and fried it on the stove. They ate the fare accompanied by buttered bread. After the meal, they all went out and sat on the step, and the rest of the men and women gathered there that evening.

John and Dinn each had a tin whistle, and William had a fiddle. They played a few slow and lonesome tunes that Erith hadn't heard before. Maggie sang a song about a sailor and his true love. Erith was not accustomed to this type of gathering. When the music picked up in speed, several of the women grabbed hands and circled around on the dirt in the lane below the step. They whirled and twirled, first one way and then the other, laughing and giggling as they followed the beat of the music. William and Tom leaped up from their chairs and ducked under the arms of the women, entering the middle of the circle, where they faced each other and step-danced. The circle continued to flow one way, and then the other around them in the opposite direction.

Erith watched the gaiety and felt an unfamiliar warmth from the happiness in this little place. Suddenly, Maggie called to her. George tapped her hand and tugged her toward the women, where she joined between Mamie and Agnes and was pulled into the excitement. She couldn't help but smile as she was dragged into the circle of dancing women. She laughed aloud when the two men merged with the circle and began swinging the women around. The whistle continued its merry tune, and Erith shrieked with glee as Tom took her by the waist, swinging her off her feet. The music ended with everyone laughing and panting for breath. There was a moment's reprieve before the next song began.

Erith was intoxicated by the music and laughter. She even took George and Tommy in the middle of the circle to dance. Their eyes sparkled with joy when they were able to imitate the men. They hugged her skirts amid their squeals of delight when the song was over, and Erith bent to gather them close. There were a few more dances and songs before everyone dispersed for the night. Dinn fetched Annie, and Agnes retrieved Stephen from where they had been sleeping on Maggie's bed.

Agnes joined her husband and sons, and they waved good night. Then it was over.

These people, with so little, had so much. That was the last thing Erith remembered thinking before sleep overtook her. She slept soundly that night and woke with a smile on her face before Maggie came to get her up.

That week, Maggie showed her how to bake bread. She took on cooking various dishes and learned to milk the cow and collect the eggs at the barn. The following Sunday she even went in the water, and two Sundays later, she swam a few strokes before she sank beneath the surface.

When high winds and rain kept the men on shore for three days, Maggie told Erith she needed to make oil clothes for Dinn. She could follow Maggie's guidance as she made the same garments for John. The men brought last year's suits from the stage. The yellowed clothing stank, and though the men washed them off regularly, they were filthy.

"We'll use them for sizes and then get them out of the house," said Maggie. "John, you forgot the linkum."

John ran back to the stage and was back in a few minutes with the oddest-looking thing that Erith had ever seen.

"What's that?"

"A linkum," said Maggie.

"Yes, but what is it?"

Maggie put it on her head. "A hat to keep the rain off."

"Oh. But what's that big flap on the back for?" Erith asked.

"Well, you'll see when we're making the suits. Most of the stitching is in the shoulders and around the neck. The flap keeps the water from getting in through the seams. It's not easy to make the seams tight."

Erith slowly nodded her head. She took the hat from Maggie's head and ran her hands over it. "This isn't like the wax cloth my stepmother sold a few years ago."

"I'm sure Kathleen ordered the special cloth when the fishing was good. She'd take advantage of either bit of extra money going around." Maggie said. "This, my dear, is made from flour sacks."

"Really? I didn't know that flour sacks could keep the rain out."

"Of course they can't. That's why we have linseed oil. After we make the clothes, when the weather is good we'll boil them in oil over on the beach."

"And that makes them tight?"

"Yes, it keeps the rain off. The oil turns the clothes a bit yellow, but it works fine."

Erith was a good seamstress. She had learned it in school and practised by making her own frocks and undergarments. Once they had the clothes cut out, she had her pants and coat finished before Maggie, and she made the linkum for John and Dinn. She was proud of her work and stitched a "D" in Dinn's clothes and, at Maggie's insistence, a "J" in John's. Maggie showed them off to the other women, who also had made similar garments.

The next day, there was good drying on fish, and the wind was off the land. They made in a fire on the beach under the bark kettle. Maggie explained that it saved on the oil if they all boiled together.

"Where did the large iron pot come from, Maggie?" Erith asked. She was astounded by the size of it.

"That's the bark kettle," Maggie said. When she saw the bewildered look in Erith's eyes, she continued. "That's kept in the stagehead over there." Maggie pointed toward the shack on the wharf. "We collect buds and bark from the spruce and fir trees on the ridge three or four times during the fishing season. The men add water and boil the pot for the whole morning. Then they dip their nets, traps, and lines in the mix for a little boil time in the dark water. After that they hang them on the fences or on the rocks to dry. It keeps the nets from getting mouldy."

"Oh," said Erith.

"It makes the gear last longer. The sea practically eats it, otherwise," Maggie continued. "Dinn and John set it up for us this morning so that we could boil the clothes."

It was a true community effort. All the women gathered, taking turns keeping the fire in and stirring the clothing. At midday, with driftwood in hand, they took the items out of the oil and laid them on the beach to dry. By the evening, the coats, hats, and pants would be cured. Erith was astonished to see that the clothing was so pliable. She expected it to be stiff, but it was easier to handle than the wax cloth her stepmother had sold.

The next rainy day, she was at Maggie's, showing George his letters on a brown paper bag, when Agnes came in. The woman looked on as Erith helped George write his name, Tommy's, and Annie's. Then she showed him how to make Agnes's name. Agnes slowly traced the letters with her finger.

"Can I try?" she asked.

Erith pushed the paper and pencil toward her. Agnes slowly made the strokes of the "A," and Erith fixed the pencil in her hand.

"It'll be easier if you hold it this way," she said softly.

Agnes smiled. "I've never made my name before."

"You can have the pencil," George said as he went off to play with Tommy.

"You're not getting away that easily, young man," Erith said with a smile. George didn't want to learn anything about writing—he thought it was better to play and learn everything about fishing.

"Take your time, Agnes, you're doing well," Erith said. "I could teach you some more, if you wanted."

"Really? That's very kind of you."

"Nonsense! You taught me to swim, so I'll teach you how to write."

Agnes stopped the pencil's movement in the middle of the "e." "I guess there's no need of me learning the letters."

"You don't know when it'll come in handy," said Erith. "The evenings are long. We can do it then."

"I've always wanted to know how to write."

"That's it, then. We can start whenever you want."

Erith was excited. She could finally contribute without having to be told or shown what to do. Agnes was smart and learned very quickly. They used up every scrap of paper they could find. The next time the merchant came for the fish, Patrick surprised his wife with a writing tablet and a pencil of her own.

Erith and Agnes grew close. One sunny day, while they were alone under the trees by the pond, Agnes asked Erith how to make Patrick's name. Agnes beamed when she saw his name on her brown paper.

"He'll be so impressed when he sees his name," she said. "And I did it."

Erith suddenly blurted out, "Agnes, what's it like to have a husband?"

"That's a strange question."

Erith blushed. "I'm sorry. I shouldn't have asked."

"It's all right, Erith. I guess you didn't have sisters you could talk to about it. I'm lucky. Me and Patrick are happy. He's a good man. He's a good provider."

Erith nodded. "You look so . . . happy."

"I am. We don't have much. We struggle sometimes, but we all have each other here in Dog Cove."

Erith felt a sudden rush of tears, and she gulped to squelch them. Agnes, seeing her distress, laid aside her pencil and paper and embraced her.

"Erith, what's wrong?"

"I don't know. I can't help myself." She couldn't hold back the sobs. Agnes smoothed her hair, whispering words of consolation and holding her until she was spent.

"Where's this coming from? Do you miss home?"

"No, no. Nothing like that."

"What is it, then?"

Erith simply wept as Agnes held her.

"Erith, we know something happened to you on the way here. Is it that?"

Crying harder now, Erith slowly nodded. She felt the embarrassment and the shame surface once more when Agnes confirmed that they all knew.

Finally, Erith said, "I see you and Patrick, and Maggie and John, and everyone else here. I think this is how it should be. Then I see the faces of those two men almost every night in my dreams. I fear they'll be here in the morning, or they'll come when the men are fishing, and they'll hurt me or you or one of the other women . . ."

Agnes grabbed her shoulders and held her at arm's length. She smiled at Erith. "Can you see anyone coming here and going up against Maggie?"

"Why couldn't I be strong like that? Why couldn't I fight harder? Why couldn't I run away?"

"Erith, you did what you could. You can't change that now. You didn't give up. Now look at you, mothering those three little children, working alongside of all of us. You are strong, Erith. You need to believe that."

They heard Patrick calling to them. Agnes got up and went to meet him, allowing Erith time to splash water on her face.

As one week tumbled into the next, Erith grew tired. She worked hard, side by side with the women, but she was exhausted at the end of the day and was thankful to get to bed early every night. Some nights she didn't dream, but others sent her in a panic until she would wake up and realize that she was safe. She wasn't eating much, and she grew thinner. Her sunken features worried Maggie, but Erith told her that she felt just fine.

11

"Erith, you're having a baby." Maggie's words penetrated her skull with the force of an axe.

"It can't be." But Maggie had confirmed what Erith feared. She had felt changes in her body. She had been tempted to ask Agnes questions but was afraid to say the words out loud. Like saying them would change her fate. Erith had prayed for it not to be true. She had even thought about letting the sea take her when she was walking the beach one day. It would have been so easy to just walk out into the foam. But she couldn't do it.

Now she fell back on the chair and put her face in her palms. "Oh, Maggie. What am I going to do?"

Maggie's stern tone surprised her and brought her from her self-pity. "You can't stay here. It'll be the death of you. You hear me? You can't stay here. Your uncle Dinn needs the help, but he doesn't need this. He won't stand for it. You'll have to go home before the winter comes and before Dinn finds out."

"What'll I tell him, Maggie? I can't just leave," Erith stammered. "What about those dear little children?"

"He has enough mouths to feed. He can't take on you and

a baby. He knows you're sick. Tell him you have to see about a doctor. The children will be fine. We'll all have time to look out for them now that the fishing's almost over."

Maggie was more of a mother to her than anything else. Erith trusted her. According to Maggie, homes were left motherless from winters bearing children, and it wasn't too many who could handle the isolation of such a small place. Erith put her hand on her stomach. Although she knew Maggie was right, she felt somehow discarded once again.

"I don't know that my stepmother will have me back, especially like this."

"I know she's been cruel to you, Erith. But she has to take you in."

"Why would you say that?"

"Your father left the business and the house to you upon his death. Your stepmother agreed to look after you until you came of age, and then the business was to be yours."

"How do you know that?"

"You might not remember, but me and John were witnesses at the wedding," Maggie said. "Your father was going to sea, and he wanted to be assured of your future in case anything happened to him. So, he married Kathleen on the condition that she fulfill his wishes. We marked an 'X' on papers that laid it out."

"Really, Maggie? I didn't know that."

"Why would you? Kathleen wouldn't have said. She probably did away with the papers and thinks we don't remember. But me and John were there and would swear to it."

Erith was devastated to learn she would have to leave, but she knew Maggie wouldn't give her bad counsel. The supply boat would be there in two days, so she had two days to break the news to Dinn and the children.

12

She looked back at the scene on the wharf as Tommy stood with his head hung low, crying, holding his father's hand. Annie was snuggled in the crook of his other arm. Maggie and John were linked, arm in arm—Maggie was stoic and straight, but Erith knew the woman would miss her. Agnes waved a tearful goodbye as Patrick consoled her. The rest of the men and women at the back waved and wished her well.

George was the most pitiful of all. He stood on the beach by the wharf, then started to run along the shore as the boat was pulling away. "Erith, come back! Please come back, Erith! Please!" He was crying and shouting to her while following the boat's progress, until he collapsed where the shore met the cliffs. Erith tried not to let him see her cry and managed to hold it in until they were all out of sight. She hadn't been in Dog Cove long, but she felt like it was the first time she belonged anywhere. Maggie, the children, and everyone else had made it a real home for her. She smiled in Dog Cove. She laughed in Dog Cove. She wanted to come back to Dog Cove more than she wanted anything else.

Only Maggie and Agnes knew why she had to leave. Dinn had understood when she told him she was sick and needed to visit a doctor. Tommy and George had cried while she sat on the floor at their house and held them. "I'll be back with you. I just have to go for a little while."

Tommy squeezed her. George held her face in his hands and said, "I love you, Erith. I loved my mama and she left, but she couldn't promise to come back." His little eyes, full of anguish, were riveted on hers. "Will you promise?"

Erith slowly lifted her hands and held his face in between her palms, and his tears leaked out between her fingers as she said, "I promise! I'm not leaving you. I'm just going for a little while. I'll be back after the winter. You have my solemn promise."

He hugged her neck as hard as he could and cried until Dinn finally had to pull him away from her. Dinn didn't say a word.

She couldn't say out loud that she loved those little ones, but she knew in her heart that she did. To say the words and leave would have been too much for them . . . and too much for her.

As she stood on the deck, the salty breeze ruffled the hem of her red coat and wafted around the fringes of the scarf loosely tied around her bowed head. She realized that she had been scared the day she came to Dog Cove, and now she was leaving there terrified.

13

Present day, March 1894

The wind blew bitterly cold as Erith stared at her stepmother's coffin being lowered. Kathleen Lock was buried with the five Sorrowful Mysteries of the Rosary at the graveside. A Mass of Christian burial would be held when the Roman Catholic priest came through later in the spring. There were a few mourners, and, as was customary, all the fishermen stayed ashore until it was over. The man was here, too. She knew he caught her looking his way, but she couldn't help herself. Her stepmother's words kept playing over and over in her mind.

She's alive, you know.

Could it be possible? The accident had been real. She had heard some of the townsfolk talk about Father Fleming's death. Nobody dared mention the baby. Her stepmother told her that little Beatrice had been in the carriage when it plummeted into the river. How could she still be alive?

But there was risk in hope, especially when it burrowed deep into her core and echoed the longing in her heart. She didn't know if she had the courage to chase what could be a fleeting falsehood, but she didn't know if she had the strength or the fortitude to stop herself from a possible elusive pursuit. Either way, she was probably damned. Either way, it was most assuredly too late.

There was only one thing she knew to do. She would ask the man Mary Rourke knew, Danol Cooper, to help her. She had heard he was some sort of police officer in Boston before moving to the south side of North Harbour. Surely he would know how to find out if Beatrice was alive. Erith was grasping for anything that would make it real. She was prepared to face her own underlying fears in the bargain. This search was not about her but about her baby girl.

She waited patiently for Mrs. Patsy and Mrs. Helen to leave. Both women had accompanied her home after the funeral and had gotten her something to eat. Erith hadn't been hungry but accepted their generosity. Mrs. Lucy's daughter had been helping in the store while her stepmother was sick. She would be back again tomorrow. For today, Erith was alone.

When both women had disappeared over the little hill on the path down the harbour, she closed the door and headed along the shore in the opposite direction. She would cross on the ice between the points, as was usual for livyers on both sides of the harbour at this time of the year.

The ice had partially formed on the harbour near the mouth of the river in late November and would break up in the next few weeks. However, a couple of the Ryans, Whalens, and Danol Cooper had crossed the ice for her stepmother's service, so Erith was sure it was safe. She had never crossed before but figured it was safest where it was narrowest. Mr. Cooper was building a house near the point on the south side. She wished she had spoken to him earlier at the graveyard, but he hadn't given her his condolences. She should have asked to meet with him, but she didn't want anyone to know what she was up to.

Erith was glad she had worn her woollen mittens and winter coat. She still sported the traditional black blouse and skirt of the mourning because she hadn't brought many outfits with her from St. John's. She hadn't planned on being here that long.

Although the day was relatively calm, the north wind had a bite to it, and the long skirts and woollen stockings helped keep her legs warm as she picked her way out the beach toward the point. Loose rocks had iced over when the tide was high earlier in the day. The tide had gone down since, and some slob ice chunks lay stranded on the beach, waiting for the wash to free them once again.

Erith wasn't paying much attention to anything around her. She was thinking back to the day her life had once again been shattered. Unconsciously, she put her hands over her ears to keep from hearing the words *That baby is dead* coming from Kathleen's stern lips, then the door slamming shut in the room to signal that that was the end of it as her stepmother left. She hadn't gotten over that. Now, maybe it had all been a lie. Still, she didn't know how that could be. Her stepmother had given Beatrice to the priest, who was taking her to the orphanage. The priest and Beatrice had been killed on the way there.

Kathleen Lock's cruelty knew no end, even in death. But if there was one chance, then Erith had to know. She almost tripped in the ladder on the beach before she saw it. A short distance away, on the other side of the ice, she saw a similar ladder, which would take her up on the beach on the south side of the harbour. She noticed a few rocks scattered on the ice and figured someone must have been testing its thickness.

Erith's mind flashed to the day she saw the two points from high on the ridge. They looked so close then, almost touching. Now, as she put her first foot on the wooden rungs, the far shore seemed to move out of reach. Or maybe her mind was trying to tell her to leave things alone—that her search was in vain. Did she really want to bring back all the pain?

Carefully, she clambered her way from the ladder onto the ice. If she counted one hundred steps, she would surely be at the ladder on the far side. She hadn't done anything like this before, but then, her life had taken so many strange turns over the last few years that she knew anything was possible. She pulled her cap over her ears and started to count as she looked down at her shoes.

Concentrating as she counted out loud, she became vaguely aware of two things: the sound of water running, and a man shouting at her. She looked up to see a man waving his arms and shouting.

"Twenty-two, twenty-three, twenty-fo—"

As she laid her foot on the ice, she heard a cracking sound and saw the ice split apart. The fracture spiralled around her. Before she could react, she sensed the shift as the pan of ice shattered, and it dumped her unceremoniously into the frigid ocean. She felt the cold grey water grab hold of her and pull her down through a symphony of bubbles. She had escaped for the last time. Her stepmother had come to take her.

Sinking, disoriented, her mouth opened from the shock of the freezing water. Her lungs contracted and sent air to meet the brackish insurgence somewhere in her throat. She couldn't right herself. Erith looked through the bubbles for an escape. There was a tug-of-war between her body and her clothing as she glimpsed a bright light in the distance. She was grateful to have learned how to swim, but she was not that strong. Her lungs battled for air as she kicked her feet and pulled with her cupped and mitted hands toward the light. She surfaced in time to spit and then gulp a breath of air. Instantly, she was dragged under once again, but this time she knew which way was up. She kicked—at least, her brain instructed her legs to move—but her body suddenly became warm, and her strength and limbs wouldn't answer with the force she demanded.

Stepmother, you'll not have me!

She struggled one last time toward the jagged hole. As she came up a second time, she threw herself forward onto the hazy glass ice pan and clapped her mitts onto the surface. The wool stuck fast to the shiny, wet surface, and Erith clenched her thumb and fingers together to hang on for dear life. She gasped and spat out salt water as she tried to get her bearings. A man was crawling toward her, pushing a ladder along before him. He was shouting at her, but she couldn't hear because of the thunderous sound of her heart beating through the cold liquid rushing in her ears.

Erith was in a precarious situation. She tried to kick, but her skirts were weighing her down, and the movement was causing the ice to crack farther. She struggled to hold on, but her hands were becoming numb, her mind was dulling, and her will alone was not enough.

She heard her father telling her to be strong, that she was a big girl now. Suddenly, she was four again and nursing a bang on her knee. She tried to kick, but her legs wouldn't answer the plea. Then her father grabbed her arms and started to pull on her, helping her out of the water. He was saying something. He was reaching past her. She felt a hand at her waist.

"Those skirts will drown you," her father said. She felt the hand tug on the waistband of her skirt. It wasn't her father. It was Noftle. Erith screamed, but her hands were trapped. She couldn't help herself. Noftle had her two hands covered and his other hand at her waist. Suddenly, the heaviness of her skirt was gone. She felt a hand grab the petticoat and the back of her jacket and then knew she was being pitched onto the ice. Her mittens remained frozen to the surface near the hole. She tried to fight—she believed she knew what she was up against this time—but her body wouldn't co-operate.

"Miss Lock! Calm yourself or you'll kill us both!"

Erith swiped at the mass of wet hair in her eyes and pushed back her cap, which had somehow remained pinned on her head. It was Danol Cooper lying on the ice next to her. Brought back to the present, she instinctively calmed when their eyes met. He was trying to save her. Before her mind could catch up, he rolled her, face down, onto the ladder and started to shimmy toward the land, pulling the ladder along with him.

"I have you. I have you," he repeated in a low and calming tone as he held her gaze. She stared at him, unable to move, silent as he snaked his way back to shore.

Here the ice was much darker, so he stood and grabbed both Erith and the ladder at the same time. Before Erith could say anything, he bolted toward the beach with her under one arm and the ladder under the other. He threw the ladder ahead of him where the ice met the beach and quickly made land. His surefootedness was remarkable.

He stood her before him and deftly undid the buttons of her soggy coat, then threw his own around her. She couldn't feel her feet and realized her shoes were full of water and were slipping on the ice-covered rocks.

"I have to warm you," he said as he swept her off her feet, into his arms, and scaled the beach toward his big house on the hill. Her mind began to function again as the heat from his coat and his body penetrated through the arctic chill that coursed through her veins.

The house, a two-storey bright yellow house with four windows across the top floor, was a massive place by all accounts. It had three chimneys, something unheard of in these parts. Six windows stood along the front on the main floor facing the ocean, and a large gallery wound clear around.

Erith went from awe to trepidation as he climbed the steps. She struggled to free herself from the tomb that encased her, panicking at the mere thought of being alone with a man and nobody else around. She wouldn't cry for fear he would see her weakness.

Breathe, Erith, breathe. She had to think, but she couldn't get free. All she had were words.

"Put me down, you big lout," she commanded. Her confidence was betrayed by a quiver.

"Now, that's gratitude for you," Danol said under his breath.

"I'm grateful, but I want to go home," she replied.

"I'll take you home once you get warmed up and dry. I have a fire going." He pulled open the door and stepped inside the porch.

Erith was stricken. She struggled in his arms, and he almost lost her on the floor.

"What's wrong with you, woman? I'm bringing you in by the fire."

Danol held her like a rag doll, her weight of little consequence to him. He took long strides across the room toward a large stone fireplace and placed Erith in an armchair close to the hearth. A pool of water on the planks near the door led to where she now sat. She bundled his coat closer around her, slipped out of her shoes, and gathered her legs beneath the thin layers of her petticoat. Her long, wiry locks were tangled around her face, and her cap was dripping icy water.

Danol reached forward, grabbed the cap, and threw it on the stone ledge near the fire. Erith had instinctively cowered. She heard a sodden plop, then hisses, as water droplets landed on the flames, but she would not be distracted by such trivial things and stared at the man before her. His vibrant blue eyes reflected the light from the fireplace as he towered over her.

"We need to warm you," he stated matter-of-factly. He reached for his coat, but she withdrew into the chair.

"Don't you touch me," she shouted hysterically.

He pulled back. "Why are you shouting?"

"Don't you touch me," she said. This time her words were a little calmer but still carried a hint of venom.

He held up his hands and backed away. "Look, you're soaking wet beneath my coat. You're cold. Your face is blue, and your teeth are chattering. You have to get warm."

"I don't need your help."

"That's yet to be seen."

"I'm fine."

"You think you're fine."

Erith stopped speaking. To her dismay, he was right. She couldn't feel the heat from the fire through the coat, she was sitting in water, and she was freezing. Her soaking clothes were probably painted on her, but she would be damned if she was taking off the coat in front of him. By God, she was alone here with a man, and half her clothes were gone! Fear settled on her heart, and she glanced around for an escape. How would she get out of there if things were to go bad for her?

"Miss Lock, I'm going to go fetch a dry shirt and some quilts for you. I can tell you don't want to be here, but there's nowhere for you to go in your condition."

Erith nodded her understanding.

"I'll bank the wood on the fire so you can dry yourself off, and then I'll leave you to do whatever you need to do to get warm."

Danol quickly went upstairs and returned with two quilts and two flannel shirts. He handed them to her, his raised eyebrows telling her that he expected her to take them.

"Get out of those clothes as soon as you can, and wrap yourself in the quilts near the fire. The sooner, the better. I have to change out of these wet things and will be down when you say so. Shout if you need something." He turned and headed for the stairs one more time. It was only then she realized that he was wet through. He had risked his life for her.

Erith knew he was trying to make her feel at ease. Her teeth clicked together as shivers coursed through her. She could feel the heat from the fire on her face, but it still wasn't penetrating through the soaking layers. Water was trickling from her unruly hair and making icy trails down her neck and under the coat. This was probably the one time she wished she hadn't rebelled against her stepmother's influence of wearing her hair in a tight bun. She could hear Danol moving around upstairs and was reluctant to change her clothes, but her body began to shudder.

"You'll stay up there till I'm ready, right?" she asked tentatively.

"On my honour," came the reply from above.

Without giving herself time to think, she threw off the coat, gathered one of the quilts around her back, and bent over to remove her shirt. The quilt would keep her out of view if he changed his mind. The beige and brown upholstery of the chair showed the damp outline of her body. Her clothes were still drenched, and her blouse was stuck to her skin and difficult to remove. Her fingers shook uncontrollably as she undid the buttons. The quilt felt heavy, but she wouldn't remove it. Steam began to rise from the patchwork.

"I can come down and get you a towel for your hair and a cup of warm tea. But only when you ask," she heard him say. There was a pause, and then he said, "Just so you know, I'm cold, too."

"I'm going as fast as I can," she retorted. She was frustrated with the blouse. Finally, it came unbuttoned. She looked at the stairs once, threw the quilt from her back, and quickly got out of the blouse and petticoat and into his shirt, then layered the second one on over it. Though they were wet, she kept her stockings on, because he had not given her anything to cover her legs. Erith quickly balled her clothes together and laid them near the fire. She trod on the wet quilt, picked up the other one, and threw it around her. Choosing not to sit in the chair again, she moved to the hearth and sat on the warmed stone.

"You can come down now."

She heard the thump of his feet on the floor above her and then on the stairs, but he didn't come back the way he had gone up. Erith was confused when she heard the scrape of the kettle on the cast iron of the stove somewhere out of view. She was startled when he spoke from the doorway behind her. He had surely heard her gasp.

"Sorry. I came down the back steps to the kitchen. The house is big enough for two sets of stairs."

Erith turned to face him. Danol was wearing a black and red plaid flannel shirt under an off-white cable knit sweater. He wore black pants, and his feet were bare. Erith just stared at him.

"What?" he asked. He looked down at his attire. "I have wool socks in the warmer for us both."

Danol disappeared again and returned with two wooden chairs and stood them in front of the fireplace, gesturing for her to sit on one. "It's better to face the heat. It'll warm your bones." He was acting as if this was something he did every day.

Erith was wary of the whole situation, and like most days, she was devising a means of getting away if she needed. Her mind was getting foggy, and she was suddenly exhausted. She wouldn't sit on that chair—she liked being able to see the whole room.

He brought her a towel for her hair, and then another when he realized that she had more hair than the towel could dry. Next, Danol brought out two steaming mugs and laid them on the stone before the fire. He left the room again and returned with two pairs of grey woollen socks. Sitting on one of the wooden chairs, he pulled on one set of socks, put his feet on the stone ledge, and picked up one of the mugs of tea.

"Now, that's better. You might want to at least put the towels on your hair to keep the water off your back."

Erith didn't speak.

Danol lifted his cup to take a drink but stopped when it was halfway to his mouth. "Miss Lock, you need to move to this chair and sip some tea. The quilt will catch fire if you stay there."

He slowly reached his hands to catch both her arms beneath the cocoon she had spun around herself, then gently guided her to the chair. He arranged it so her feet could reach the ledge and helped guide her to put them up, then grabbed the socks and pulled them on over her wet stockings. The wool would help wick the water away and keep her warm. He hurried to the kitchen with her mug, and Erith heard the spoon tinkle on the porcelain before he returned. Danol brought the cup to her lips and told her to have some.

"The sweet tea will help revive you." He smiled as he

helped her drink it. "That's the thing about having friends who are doctors. You learn some basics."

Erith sputtered at the sweetness, but he urged her to drink more. After a few swallows, she could feel heat rise in her cheeks. Why was Danol holding her tea? What was in it?

She shook her head. "What's in that?"

"Just tea and sugar."

"Is there spirits in that?" She tried to move her arms out of the quilt.

"There's no rum. Mary Rourke, I mean Mary Nolan, beat that into my head. Rum is bad for somebody who's cold. It doesn't help."

Freeing one arm, she took the cup from him and put her nose to it first before taking a tentative sip. Both shirts were buttoned to her neck, and the arms were rolled up over her wrists. She was fully covered yet felt exposed. The quilt was firmly encased around her waist and around her legs to the woollen socks. Her stockings were wet and itching against her skin. She was beginning to warm up, but she wouldn't allow her mind to settle.

"Miss Lock, I can assure you that I mean you no harm. But somehow I don't think that's enough."

She stared wide-eyed at him as he spoke. His voice had an odd twang tailored by his foreign birthplace. She had no reason to be scared, but she'd had no reason before, either. Erith was older and wiser, but that didn't mean she wasn't vulnerable.

"Once I know you've your wits about you, I'll get some things for you. As you can tell, I have nothing here." Erith guessed he was talking about clothing. "I'm going to run to Whalen's house. They have girls there."

Danol went on to tell her he would send somebody to the other side of the harbour to let them know she was here. She hadn't thought that anyone would be looking for her, but now she guessed that maybe somebody would.

"What about the ice?"

"If you'd followed the markings, you'd have been fine. You went as the crow flies and walked right into the river current." There was an expectant pause, but she didn't say anything. "If I hadn't seen you when I did, you could've disappeared without a trace." There was another expectant pause before he said, "Miss Lock, why were you on the ice?"

She had been momentarily distracted from her mission. Now was not the time to ask him for help. She was afraid to speak the words aloud.

"It'll keep," she said quietly.

He didn't press her. Instead, he waited, wiggled his feet in front of the fire, and sipped on his tea. She drank hers as well. The fire crackled, and her feet warmed, but she wasn't thinking of anything now except Beatrice. She bit her lower lip. Why did her stepmother have to torment her so? What had Erith done to deserve the purgatory she had been living, seemingly since she was born? Was Beatrice suffering the same fate? Was death really worse? She couldn't stand either thought. She had to know one way or the other.

"I came to see you."

Danol didn't speak. He must have guessed as much.

"Aren't you going to ask me why?"

"No."

"You were a policeman, right?"

"Yes, I was. I left that life a few years ago. I believe you already know that."

"Yes, I do," Erith said. She knew he had worked with the police in Boston before he was shipwrecked in John's Pond. She also knew that there was some kind of crime—kidnapping and murder, she believed—that he'd been hurt, and that Mary Rourke had saved him. He had convinced her to go to Boston to become a doctor, and he now took Mary and her doctor husband, Peter, to the outports on his boat. The duo had brought medical care during the summer to those who would otherwise do without. Erith wasn't clear on what had actually happened, but the news had reached St. John's at the time. She remembered reading about it in the *Evening Telegram*.

"When you were a policeman, did you have to look for people?"

"Sometimes. If somebody was reported missing, we'd try to find them."

"Could you find somebody for me?" Erith asked. He turned in the chair and stared at her. While she still had the nerve, she blurted out, "I want to find out if my daughter is alive. I need to find her."

He opened his mouth, but nothing came out.

"I have money. I can pay you."

"I don't want your money," Danol said. He seemed a little annoyed that she would think he would do anything for money. "I have freight runs to make when the ice leaves the harbour. I have to go to Boston for Mary and Peter Nolan at the end of April, and then I have the medical business to take care of in the bays. I don't do that kind of work anymore, Miss Lock. I'm afraid you'll have to find somebody else. What about the Newfoundland Constabulary? Try them."

"I need to do this privately."

"I'm afraid I don't understand."

Erith squirmed in her chair, and she stopped breathing as she felt the world closing in on her. She hadn't spoken of her baby in almost seven years. She didn't know if she could even say her name.

"I had a baby girl. My stepmother wouldn't allow me to keep her, so my baby was sent to the orphanage. Only she didn't end up there. I've checked. The priest who took her was killed on his way to St. John's, and little Beatrice was assumed to . . ." Erith couldn't speak the words that she had heard over and over in her head almost every day since it happened. "On her deathbed, my stepmother told me she hadn't died. I want to confirm that."

Danol reached out and touched her arm through the quilt. Strangely, Erith didn't pull back this time, though the warmth of his fingers on her arm was unsettling. She wouldn't tell him the whole story. He didn't need to know the circumstances around her baby's birth. He wasn't going to help her, anyway, so she didn't need to tell him anything else. She didn't know why she thought he would help. Maybe she should leave it alone.

Sipping her tea, she thought about Beatrice and the few short months that she had been alive.

"Miss Lock."

"No. Forget about it. I must forget about her. She's gone, and I have to accept that."

Erith straightened in her chair. Her stepmother's cruelty was evident in her tone, and that made Erith mad. She didn't want to be like Kathleen Lock. But right now she needed that hardened shell to get her out of here and back to the house.

"Did you say you were going to Whalen's?"

Danol felt like a heel. He was lucky to have spotted her. Knowing everyone followed the markers on the ice, his heart came up in his throat when he saw her making a straight cut between the two sandy, ice-covered points. He hadn't recognized the long, wild tresses and paused for a second to see who it was. When he realized she wasn't following the path, he panicked. Thankfully, he had made it in time.

Now she was hurt, and not in a way that would heal quickly. There was nothing he could say to ease that. He stared at her as she looked forlornly into the flames and drank her tea. He got up and stoked the fire, added a few logs, and left without saying a word.

For the next several weeks, Danol Cooper couldn't get the girl off his mind. She had left the day after her visit with him and he knew he wouldn't see her again, yet her circumstance bothered him. He didn't get much information out of the Whalens, except to say that she had left the community when she was in her mid-teens and that her stepmother was a cruel woman.

The spring was milder than usual, and Danol left for Boston a week earlier than planned. He wanted to pick up some items for his house: a few stained glass windows for the third level he intended to add, some maple plank for the floors, and a few indoor plumbing items, to name a few. He would also get to see acquaintances he had made while policing and, of course, spend some time with Mary Ro's Boston family. Mary's sisters had made him feel welcome from the time he had first met them. He was looking forward to seeing them and could hardly believe it had been two years.

Danol couldn't explain the connection he had with Mary and her family. She had saved him in more ways than one. Her innocence, strength, and her trust in him had changed his life. After his father had been murdered, Danol was alone. His mother died before he knew what a mother was, and he had no siblings. Really, there had been nothing holding him in Boston except the career he no longer wanted.

At first he believed there might be more between him and Mary, but now that he was testing his life on the sea, he liked the solitary existence. He didn't think he would ever be ready for anything romantic, and he didn't miss it. Mary had become family. That's where she fit in his life, and he would do anything for her. She was happy, and that was all that mattered to him. She would graduate in two years and be a full-fledged doctor, and he was proud of her.

Danol was content in Newfoundland with his boat and his lucrative business. He was thinking about buying another schooner, or even two. Maybe he would even build one after the house was finished. As a young boy growing up in the city, he had dreamed of a big yellow house on the bay. He was doing his best to build that house with his own hands. Danol didn't know he had the skill, but it came naturally to him, much like being on the water.

He liked his own company and figured he would spend his life alone. Danol had enjoyed a few short- and long-term relationships but nothing that meant anything to him. Mostly those girlfriends accompanied him to police or city functions, but he had no desires of anything permanent beyond that. Once a woman got serious and wanted something more, Danol would break it off as gently as possible. He was always clear upfront, but sometimes women got other ideas. He couldn't quite figure them out.

Now this wild-haired woman was keeping him awake at

night. He couldn't quite shake the feeling that he should help her. Danol didn't know if it was the former policeman in him that had him hooked or if it was something else. But that something else bothered him. He couldn't put his finger on it. His lack of sleep and his preoccupation with her were wearing on him.

On the return voyage from Boston, Mary cornered him in the galley.

"Danol, is something bothering you? Are you in any kind of trouble?"

"Busy, that's all."

Mary thought about that for a moment. "Danol, do you want to get out of our agreement? Are Peter and I interfering with your business? We can make other arrangements."

"Don't ever let that trouble you, Mary. Why would you think that? I'm committed to your medical trips as much as you are," he said with some force.

"So, it's not that. But it's something."

Danol paused, and Mary waited. She had all the time in the world. He knew she wasn't going to leave this alone.

"Do you know Erith Lock?"

"Erith Lock. Yes, I remember her. She was reared up by her stepmother at the store in North Harbour. Why do you ask?"

Danol told her about the incident on the ice and about Erith's request. He asked her not to mention it to anyone but Peter. Mary assured him she wouldn't.

"You told her no, I take it."

"Of course I did. You know about the baby?"

"Yes, quite a sad affair."

"What can you tell me about the situation?"

"I can't tell you anything more than Erith told you herself."

"You must know something?"

"Danol, anything that I know will have to come from Erith. I'm sorry."

Danol didn't press her. Nobody seemed to want to talk about Erith Lock, and that couldn't be good. He knew Mary—she wouldn't say another word, and she certainly wouldn't say anything disparaging. Now he was more intrigued than ever.

"I don't feel right having told her no."

"Danol, Erith Lock lost her parents at a very young age, and she didn't have it easy growing up. She was allowed to do very little. She tended the store and the mail from the time she could see over the counter. She left several years ago, and we haven't really heard much about her. Apparently she came into some money."

"She reminded me of some of the high-society women in Boston."

"She must have changed, Danol. I don't recall her being like that from the few times I met her. Remember, she didn't have it easy, and she had few friends, if any."

"She must have had a boyfriend. She had a baby."

Mary didn't answer.

"You have freight for St. John's and are heading there once you get us home. You have lots of time to at least meet with her before we head for the bays," Mary said. "She deserves a chance, Danol. God knows she didn't have much of that growing up."

14

Two weeks later, Danol found himself on Devon Row in St. John's looking for Erith Lock. He knocked at number sixteen, an ochre-red brick house with a yellow door. He hadn't realized he was holding his breath until the door opened. A young girl's voice drew his attention downward. She had light-coloured hair in pigtails and looked to be about eight or nine years old.

Danol immediately thought he was at the wrong house. He wasn't expecting a child to be there. Then he saw Erith in the hallway coming toward him.

"Annie, how many times have I told you not to answer the door?"

"I'm sorry, I couldn't help it," Annie replied.

"I know, darling," she said as she patted Annie's head. Then she looked up. "How can I help . . . ?" Her voice trailed off as recognition set in, and her tone changed. "What do you want?"

Annie tugged on her apron. Erith stooped to eye level with the girl. "How about you go and make sure Tommy and George don't eat all the cookies on the sideboard?"

Annie smiled and skipped off down the hall. Danol could hear her squeal after she went out of sight, and he couldn't help but grin. Erith stood up and asked him again. "What do you want?"

"I'm not sure. I came to hear you out."

Erith stared at him a moment, then stepped aside. "Well, come in out of it, if you must." She held the door, and he noticed that she backed up to the wall until he passed. Erith motioned for him to continue down the hallway, and he entered a small, bright kitchen. The smell of molasses cookies was tantalizing.

Three children stood facing the cupboard and focusing on the brown delights. Near the edge, dark crumbs on the white tea towel spun the tale that they had already been into the cookies. The three turned, their full cheeks further telling what words didn't need to express. They tried to chew quickly, naively thinking it would erase the evidence before them. Danol chuckled at the sight and felt a sharp poke in the arm from behind, then heard a sudden intake of breath. He was sure Erith hadn't meant to do that.

The children swallowed in chorus, their faces portraying an innocence that only children knew how to fake. Danol couldn't suppress his snort, but this time there was no jab.

"Now, what have you three been up to?" Erith's voice was soft and melodious, and Danol almost had to turn to make sure it wasn't somebody else behind him.

"Nothing," came the reply.

"We're waiting for the cookies to cool off," said the tallest and, Danol assumed, eldest of the two boys. His grin broadened even more. Then he eyed Danol, and his features changed to a grimace.

"I see," said Erith. "I think they should be fine by now. Would you like to take two each and a glass of lemonade and go out in the garden for a while?"

Annie and the youngest boy, who was about a year her senior, nodded and eagerly turned to take the cookies. The eldest of the three stepped forward in a gesture of protection. Erith crossed the kitchen and poured three small glasses and carefully handed them out. "I have to speak to Mr. Cooper and will call you in when I'm done. George, you look out for Annie and Tommy, you hear? Don't go too far. Supper will be ready soon."

"Yes, ma'am," said the eldest boy. His attempt to protect her wasn't lost on Danol.

"I'll be fine, George. I know this man."

She offered Danol tea, but he said a glass of lemonade would do. And a warm cookie. They both sat across from each other at the small hardwood table.

"I'm sorry to just drop by like this."

"I wasn't expecting to see you again," Erith said.

"Me, either. Is your husband about? Does he know?" Danol didn't want to impose or cause her to have to answer questions if that were the case.

"I'm not married."

"Oh!" Danol was surprised. She had at least four children and no husband. His mind went to one obvious reason for her to be in such a situation, and he didn't like it. Now he was mad at himself for thinking about her for the last few months. He made an attempt to push back his chair, intending to leave, but her hand on his arm stilled him.

"Please. Give me five minutes of your time?"

Danol didn't know why he felt compelled to stay, but he

nodded and sat back on the chair. Erith's hand shook as she poured herself a cup of tea. His eyes followed her as she moved about the kitchen. She took a quick glance out the back door, straining her neck, before returning to her seat.

"These are not my children. They came from the orphanages. I knew their father," she said as she stared into her tea.

"My God, Miss Lock, you took this on all by yourself."

Danol couldn't explain the relief he felt. He could tell by the way she spoke that she loved the children and was good to them.

"I bought this place so I could have the children with me. Now that my father's house is vacant and the shop needs tending, I will return to North Harbour with them. It may be better for the children."

Erith wrung her hands and shifted in the chair while she talked. "George is spending more time down by the docks. He wants to get a job. He's barely twelve. Tommy doesn't talk. Annie wets the bed and is afraid she's going back to the orphanage."

"Just keep them off the ice in winter. Or at least teach them how to follow the markings," Danol said, hoping to bring some levity to the conversation.

Smiling hesitantly, Erith said, "Yes, there's that."

He offered passage to North Harbour aboard his boat for her and the children when she was ready to make the move. After all, it was his home port, and he would be returning several times within the month and could easily land them at the same time. His business was thriving. Except for the few weeks that he would be gone with the doctors, he could make sure they got to North Harbour safely. Erith agreed and set the date. She spoke of her plan to take the train to Whitbourne and travel by land to North Harbour, but in the end she agreed the boat would be easier.

"I guess you know that's not the only reason I need your help."

"It looks like you have a lot of responsibility here, Miss Lock. I don't envy you your position. You're a young woman who could have any kind of a life you want, yet you chose to take on a family by yourself. I don't know what you have in mind, but I'm intrigued enough with your situation to want to help."

"Thank you, Mr. Cooper."

"Danol, please," he said.

Erith didn't return the offer of a first name.

"Mr. Cooper," she said. "I'm not interested in anything beyond moving my family to North Harbour and finding out if my daughter is alive and if she's happy."

"That's fine with me. I'm a confirmed bachelor and have no intentions otherwise." His face reddened as he spoke. Why the hell had he said that?

She nodded and went on to tell Danol more details about her daughter's presumed death and about her stepmother's deathbed confession.

"Perhaps my stepmother wanted me to suffer for the rest of my life, and perhaps the baby's dead and I'll have to deal with that once more. However, if she is alive, I want to make sure that her life is a happy one and not the life that I lived. If she's not being well taken care of, I plan to take her with me. I have money for the court costs, if that's the case. I owe her that much, since it wasn't her fault she was born."

Danol thought that an odd thing to say, but she didn't elaborate. Erith Lock was an interesting woman, to say the least.

"Let's get down to business," Danol said. "So, you know for a fact that she wasn't in the orphanage that Annie was in, but you haven't checked anywhere else?"

"No, I didn't think to do that."

Danol asked her what she knew about the priest who was killed, where it happened, and when it happened. He wrote all the information in a notebook, which he returned to the inside pocket of his jacket when she was done.

A short time later, Annie came looking for another cookie. Erith told her she could have another after supper. The girl shrugged and returned to the garden.

"I think that's about all I need to start. I must tell you, though, that I have commitments and schedules that I must keep with my schooner."

"I understand," Erith said. "I'm glad you've agreed to look for . . ."

"No promises, but I'll do what I can."

"I'll pay your price."

"No, I'm not in that business. I'll see what I can find out. That's it."

"Then why are you doing this?" Erith asked.

"I'm not entirely sure."

15

Four weeks later, at their agreed-upon time, two horse-drawn carts and a carriage pulled up to the door. Danol and several men quickly loaded boxes, crates, and canvas luggage into the carts, and Erith and the children climbed into the carriage. He helped the two boys onto the back seat of the wooden buggy and guided Erith and Annie to the front seat next to him. He was the driver.

George and Annie talked incessantly about their new adventure while Erith quietly listened and answered their questions. They had many for Danol, too. Erith noted his patience as he explained the particulars of their journey to North Harbour.

The sun was fresh into the day and painted the houses with wide, golden strokes as they travelled from one street to the next. Danol promised breakfast on the boat. "There might even be molasses cookies," he told them. They all seemed happy to be going on a new adventure.

There was ordered mayhem at the crowded docks as ships readied for the tides. Danol jumped from his perch to the ground with ease and came around the wagon to help Annie and Erith. Within a few days, he would have them all in their new home in North Harbour, and he felt satisfied with that. There was something about Erith that stood out, much like Mary had a few years back. But this time the feeling was significantly different, and he couldn't put his finger on it. Maybe it was the mystery of the child and not the woman.

He reached for Annie but stopped when Erith suddenly let out a gasp and pulled the child back. Danol had his arms up, but Erith was staring past him. Her face had gone ashen. She was swaying in her seat, and Annie was still leaning out, giggling and reaching down toward Danol's arms.

"Miss Lock! Miss Lock, let the child go."

Erith's fingers complied, but her eyes didn't move. Danol grabbed Annie and reached for Erith, but she seemed frozen in her seat. A look of pure horror was etched on her face. Danol turned but was met by a sea of faces, and he couldn't tell where her gaze was focused.

Peter and Mary Nolan were on the deck of his schooner and came to greet them. They were in St. John's to pick up the last few supplies for their medical trip in St. Mary's Bay and Placentia Bay and along the southern shore of the island. They had brought their sons, Petie and Eddy, knowing that Erith would be on this trip with her three youngsters.

Danol asked Mary to see to the children. Mary took Annie's hand and looked at Erith.

"What's wrong, Danol?" she asked softly.

"I'm not sure. Something's the matter, though."

He raced around the wagon and got up in the seat next to Erith, trying to see what she was looking at. When he put his hand on her shoulder, she flinched. She continued to stare at the crowded wharf, where many boats were preparing to leave on the morning tide.

Danol could see sweat form on her brow. Her hands were clenched on either side of the seat, her knuckles white. She was terrified of something.

"Miss Lock. Erith, are you afraid of leaving?" he asked. He knew what he said sounded absurd.

She softly spoke the word "Noftle."

"Erith, I don't know what that means."

"Did she say 'Noftle'?" Mary asked.

"I think so," Danol said. He raised his eyebrows at Mary, framing the unasked question.

Mary told Annie to go with Peter and asked her husband to get the kids on the boat. She climbed the step and moved in beside Erith. The seat felt cramped with three adults aboard.

Mary pried Erith's hand from the board and held it between hers. "Erith, it's me. Mary Ro. Remember me? I'm here, Erith. Where is he?"

Mary slapped her face. Not hard, but enough to sting. Danol's jaw dropped, and he gave his head a slight shake.

"Mary, what are you doing?"

"I won't hurt her." Erith shook her head and blinked several times. "It's Mary Ro. Danol and I are here, Erith. We're here. We won't let anything happen." Mary kept repeating this.

Danol scanned the dock for something out of place, but all he could see were faces of ships' crewmen loading supplies. Nobody stuck out. Erith seemed focused on the second wharf, but he didn't know what he was looking for. She trembled beneath his hand, and he instinctively squeezed her shoulder to let her know he was there.

"Mary, what's happening?" Danol asked. He was poised for action. Every nerve in his body was ready to move.

George was calling out to her from the ship. He was becoming frantic, and one of the crew was having a job holding him back. The boy knew there was something wrong. Erith glanced toward his voice. He was screaming her name now, and Tommy was openly crying. Both were struggling to get free of the men who held them.

"The children," she said as she stepped around Mary, jumped down, ran toward the ship, and bounded up the gangway. Peter Nolan motioned for the crew to let the children go, and the young ones met her as soon as she stepped on deck. Peter tried his best to keep them from knocking her overboard.

Erith immediately fell to her knees, put her arm around both boys, and hugged them while Annie came around behind her and hugged her neck.

"I didn't mean to frighten you. Please forgive me," Erith said. She held the boys at arm's length and looked them each in the eye. "I'm sorry."

Tommy said, "Mama, I thought you were sending us away."

Erith gasped and struggled to catch her breath. Tearfully, she stared at his upturned face and slowly drew her forehead to the boy's. She closed her eyes and gently cupped the back of his head with both her hands and tenderly kissed his brow.

"Tommy, Tommy, Tommy, I will never, ever send you away." She spoke slowly and emphasized each word. "You're all stuck with me, you hear?" She hugged them fiercely as she looked from one to the other.

Erith stood up while the boys clung to her, their knuckles white and eyes shining. Annie calmly reached for Erith's hand. The young girl kissed her fingers and laid her head against the back of her hand. Mary came up behind her and laid a hand on her arm.

"Erith, what will we do?" she asked. Danol stood next to Peter and knitted his brow. He looked from one to the other, hoping to make sense of what had just happened.

Mary took her hand. "I told you a long time ago, if you ever needed me for anything, I'd be there. I'm here now and will be with you every step of the way."

"Then we need to fetch the police. I'm tired of living in fear."

"Somebody has to tell me what's going on," Danol said as he shifted anxiously from one foot to the other. "Why do we need the police?"

A young, dark-haired boy not much older than George came on deck from below. Mary asked him if he could take little Petie and show the Ryan children to the galley and get some breakfast. After Erith's reassurance that she would be down shortly, they scooted below behind the lad, anxious to have their bellies filled. The eldest looked back several times, but she motioned for him to go.

Erith turned to face Danol and Peter. Mary stepped up next to her and linked her arm in around Erith's. "Erith, this is my husband, Peter. Peter Nolan."

"We've met before," Erith said as Peter nodded. "Doctor Nolan used to see the children from time to time a few years ago."

She took a deep breath and straightened her back. Her voice trembled when she spoke. "There's a man on the dock loading crates onto a vessel. He's wearing a brown jacket, black pants, and a brown knitted hat. His hair is dark brown. He's pudgy and filthy. That man, whom I know as Noftle, and his partner, interfered with me when I was barely sixteen years old. They left me for dead in a meadow near Dog Cove."

Erith stared off above their heads, not making eye contact.

"I'd like that man arrested and held accountable for what he did to me."

Danol was shocked. He was speechless. None of his police experience showed itself in that moment. He hadn't quite recovered by the time Peter asked Erith to point out Noftle. She turned to face the boats farther down the quay, at which point Peter pushed Danol ahead to stand near the two women. That jolt forced the breath back into him. So many things made sense now: her hesitation and jitters when she was around him, her panic at his house after she fell through the ice, her abruptness with him. The woman had been raped. Correction—she had been raped as a child. Her baby girl . . .

His world shifted. Danol tensed as his emotions did an about-face. He could feel the heat rising to his face. There was a man somewhere before him who had hurt her. He would see that the man answered for the crime—if he didn't kill him first. Danol had seen many cases like this in Boston. This was not new to him . . . but somehow it was. He was feeling something he hadn't felt before. Danol couldn't fathom why men were abusive to women. He had always paid special attention to those cases and those women. Yet now he was awash with something new that he couldn't seem to control—a fury that was getting away from him.

Through clenched teeth, he told one of the crew to fetch the constables. Once she pinpointed Noftle near the *Vagabond*, Danol, Peter, and four more of the crew strode off the vessel. He tried to grind his anger into the paved stones beneath his feet. They would bring the cad back to the dock near their own boat to avoid any confrontation with the man's crew. Noftle could have friends with him, so they would have to be careful.

Danol was out in front of the group, his gaze fixed on

the man Erith had identified. Peter caught up to him and said, "Don't do anything foolish."

"I'll kill him."

"That would be foolish."

Danol tried to control his rage. He really could kill the man. "What if it were Mary?"

"Then we'd both kill him," Peter said matter-of-factly. "Not with all these people around, though."

Danol slowed. Peter was right. He had to rein in his anger or it wouldn't end well for Noftle or himself. They turned right to go along the wharf where the man was working. Four boats were tied up, but their attention was fully on the *Vagabond*.

Danol grabbed Noftle from behind. He turned the man around, spat out a curse, then struck him in the face. He felt a sudden wildness inside himself that he couldn't control. The man fell, but Danol picked him up by the coat and hit him again. Peter grabbed Danol before he could pick up Noftle a second time.

Several of the crew from the *Vagabond* gathered around, and the man who appeared to be the captain came forward to see the cause of the commotion. Peter talked to him, and within a few minutes the skipper was motioning for the rest of his crew to back off. He returned to the vessel and told the men to get back to work.

Danol picked Noftle up off the dock and flung him ahead of him on the wooden planks, keeping him balanced with a deathly grip on the man's coat. Noftle almost fell from the force of the push and stumbled ahead of the group.

When they neared his boat with Noftle, Danol saw Mary and Erith coming toward them. They met at the bottom of the gangway. Immediately, Erith lunged forward and struck the man in the face. Danol saw a slight flicker of pain cross her face and knew she had hurt her hand. He held the man in place, fully prepared to let her hit him as often as she wanted, but Mary grabbed Erith and told her to stop.

Noftle seemed surprised by the blow and absently rubbed his fingers over the red blotch that was forming on his cheek. The expression on his face changed. "Why, Miss Erith Lock, I heard you were dead," he drawled. In an instant, Danol's fingertips flicked across the top of his ear, and Noftle cringed.

"Better for you if I were."

"Why, Miss Lock, whatever do you mean?" he retorted. "I'm sure there must be some misunderstanding."

Before Erith could respond, a caped officer from the Newfoundland Constabulary pushed his way through the gathering crowd. Erith turned toward the gangway and moved away with Mary while Danol explained the offence. He noticed Erith watching from the rail as Noftle was taken away.

As he came aboard the boat to tell her she would need to file a complaint at the office, he heard her tell Mary, "I regret I've not been afforded the strength to hit that man as hard as I wanted."

Danol cleared his throat. He wanted to reach for her but held himself back.

"I'm keeping you from leaving," Erith said. "Oh no! I've no place to go back with the children."

"We're in no hurry," Mary said. "You'll stay here with us."

"Yes, you can stay here," Danol said. His tongue felt like it was tied, and the words were hard to get out. He nodded to Mary, who returned the gesture. "You should go below to have some breakfast with the children. I'll take you to the station shortly thereafter."

Mary tugged on Erith's arm and led the way.

Danol couldn't believe it. He was losing control over his emotions. He helped the crew load the items from the wagon and other crates from the wharf, but even manual labour did nothing to calm him. The men gave him a wide berth while he worked. He felt the need to protect Erith Lock, but it was too late for that. Nobody had protected her when she needed it the most. Then he had thought the worst of her, and that made him more angry at himself.

By the time everything was aboard, he informed the men they would be staying another night. He told them they would be leaving on the first tide the next morning. The younger crewmen were happy to have a night in port, and they were probably glad to get away from him, given the temper he was trying to work off.

Danol heard laughter coming from the galley. This lightened his mood a little as he joined the group at the table. Mary laid a plate before him and told him to eat. The young girl looked at him from across the wide plank surface and smiled. Danol couldn't help but smile back at Annie's beautiful little face. He found it difficult to take part in the lively banter. He glanced at Erith often and could tell that she was smiling, but it hadn't yet reached her eyes.

16

Later that morning, Erith and Danol walked in silence up the Cathedral Street hill toward the Roman Catholic Cathedral of St. John the Baptist. Erith could sense a change in the man. He seemed to be brooding since hearing about her past. She wasn't surprised by that, but it hurt a little just the same.

It was a short distance to the constabulary headquarters in Fort Townshend, which was just beyond the massive stone church. Erith had insisted on the walk to clear her head. She had started something that she couldn't back away from now. Maybe, if she were lucky, this would bring her peace, and the queasiness in her belly and the bleakness in her head would go away.

She knew she was responsible for the boat being docked a day late, and that weighed on her, despite Mary's assurance that it was of no consequence. Erith was relieved that Mary had agreed to stay with the children, even though she had first insisted on accompanying Erith. It was a very sensitive time for Tommy, now that he had found his voice, and Erith believed that a female presence would help her youngest boy.

Danol had decided to go with her, although at this time she wasn't sure why. She believed Mary might have suggested it. This feeling was new for her, but Erith was somewhat disappointed that he may have come for Mary's sake and not for hers. However, though Danol was unusually quiet, his presence put her at ease.

"I can bring Annie and the boys to a hotel for a few days. You can take my furniture to North Harbour, and we can catch the train to Whitbourne when things are straightened up here," she said rather sternly. Kathleen Lock came through when Erith became defensive. This bothered her more than she cared to admit, but it seemed to happen most when she was around Danol.

"What?" asked Danol.

She repeated herself.

"I thought we had already agreed that you would all stay on the boat. The children seemed excited about it."

"I know." Her voice softened. She hated to disappoint them. "But we're keeping you from leaving port."

Danol looked up at the sky and said, "It's near midday, and even if everything was ready, we'd barely have time for our first stop."

They strode in silence across an intersection before Erith said, "I'm sorry for the delay."

"Don't let it trouble you." Danol's words sounded harsh. He walked two steps ahead of her and stopped to turn and face her. "It's me who's sorry. We rarely get out of the city without a delay. My crew are delighted to have the day to themselves. Really, I mean it. You have enough to worry about."

He sounded sincere, but in truth Erith hated depending on anyone. She had been alone for a long time—most of her life, when she really thought about it. Now she had to rely on somebody besides herself, and it was hard for her to admit. She nodded as if to say that was the end of it. Danol blocked her way until she looked him in the eye. He raised a brow. They exchanged smiles.

She nodded again. "All right."

Danol asked if she knew the history of Fort Townshend. As they walked toward the offices, he explained that the British had used the fort to protect the city, primarily from the French, until 1870, when the constabulary took over, expanded, and reorganized to meet the needs of the city.

"How do you know so much about them?" Erith asked.

"I had to do some work on their behalf a few years ago. When I returned to the island to live, they reached out to me to see if I'd be interested in joining the force. They knew my background in Boston and wanted to add me to the ranks."

"Really!" Erith blurted. She hadn't meant to say that. She wanted to know more but still didn't want to know him, or any man, for that matter.

"Yes. However, I chose to stick with my new business. I like the sea, and I'm committed to the medical trips in the summer with Mary and Peter."

He led her along a street toward the building. "We're almost there."

Before long, she was sitting at a desk with a uniformed officer about twice her age. He was kind and asked her to recount the circumstances of her assault. The man allowed her to take her time, and he wrote down her complaint as she spoke. To keep her sanity, she told the story as if she were talking about someone else. She was able to get through it without breaking down. Somehow, saying it out loud began to cleanse her. It wasn't her fault. There wasn't anything she could have done at the time to keep it from happening. She had been innocent to the ways of the world. She had been given no reason not to trust.

The officer confirmed that the man's real name was Peter Simmons. He had a criminal background and had spent time, on two different occasions, at the St. John's Penitentiary. She described her other attacker, Hand, but there were no records to tie Simmons to anyone matching her recollection.

When she was finished, the officer told her she would have to go before the magistrate and face Simmons in court. He said it would be a month or more before she would be called. She would be notified of the date by telegram if she was moving to North Harbour. He asked if she had a barrister, and Erith gave him the name. She would inform her legal counsel today of the pending court appearance.

Erith thought she would be scared at the thought of going to court, but she wasn't. She realized she had suffered enough and would face the man one more time to be done with it. She would see this through and make sure that he was punished for what he had done to her. The thought of Annie growing up with the likes of that man on the loose only strengthened her resolve.

She held her head high as she entered the reception area. Suddenly, Erith felt no shame in being the victim. She didn't even know why she had before this. Now, saying it out loud, telling her story, helped her forgive herself.

Danol was speaking with an officer when she came into the room. "This is Constable Jeffries," Danol said.

The blond-haired man extended his hand and shook hers. "Pleased to make your acquaintance, miss," he said. He nodded to Danol. "Nice to see you again, Danol."

They left the office and made their way back toward the boat. Erith told Danol she needed to visit her solicitor, William Horwood, on Duckworth Street to let him know about the morning's events. The office was almost directly on their route, and she wouldn't be long. It was a bright day. The sun was behind them, and the city's downtown stretched out before them from their vantage point on the hillside. The streets were lined with row houses of various colours. They were all new, having been rebuilt after the Great Fire in 1892. The house that Erith had bought and was now selling had been spared during the fire. Regardless, she and the children had taken shelter at the orphanage during the cleanup.

Danol waited on the street while Erith met with her lawyer. He was going over his conversation with Jeffries. The constable had told him that Simmons would most likely get seven to ten years at the penitentiary for the crime. When the British had been in charge of the courts, anyone convicted of rape or murder was most often hanged. In more recent years, however, the courts had shown mercy in such cases, depending on the circumstances and the person's criminal history.

He didn't know if Erith had thought about that, nor how she would feel about it. In fact, he wasn't sure if he would tell her or not. His ire had risen again. Danol was glad that Simmons was behind bars—he would wring the man's neck if given the chance.

They got under way again in silence. As they neared McCallum's Lane, Danol was two steps behind Erith. There wasn't much foot traffic on this part of the street after lunch hour, but he had moved behind her to let two ladies pass. Just then, a slight movement caught his eye. Something seemed out of place, or at the very least not quite right. Danol had seen the movements of a shadowed figure moments before but hadn't paid much attention, thinking somebody had turned back, but now it seemed like somebody was skulking in the lane. It was probably a pickpocket waiting to grab Erith's wallet.

The houses and businesses fronted on the street, and Erith was almost at the corner when he reached to pull her back. Too late! He caught the glint of a blade in the sun's rays as it came down toward her head. Danol's warning shout left his mouth as he pushed her to the ground. Instinct kicked in, and he grabbed the arm while it was still in motion and pulled hard toward the corner of the building. He was off-balance, but he heard the dull thud on the clapboard before he also hit the wall. The man was clearly stunned and hadn't expected to be confronted.

Danol pushed off the wall with his free hand and held the man by the wrist in a death grip. As he stepped into the lane, the man recovered and threw his whole weight into a punch aimed at Danol. He ducked and pushed himself hard into the man's midsection while pulling back on his arm. He heard a snap and a yelp and the sound of the knife clattering to the ground as the man flew over his back and landed face down on the street. He was sure he had broken the man's arm.

Danol kicked the knife away and gulped in air as he turned his assailant over to get a look at him. He guessed him to be about fifty. His long, thin grey hair, meant to hide the balding area on the top of his head, was now matted red on the cobblestones. He must have suffered a broken nose when he hit the ground, judging by the look of the blood covering his face. The man tried to reach for the knife, but Danol stepped on his wrist. Whistle blasts sounded, and Danol looked up to see two constables running along Duckworth Street. He heard one of them shout, "You there! Unhand that man!"

A merchant from the store a few doors away shouted back, "He was defending the lady from the fellow on the ground! I saw it all!"

"That's right, Constables. That man had a knife," Danol said as they approached. He straightened and turned toward Erith, who was on the ground. He must have pushed her harder than he thought. Quickly stepping over the assailant, he went to her. There were a couple of women in his way, and one shouted, "She's hurt!"

He moved around a portly woman and extended a hand to help Erith up. She wasn't moving. Then he noticed blood slowly seeping out from beneath her. "God, no," he said. He gently took her shoulder and turned her over. He hadn't saved her after all. The knife had found its mark.

One of the constables came behind him and bent to look at Erith. Danol scooped her up in his arms as he spoke. "I'm Danol Cooper. Constable Jeffries can vouch for me. There are two doctors on my ship, *Angel Endeavours*. I'm bringing her there."

The look on Danol's face told the constable not to argue. He turned and sprinted to the waterfront with Erith limp against his chest. The dock was crowded. Danol yelled for people to get out of his way and made a straight cut for the boat, then shouted Peter's name over and over as he neared. He couldn't remember touching the gangway at all as he leaped on deck.

Danol wasn't fully sure what happened after that. Peter tried to take Erith from him, but he wouldn't let her go, so instead Peter grabbed his shoulder and pulled him down to the medical room. *Thank God the ship is fully supplied*, he thought as he laid Erith on the examining table.

Mary rushed in. "The children are all upset in the galley. You have to go to them," she said. She took Danol's face between her hands and made him focus on her. "Do you hear me, Danol?"

"Yes," he said flatly.

"Danol, I have to help Peter with Erith. You have to go to them."

"Save her, Mary." He felt panic rising in him.

"Danol, go! We'll do our best. Every moment counts. Get out of here," Peter said. He was already working to expose the wound.

"Change your shirt, Danol," Mary said before she joined Peter.

Danol looked down at himself. His clothes were covered in blood. He stopped in his cabin to grab a shirt and quickly changed before going to the galley. He could hear the havoc before he opened the door. Peter's son, Eddy, was trying to keep control of the situation. He was a fine boy who looked very much like his father—tall for his age, with his short black hair gleaming in the daylight that shone in through the portholes. George and Tommy's eyes were as big as saucers. They looked to him for some sign of Erith's well-being. Annie was holding Mary's baby and staring at him.

Danol had to get control of his emotions. They needed him now. "She'll be all right. I promise," he said. He had to believe that. George ran to him and struck out at Danol's face. His heart hurt more than the force of the blow. Danol grabbed the two small hands before the boy could hurt himself.

"I'm sorry, son. I should have kept her safe." The strength went out of the boy's arms, and he collapsed into Danol, who awkwardly patted him on the back.

"Can we talk to her?" George asked.

"Not right now. Mary is helping her get better."

"Will she leave us?" Tommy asked from across the table.

"Not if she can help it," Danol said. A lump as big as an apple formed in his throat. "Let's all go up on deck in the sun and let the doctors do their work."

With Eddy's help, he led them from the close quarters, while Annie stayed with the baby. Danol tried to distract the boys as much as he could, but it was difficult to concentrate. His mind was on Erith and what he could have done better. If he hadn't been preoccupied with his own anger, he might have been able to keep her out of harm's way. But this wasn't about him, he quickly admonished himself. She was fighting for her life.

Constable Jeffries came aboard and inquired about Erith's health. Danol couldn't tell him anything. The constable told Danol that he didn't believe this to be a random act. The man who had attacked them was now in the prison infirmary. A guard remembered that he had also been to the prison earlier that morning and met with Simmons. Jeffries believed this was the man who Erith knew as "Hand."

"Do you think he was trying to kill her so that she couldn't testify against Simmons?" Danol asked.

"Too early to say for sure, but it looks that way," the constable said. "These are bad men, Danol. I came to warn you of the threat in case Simmons has other friends."

"I'll call the crew back and have them stand watch for the night."

"That's a good idea. I'll stay around on the wharf until you get your men in place."

Danol gave a few coins to two young boys who were hanging around the dock and sent them to fetch some of his crew. He then paced the deck while he waited for news of Erith. In time, Peter came on deck. George and Tommy ran to him with Danol close on their heels. Peter's smile said it all. He nodded at Danol.

"She's a stubborn woman," Peter said, looking at Danol over the boys' heads. "We have her set up in your cabin."

Peter bent to talk to the boys.

"Erith wants to see you, but you have to be very careful. Promise?"

"Promise," they said in chorus, their faces beaming.

"She's well enough to see the boys and Annie?" Danol asked.

"Yes. She insisted. That's what took us so long. We had to get her propped up in your bed."

"I'll get Annie and bring her." Danol wanted to see her, too, but didn't want to sound over-anxious. By the time he fetched Annie, Peter had disappeared with the boys.

His breath stopped when he opened the door. Erith was lying in his bed with her back propped up by several pillows. Her long, wild hair was splayed out against the white backdrop, perfectly framing her beautiful face. Her right arm was in a sling, and her left hand was busy moving from one boy to the other as she tried to assure them she was fine.

She smiled at Annie. "There's my girl, now."

Annie squealed her delight at seeing Erith. Erith extended her arm for the young girl to come to her. Danol passed little Petie to Mary. Erith locked eyes with him as Annie delicately leaned in for a kiss. She smiled at him. He felt he was not deserving and looked away.

Danol was overcome. His insides were in turmoil, so he left to attend to things on deck. He didn't realize his legs were shaking until he stumbled on the stairs. Some of the crew had returned, and Danol quickly filled them in on what had happened. He had a great crew. They promptly went into action to ensure everyone was safe and that supper was cooked. It was late, and he didn't think anyone had eaten since breakfast.

Danol was leaning on the back rail of the boat, gazing into the ocean and thinking about the day's events, when Peter came to stand beside him. He didn't say anything, just stood there in silence. He laid a hand on Danol's shoulder and leaned on the rail beside him.

Despite Danol's initial dislike of the man, Peter had become a good friend. He suspected Peter knew the direction of his thoughts better than he knew himself.

"What should I do?"

"I can't tell you that. You need to figure it out on your own," Peter said. "In the meantime, the kids are in the galley, and Erith wants to see you."

Danol straightened immediately. "Why didn't you say that earlier?"

"She said she needed a few minutes with Mary first."

Danol let out a long breath, and Peter grinned. "You poor man," he said. Then he clapped Danol on the shoulder.

Danol and Peter talked about the events of the day before Danol made his way to the cabin. When he knocked, Erith told him to come in. Mary was straightening the sheets around her.

"She was trying to move to another cabin, but I won't let her," Mary said. "She doesn't want to put you out of your room. I told her that this one wasn't yours and that you'd move to another." Mary and Peter had the main cabin, Danol's room, any time they were on the boat. It was the biggest and could accommodate the doctors as well as Petie. Eddy believed he was old enough to sleep in the forecastle with the men, so they allowed it.

"Mary's right. I can go anywhere to lie down," Danol said.

"Now, if you'll both excuse me, I have to get something to eat. Erith, I'll bring you back something shortly," said Mary.

"I'm not hungry."

"You will eat," Mary said matter-of-factly. Erith didn't argue.

When Mary left, there was an awkward silence.

"You wanted to see me?"

Erith didn't answer at first. Then she started to cry. Her hands automatically went to her eyes, and she doubled over in pain when she moved her right arm. Danol came around the bed but stopped short of touching her. She moved back to lie on the pillows and wiped her eyes with the sleeve of her nightshirt before settling her slinged arm back to where it didn't hurt.

"I'm sorry. I didn't mean to do that," she said. Her eyes were hooded as she looked at him.

"You have every right to do that. Do you need me to get Mary?"

"No. I wanted to speak to you alone."

Danol waited for Erith to say something else. Then they both blurted out each other's names at the same time. Danol motioned for her to go first. He wasn't sure what he was going to say.

"Mr. Cooper . . . Danol . . . I want to thank you for saving my life."

"I almost got you killed. I should have protected you," he said hurriedly.

"You didn't have anything to do with what happened. You pushed me away from the knife."

"I saw him too late to act."

"You saw the man and acted," she replied softly. "He would have killed me. I got a glimpse of him. It was Hand."

"The constables guessed as much."

"They were here? Did he get away?"

"No, he's in the prison infirmary." Danol explained the man's condition.

"Good. He won't hurt anyone else. Mary said you ran all the way here with me."

"I figured this was the best place for you."

"You saved me, Danol. Mary said I was bleeding and could have died."

"It shouldn't have happened," Danol argued.

"You're right. It shouldn't have happened. People like Hand shouldn't be in the world, but they are. If I had to go on my own, like I wanted this morning, I wouldn't be here now."

"But you are."

"Yes, I am, thanks to you." Erith held her hand out toward him, and he grasped it in his palm. She mouthed another *Thank you*. She seemed different now. More relaxed. Perhaps it was the medication. She let go of his hand.

"Now, let's talk about what's going to happen tomorrow."

She told Danol she was going to a hotel and hiring a nanny for the children until she was well enough to travel. Mary had said she would get her stitches out in about ten days, and she figured she would be as good as new in two weeks. Danol listened in silence as Erith said she was going to pay him for the loss of wages for him and his crew for the day and for delivery of her furniture and baggage to North Harbour.

"Are you finished?"

"Yes, I believe so. Oh, wait, I'll book passage with you again in a few weeks or we'll go on the train to Whitbourne and get a horse and cart from there."

"Are you finished now?"

"Yes."

"Well, let me tell you what's going to happen tomorrow."

Danol told her she was remaining on the boat and he would deliver her to North Harbour in a few days, where she could remain in the care of Mary and Peter. Erith opened her mouth as if to protest, but she didn't say anything when he continued with his plan. He would hire a housekeeper in North Harbour and somebody to care for the kids while she healed. She could pay for that if she felt the need. He knew that somebody was already working in the store, so she would be fully covered. Danol said he would stay around during the day and that Peter and Mary had volunteered to spend the nights with her until the trial.

Erith stared at him. "Why are you doing this?" Tears stung her eyes, but she didn't try to stop them.

"You'll be safer in North Harbour."

Danol spoke to Constable Jeffries later that day, once Erith had confirmed her assailant was Hand, and they agreed to get the trial date set as soon as Erith was well, to get ahead of any other "friends of Simmons." Jeffries confided that there might be one complication to setting a date for the trial. The courthouse had been destroyed in the Great Fire of 1892. Since then, court was held at the Colonial Building when the government of Robert

Thorburn wasn't sitting. However, because talks with Canada regarding confederation were heated, the House was sitting longer than usual, and trials were backed up. The government was in the process of renting the new Star of the Sea Hall on Henry Street, which had recently been rebuilt after the fire, but the interior hadn't been quite finished. That could potentially cause a delay of proceedings, but Jeffries would keep him informed. Danol wouldn't bother Erith with those details.

For the life of him, he couldn't tell Erith why he wanted to be so involved. He wasn't going to leave her on her own, and he felt guilty about what had happened, but it was more than that.

As Danol sat in silence with Erith, Mary came in with a tray laden with soup and crackers.

"I guess you told her she was going to North Harbour."

"Yes."

"Did she argue?" Danol shook his head in answer. "Good. Now, if you'll excuse us, I have to feed the girl."

Danol grinned. That was Mary. Not one for mincing words. He grabbed his soap and razor, as well as some clothes, and made an exit. As he packed his stuff in a cupboard above an empty bunk in the forecastle, he was joined by two others who were giving up their privacy for the sake of the children. The two boys would sleep in the room next to Erith, and Eddy would stay with them. Annie would sleep with Mary and Peter, and little Petie would stay in the main cabin.

Danol doubted he would get much sleep himself. So much had happened since he had left the boat that morning. He couldn't imagine how Erith had lived under such a shadow for so long. She was really something.

17

A constable came to see them early the next morning and took an account of the assault. Erith confirmed the culprit to be Hand and was assured that he would be tried with Simmons for her initial complaint. Erith was relieved that it would be over soon.

More than once the thought crossed her mind that she should have said nothing. She wouldn't see the men again. Then she reminded herself that she saw them everywhere. Every time she stepped outside her house, they were there. Too often, when she closed her eyes, they were there. They took days and weeks from her at a time when she was consumed by fear and a blackness that was hard to describe. If not for the children, she didn't know what would become of her.

Erith didn't know if it was the laudanum that Mary gave her, or the feeling of being safe, but she felt well-rested. She had worried about putting everyone out of their way on the trip, but all hands assured her it was the best thing to do. The more she protested, the more they ignored her.

She sat alone in the room after the constable left and once

Mary had cleared away breakfast. The subtle movement of the boat beneath her as they left St. John's harbour was comforting. Two days before, she had only herself and three children and the thoughts of Beatrice for company. Now she was in a whirlwind of people who wanted to help her. Despite the looming trial and knife wound in her shoulder, Erith felt strong.

She had met evil for the second time and survived. Erith hadn't given up, and she wouldn't now. Just like she wouldn't give up on Beatrice until she knew for sure. She prayed Danol would still help her find the truth, though after the trouble she had been for the last couple of days, he might decide differently.

Now she couldn't stand being in bed any longer. Mary said she had lost some blood but that she should recover without any lasting effects. The knife had gone deep but hadn't hit anything that wouldn't heal. She shivered when she remembered seeing Hand. The knife was aimed at her head. If Danol hadn't pushed her out of the way. . . . She didn't even want to think about that.

With great care, she wormed her way out from under the covers, rolled to a sitting position, and put her feet on the floor. How was she going to do this? She pulled the grey canvas bag, her clothes trove, onto the bed, feeling the sting in her shoulder. Erith waited for the pain to settle before rifling through the bag for a loose blouse and comfortable smock. The stockings were hardest to get on. She contorted her legs and her toes until her feet were inside, then pulled them up with her good arm. A few times she bent too far and winced, but she was careful not to burst a stitch.

She cautiously manoeuvred her head out of the sling and her arm from her nightclothes and gasped when she saw the enormous bruise reflected from the mirror attached to the storage locker door. Sitting back on the bed in shock, she probed the bandaged area with her left hand, her fingers gently grazing the purple and yellow marks above and below the white strips that ran around her neck and under her arm.

Working carefully, she put her hand in the sleeve of her blouse and wove her arm through. She set the blouse across her shoulders and quickly finished dressing and fixed the buttons. Her long grey skirt had an elastic waist and was easy to pull on over her small hips. She shoved her head through the hole in the sling and settled her arm, then rooted her shoes out from under the bed and slipped them on. Now she was ready to get out of the room.

Erith stood slowly, fully intending to sit back on the bed if she became dizzy. She wanted to get out, but she didn't want to injure herself any further. That was a setback she couldn't afford. She shuffled toward the door and carefully turned the knob. The passageway was empty, so she used her good shoulder to guide her way along the wall to the stairs. She was on the third step when she saw Mary at the top.

"Erith Lock. My God! What are you doing out of bed?" Mary came down the stairs and grabbed Erith's arm to help her up the remaining steps.

"I was going crazy being cooped up."

"But you haven't been there that long."

"Long enough!"

"I can see you're going to be a difficult patient," Mary said with a smile.

One of the crewmen spotted her from the wheel. "Glad you're feeling better, miss."

Erith thanked him and, with Mary's assistance, walked out on deck into the sun. George and Tommy raced toward her, shouting her name.

"Careful, boys," Danol called from behind them.

"I need to sit," Erith said. She was suddenly exhausted.

Danol took her arm and led her to the bench that ran along the front of the wheelhouse. Erith sat and gathered Tommy into a hug on her uninjured side. George was hesitant, as he had decided he was getting "too old for that" after spending time with Eddy. He merely nodded and smiled. Erith learned that Annie was helping Eddy with Petie, who had gone for a nap. That was where Mary was heading when she met Erith. The doctor left again, and Danol remained with Erith.

"I'm sure you have something to do besides looking out for me."

"Actually, I don't," Danol said as he sat on a coil of rope. "Should you be up?"

"Mary's mother, God rest her, once said that there's healing in the sun."

Erith shivered at the slight breeze, and Danol took off his coat and covered her. The residual warmth from his body transferred to her. She protested, but he wouldn't hear of it, so she snuggled beneath the jacket with her back to the rough wood and closed her eyes to face the sun. Soon she nodded off, then just as quickly startled herself awake. The jolt caused her to wince, and she cried out.

Danol immediately moved to her side and cradled her against him. "I'm bringing you below. This is too much for you."

"No, please, just a little longer." She felt like a child asking permission and stiffened against him.

"Fine," he said. He pulled his arm back. "The only way you'll stay here is if I sit beside you. We don't want you hurting yourself."

There was no panic—she was too tired for that. Erith would

let her guard down just this once. She would briefly expose an unexplored part of her that had been buried beneath a cloak of so many hurts. The warmth from him, the lull of the tide, and the sun shining on her face were heaven. Erith felt . . . safe.

Danol put his arm around her again and carefully covered her with his coat. Mary returned moments later. She sat on the coil of rope and smiled.

"We really need to get her back into bed, Danol."

Erith groaned in protest.

"You think you're tough, but your body is weak. I don't want you getting cold or bursting your stitches," Mary said.

"Thank you, Mary. You seem to be with me when I need you the most," Erith mumbled. She was finding it difficult to keep her eyes open.

"We tended to her. You know . . . when it happened," Mary said.

Danol nodded. "I'll take her down."

Erith didn't want to fight back. Just this once she would allow herself to feel . . . safe . . . whole.

Mary took Danol's coat and helped him ease Erith into his arms. He gently hoisted her, and as she laid her head into the crook of his neck, her hair blew up around his face. Mary covered her with the coat, corralled Erith's hair and poked it beneath, and followed Danol to the cabin. He laid Erith in the bed and left Mary to cover her up.

18

Although the medication took away her physical pain, once she closed her eyes, Erith's dreams transported her right back to one of the worst days of her life.

"Please don't do this. I'll keep her upstairs. I'll do whatever you want."

"Too late, Erith. What's done is done. I've made the arrangements," Kathleen Lock said.

"Unmake them. Please. I won't ask for anything else."

"They can't be undone. It's asking more than I'm prepared to give. Father Fleming will be here tomorrow."

"I won't give her up."

"You will or you'll leave. I mean it, Erith. I did my duty to your father by keeping you. I'll hear no more of it."

"But where will I go?" Erith implored.

"That's up to you. You got yourself in this predicament, and I won't be paying for it."

How could she blame her for this? Erith sat on the top step, facing the unrelenting woman below. She heard the baby stir. How could she give her away?

"Please!" Erith cried. Then more gently, "Please."

"Enough!" her stepmother roared from the front hall. "I won't discuss this. Have that baby ready to leave by tomorrow after Mass."

Erith's face fell into her hands. She was desperate. Time was running out, and she had nowhere to go and no money to go anywhere. She had seen how hard it was to raise a family while she was in Dog Cove. It would be worse for her and the baby. But how could she give up little Beatrice? And how could she not? She wasn't foolish enough to think things would turn out well for her if she left with the infant. She would just prolong the inevitable and put the little one in danger, and she knew she couldn't do that, no matter the cost to herself. Beatrice had paid enough by being born.

So, this was it. Sometimes she wondered if it was a kindness or a cruelty that Beatrice was born during the winter months, when the priest didn't travel to the harbour. Erith had less than a day left. She stood and went into the room where the baby lay napping. At three months she was already sleeping through the night and barely cried. They had been exiled to the upstairs, and Erith was not allowed down when anyone came to the store or for mail. This was no life for her little one, and she was sure that this was how it would remain if her stepmother gave in. What would she do when Beatrice started walking? She couldn't keep her upstairs forever. Although she would love to do just that, it was no life for her baby.

Erith picked up her baby girl. She lay on the bed and placed the precious child on her chest, staring at her. Despite the circumstances of her coming into the world, Erith loved her. The tiny nose, the dark eyes that had not yet come to full colour, the little tufts of light hair that tickled her neck whenever Beatrice turned her face, and the cherub lips. Erith gulped back the pain of what had happened and what was to come. She chose to stare at the beautiful face, to etch her baby into a place in her memory that couldn't be touched. She would drink in every second of her, every breath, every sigh—until she couldn't.

Erith wasn't sure how she would get through tomorrow, but she wouldn't ruin the precious moments of this day with Beatrice by thinking about it. Though she gave the baby milk, she, herself, refused to eat. That would take time away from her vigil.

The oil lamp sputtered, and darkness fell on the room while Erith stared at the baby. Morning came too quickly. She hadn't slept, nor changed her clothes, for fear of missing a precious second with her child.

She could hear her stepmother getting ready for church service. Kathleen would be staunch and upright in the third pew from the front with the rosary beads draped between her thumb and forefinger. The woman made a mockery of the church just by going.

This time a year ago, Erith was a child herself. Now, forced to be a woman, she had to make the ultimate sacrifice for her child. She had to give her away.

Erith fed and changed Beatrice, then folded the remaining diapers and collected the few items belonging to her child. Picking up a doll she had knitted over the winter, she placed it by her feet to keep her warm. She wrapped her in a flannel sheet on which she had stitched THIS IS BEATRICE, SHE WAS LOVED so the child would know she was given, not thrown away. Erith quickly swaddled her in two more blankets and tenderly placed her in the small wooden cradle that had once been hers. She kissed her forehead and said, "Goodbye, little one. I love you enough to let you go." Tears formed in her eyes as she heard her stepmother enter the foyer.

"Erith, dear!" Kathleen called.

The priest must be within earshot, Erith thought.

Erith didn't answer. She couldn't. She heard the footsteps on the stairs and the scrape of the cradle behind her as her stepmother picked it up. Each step of Kathleen's descent sounded like a gunshot in Erith's ears. She didn't realize she was clenching her hands until she felt a trickle of blood from where her nails had pierced the skin.

From her room upstairs, Erith couldn't make out the words spoken in muffled voices outside, but she heard the whinny of the horse and the sound of the mud sucking on the wheels of the cart. Her baby was leaving. The priest would go back the way he came, from the harbour wharf to the south side, then over the hill to John's Pond, and on to his final destination—the orphanage in St. John's, from where Beatrice would be adopted.

The door closed below, and her stepmother went to the kitchen. Instantly, Erith let out a blood-curdling roar and burst from the room. She ran down the stairs and threw open the door in time to see the cart going out of sight toward the wharf. She screamed Beatrice's name over and over into the still March air and began to run after the cart.

Erith tripped on the doorstep, fell, and hit her shoulder on a rock. Pain shot through her body, and she couldn't get her feet under her. Something was holding her down. "Beatrice! Beatrice! Beatrice!" she cried as she struggled to get up.

"Erith, stop or you'll break your stitches! Danol, keep her still, she'll hurt herself. Erith! Erith, honey, you're on the boat. Beatrice is gone."

Erith was confused. She opened her eyes to see Mary and Danol on either side of her and Peter at the foot of the bed.

"Beatrice," she said softly as reality sunk in. She lay back on the pillows. "Beatrice is gone."

"I knew getting up was a bad idea," Mary ranted at nobody in particular. "You suffered a near-mortal wound yesterday and then went traipsing around on deck this morning. I'm going to get you something to eat. Danol, you stay with Erith."

Peter came around to the space that Mary had vacated and told Erith he needed to look at the bandage. He peeked inside the shirt. "There's no blood. That's a good sign. Do you have any pain?"

"Not in my shoulder," Erith said softly as she twisted her hands together.

"I'm sorry, Erith," he said.

"I know. It's been a long time since I've had that dream."

"We'll be on the boat for quite some time, so I'll go get you something to help you sleep." Peter didn't wait for her to answer.

Danol was alone with her for the second time that day. He covered her hand with his.

"I promise I'll do my best to find out what happened to your Beatrice, no matter how long it takes."

"Do you promise to tell me the truth, no matter what that is? I want to put my hand on the ground over where she lies and make sure she has a proper stone, if it comes to that."

"On my word of honour," Danol said. He let her go when Peter came in.

Erith slept once more. Mary returned when the crew were readying the boat for their stop in Ferryland on the southern shore of the peninsula. The doctors would see patients for the afternoon and into the evening. Mary and Peter would sleep on the boat while it was moored at the community wharf. The next day they would move on to Trepassey Bay to help there before going into St. Mary's Bay and heading for home the following morning.

Erith was getting stronger each day and spent some time on deck. The fog had rolled in by the time they reached Trepassey, so Mary was adamant that she stay below. She gave Erith a couple of books to read and keep her mind occupied.

She started *The Count of Monte Cristo* by Alexandre Dumas. Mary said it was her favourite. But when Erith realized there was a prison escape involved, she quickly closed it and picked another. She determined that *Black Beauty* by Anna Sewell was much more appropriate to her taste.

19

Erith was on deck when they docked in North Harbour. Coming in through the harbour, she couldn't help but recall the day she had left, supposedly for good. She remembered as if it were yesterday.

Confined to her room, Erith had been in a state of oblivion. She hadn't seen nor spoken to anyone in weeks. She was adrift on an ocean, but it refused to take her. Instead, it taunted her. Wave after wave overtook her, stopped her breath, and salted her wounds, keeping them fresh, open, and sore. There was no mercy. The vast sea of anguish wouldn't claim her, and there was no shore in sight.

Then, one day she'd heard voices downstairs. Her stepmother's raised voice was common, but there was a man who was shouting back at her. It sounded like Maggie's son, Patrick, but Erith must have heard wrong. She began to pay attention to the voices, and then she heard Agnes ask about her.

Erith quickly pulled on a clean smock, ran her fingers through her dishevelled hair, and made her way downstairs.

"How dare you!" Kathleen cried. "I've enough to deal with. I wasn't taking on three more mouths. I owed him nothing."

"That *him* was your brother," Patrick shouted in frustration. "My God, woman!"

Erith pushed open the door. Patrick saw her and said curtly, "Erith."

"Patrick, Agnes, what are you doing here? Shouldn't you be fishing? Where are Steven and the boys?"

Agnes gasped, clearly shocked by Erith's appearance. She ran to Erith and gave her a hug. For a second Erith was taken aback by this sudden human contact. She hesitantly hugged Agnes in return. "What's going on?" she asked.

"We've just moved to the south side of the harbour," Agnes said. "We're here to get a few items to tide us over."

"You're moving here? Maggie will miss your help this year."

"Honey, Maggie isn't in Dog Cove."

"She isn't? Where is she?"

"Erith doesn't know," her stepmother growled from between pursed lips.

"Doesn't know what?" Erith asked.

Patrick shook his head. "How can she not know?"

"I didn't tell her, that's why. She didn't need to know," Kathleen spat.

"I didn't need to know what? Will somebody tell me what's going on?"

"There's no easy way to tell you this, Erith," said Agnes.

When Agnes told her that Dinn and John had perished

weeks ago, Erith fell back on a barrel of flour. Dinn had gone on the ice to retrieve a seal, and the pan had overturned. When he didn't surface, John grabbed a stick from the woodpile in an attempt to rescue him. A wave jostled the ice, and he lost his footing and was jammed between two pans before going under. Their bodies washed ashore days later. Maggie was distraught. They were brought to St. Joseph's, on the other side of the bay, for burial. Maggie remained there with her daughter's family. By summer's end, the community would be abandoned, the life snuffed out of it as if someone had pinched its wick.

Erith went white. She had expected her stepmother to come for her and tell her she was going to Dog Cove once more. Instead, the reprieve from her grief over Beatrice hadn't come, and she hadn't been in any condition to ask why.

When she recovered from the shock, she asked, "Where are the children?"

"Their so-called aunt refused to take them. They've been sent to an orphanage in St. John's," Patrick said with such ferocity she thought he was going to beat her stepmother senseless. Erith hadn't known him to have a temper.

"No, no, no, no," Erith said. "That can't be." Kathleen had refused to take the children.

"I guess she doesn't know about Dinn's letter, either?" Patrick inquired.

"Dinn's letter?"

"Yes, Agnes wrote it for him and sent it here months ago."

"I don't know what you're talking about," said Kathleen. Her stoic face was betrayed by the slight colour in her cheeks.

"My God," Patrick said slowly.

"What is it?" Erith asked. How much more could she take? What more could there be?

"Don't, Patrick," Agnes said. "Nothing can be gained from it now. Let it lie."

"I want to know," Erith said.

"She has the right," said Patrick.

"Not while she's under my roof," Kathleen replied.

Patrick grabbed the woman by the arms and lifted her up so that she was face to face with him. "We're telling her." He laid her down again, barely controlling his temper. "You're lucky I'm not in the habit of hitting women."

"Do what you must," Kathleen replied under her breath, clearly shaken by the manhandling. "It won't change anything now." She left the store in a huff and slammed the door to the kitchen behind her.

Patrick pulled a chair over and motioned for Erith to sit. Agnes took Erith's hands in her own. She told her that Dinn had learned of Erith's predicament. Maggie had told him.

"He blamed himself for what happened to you," Agnes said. "He figured he should have come in and got you that day. He was mad with his sister for sending you out with strangers."

Dinn had sent a letter telling his sister, Kathleen, that he would take Erith and the baby to Dog Cove and that he would marry her when she turned eighteen, if she would have him. Erith's mouth dropped open. She had been afforded an option after all—she could have kept Beatrice! She would be alive now. Her stepmother had done this.

Erith would have married Dinn, though he was more than twice her age. She loved his children, and she had loved Beatrice. Life would have been hard, but it wouldn't have been any harder than it was now. She would have something more than a petrified heart. Now it was all gone—Beatrice, the children, and Dinn.

The shocking news brought her back from the hopelessness she had felt at the loss of her child. Erith knew what she had to do. She gave Patrick and Agnes the supplies they needed and thanked them for telling her about Dinn. She told Patrick she was sorry for the loss of his father. Agnes hugged her again, saying she didn't want to leave her, but Erith told her to go.

Erith had lovingly placed every memory, every sound, every smell, and every feeling of Beatrice in a room within her heart, expecting that someday the space her baby occupied might have a chance to grow. That had lasted only two days. Once she got the terrible news that Beatrice had died, Erith had sat with Beatrice's memory in that room and cloaked herself in despair. She had stayed inside herself with her little girl. Unwilling and unable to get out. The terrible news from Patrick and Agnes was the catalyst that brought her back.

So as not to betray her daughter, and in order to keep her own sanity, she locked the door on Beatrice's room to preserve every morsel of the child's existence. She swore an oath that, unlike Beatrice, the lives of Dinn's three children would not be lost to her. Somehow, she would make it right.

When she lived in Dog Cove, she had made a solemn promise to George that she would come to him. She looked at her hands and felt his tears on them. It didn't matter that it wouldn't be in the way it was intended—what mattered was that she would keep her vow. Her word was all she had. Nobody could take that from her. She had to keep it for the little boy crumpled in anguish on the seashore, the speechless little boy sobbing silently on the wharf, and their little sister, who would forget them all if Erith didn't intervene.

Two days later, when the mail boat came, Erith grabbed a

bag from under the bed, her coat from the hook, and while her stepmother was tending to the mail, every cent of money that was in the store's till. She calmly walked out of the house as if a perfect future lay ahead of her. The following day, she stepped onto the dock in St. John's.

Erith didn't return to John's Pond until she heard her stepmother was dying. She wanted to see for herself what it was like for the devil incarnate to die, and she wasn't disappointed. Erith made sure Kathleen knew that she had survived and prospered, despite the woman's every effort to bring about the opposite. She told her she knew what her father had done and only let it continue out of respect for him.

Kathleen's final utterance might have been her last attempt to make sure she destroyed Erith's bittersweet semblance of peace. That was why it was so hard to believe that Beatrice was alive. On rare occasions, Erith sneaked a peek in Beatrice's room. She dared not fully open the door for fear she would be sucked in and swallowed in the nothingness. The pain in that place was her penance for sins she guessed she had committed. If she listened to Kathleen Lock, it was for being born.

Her desperate need to save George, Tommy, and Annie from an existence akin to her own unwanted and unloved youth had eventually saved her. However, when the blackness came, sometimes it was hard to tell if she had truly been saved.

20

When she arrived in St. John's the first time, Erith felt more alone than she had the day she went to Dog Cove. She could as well have been in a foreign land. Dockworkers stared at her when she got off the boat, some making shocking remarks that brought back the terror of the distant cove. She blindly ran away from the wharves to escape the jeers and taunting. Fear mocked her, and panic pulled her onward.

Erith thought of Kathleen's rage once she found out what Erith had done and wondered if her stepmother would send constables after her to retrieve the money—and possibly put her in jail, if there were any such place for young girls. She ran out of breath before she could rein in her growing fear. Her body heaved under the need for air. She gasped and coughed uncontrollably and leaned on a white picket fence to keep herself upright. A woman shouted at her from a doorstep just beyond the palings. Erith couldn't quite make out what she was saying. She wasn't able to straighten up.

The woman strutted toward her with a straw broom. "We don't want your kind around here." Erith wasn't sure what she meant. Did she know it was Erith's first time in St. John's? "Be off with you," the lady said as she waved the broom at her.

"I'm sorry, ma'am. I just came from the boat . . ."

Before she could finish, the woman said, "I know where you came from, and like I said, we don't want your kind around here."

Erith was petrified. What was it about her that made this woman despise her? She hurriedly left the fence and continued up the hill away from the docks and the angry woman.

She was looking backwards and failed to see two black-dressed figures step onto the street in front her. Erith slammed into one of them, and both almost fell to the ground. Her arms flailed to keep from falling. "I'm so sorry! I wasn't paying attention," she stammered.

Two Sisters of Mercy, Sister Mary Joseph, a woman of about forty, and Sister Mary Clement, a girl not much older than Erith, were coming from a sick call when she reeled into them. Erith later discovered that the nuns had taken these names when they joined the convent. The older, Sister Mary Joseph, was the niece of Anastasia Tarahan, who was the first Sister of Mercy to hail from Newfoundland.

The older nun put her hand on Erith's arm and smiled. "It's all right my child. No harm done."

"Where are you trying to go in such a hurry?" Sister Mary Clement asked, her kind voice matching her warm smile.

Erith couldn't hold back any longer, and tears spilled down her cheeks. The two nuns stood patiently with her on the side of the street until she was ready to speak. The older nun gave her a handkerchief. In between sobs, Erith managed to tell them she had just arrived in St. John's and had nowhere to go. She said she came looking for three children from Dog Cove but hadn't made any plans and didn't know what to do next.

"Well, it's a good thing we were here," Sister Mary Joseph said. "Come with us, child. We'll get you something to eat and then figure out the rest of it."

They guided her along mucky lanes on the west side of town. The houses looked like they had been hastily put together and attached to one another in long rows on narrow streets. In the gutters, horse droppings and human waste discarded from the front doors in the early morning smelled to high heaven. The older nun explained there was no running water in this part of the city and poverty and pestilence were rampant. Folks were very poor but proud and hard-working.

The nuns were familiar with this clustered part of the city. They brought education to the young and nursing care in the way of medicine, food, water, and company to many in the area. Although there were eighty Sisters of Mercy in Newfoundland, only a few were stationed in St. John's at that time. They knew many of the residents and were respected for their charity and kindness, which they delivered any hour of the day or night, whenever they were needed.

En route, they asked questions about the children Erith was seeking. Sister Mary Joseph informed her that a child named Anne Ryan had been delivered to the Belvedere Orphanage over a month before. After a few weeks of adjustment, she was doing well. The nuns offered to take her to Annie. Erith couldn't believe that she might be able to see the little girl so soon!

They arrived at a four-storey red brick building. There was a porch that seemed to stretch from street level to the roof, and each floor had nine windows, one on the porch and four on either side. The top floor had gabled windows and looked like it was built into the attic. The nuns led her around the back to another two-storey wooden building. The white painted structure gleamed in the afternoon sun. It was attached to the rear of the brick building, and Sister Mary Clement told her this residence was St. Michael's Convent.

Erith wanted to go to the orphanage, but Sister Mary Joseph asked her to come into the convent with her first. After getting her something to eat and a cup of tea, Sister Mary Joseph asked Erith her intentions for Annie. Erith told the nun she planned to take Annie and find the boys and get a place to live. After much questioning, Erith realized that she was a seventeen-year-old girl with little money, no job, and no home. She didn't know how she was going to look after herself, let alone the needs of three children. What had she been thinking? Then again, she hadn't been thinking. Her actions over the last few days told her that.

Erith saw herself in the children. She didn't want them to suffer the same fate that she had—unloved and alone. She had seen herself in Beatrice, too. . . . Erith put her hands in her palms and wept once more. Sister Mary Joseph moved beside her and held her while she cried.

"What am I going to do?"

"What of your parents? Can you go home?" the nun inquired.

Without going into too much detail, Erith explained her parents had died and she was no longer welcome at her stepmother's house.

"Well, the streets are no place for you." Sister Mary Joseph went on to tell her about St. Clair's Boarding School. "It's a lovely place for young girls. It was once the Mercy Convent and Immaculate Conception Orphanage before we moved to Belvedere." Erith could live there until she was able to manage on her own. She could find work. Many good homes were looking for housekeepers and nannies for their children. The older nun said she would make inquiries. Erith could work every day at the orphanage in lieu of payment for her room, and that way she could see Annie more often. The nun said she would check Annie's records to try to find out where the boys were located.

Erith was disheartened. She had foolishly thought she could come to St. John's and reclaim the children—but she had no right by birth to do so. Sister Mary Joseph was talking, but Erith had trouble focusing.

"Miss Lock, can you read and write?"

Erith nodded. She had gotten her grade eight education, mostly because the teachers boarded at their home. Erith suspected her stepmother wouldn't have let her go to school. She constantly told Erith she was stupid and couldn't learn. The teachers had been kind and patient, and Erith hadn't given up.

"Good. That might help you get in a good home. Where are your belongings?"

Her bag! Erith had left it on the boat. She didn't have much, but it was all she had. Luckily, she had kept the money on her person and not in the old canvas tote. The nun patted her hand and told her not to worry. She got the particulars from Erith and said she would send the groundsman to retrieve her belongings.

By that night her emotional turmoil had come to rest in a little butter-yellow room on the third floor at St. Clair's Boarding School. She had a narrow bed, a maple wardrobe, and a small matching table to keep her company for however long it would take.

Annie didn't recognize her right away, but she cried when it was time for Erith to leave. She assured her that she would be back. She refused to let the baby girl see her own tears and cried herself to sleep that night. Now that the drama of the last few days had calmed, the blackness began taking hold of her mind and settling in.

By the following week, Sister Mary Joseph had found her a housekeeping job at the home of a prominent family on Circular Road. More importantly, she had also found the boys at the Villa Nova Orphanage in Manuels, Conception Bay. Sister Mary Joseph booked tickets on the train for the following Sunday afternoon. She would accompany Annie to see her brothers. It would become a weekly trip for Erith until she could take the boys to live with her.

Erith couldn't contain herself as they strode toward the train station, the nuns in black, herself in her red coat, and little Annie dressed in a pink cotton dress, red velvet coat, and black shoes that Erith had picked out of a box of clothes that had been donated to the orphanage. According to the nuns, it was common practice for the well-to-do to share their discarded clothing with the orphans.

As the group made their way toward Fort William, near the harbour and the base of Signal Hill, Erith was amazed when she saw several trains lined up side by side. A big crowd had assembled. The little stone and brick building that served as the station was bustling with people. Many waited on a wooden platform that sidled the track, some sat on benches, while others stood alone or in groups chatting while they waited. She noticed people were quickly crossing the multitude of tracks from the opposite side to join the throng. She wondered about their safety, but Sister Mary Joseph and Sister Mary Clement didn't seem worried.

She heard the train whistle and became nervous about her first ride. Sister Mary Joseph had travelled a few times as far as the Villa Nova in Topsail and even farther to Holyrood. Erith had overheard a conversation at work about the train. Within a few years, it would be able to cross the island. Erith didn't understand how far that actually was, but she heard that it was almost 550 miles.

Her heart pounded as she caught a glimpse of the big black iron machine heading along the tracks toward them. Annie grabbed her leg and hugged hard, burying her head beneath the folds of Erith's skirts. Erith laid her hand on the child and told her it was going to be all right. The engine churned louder and louder, and there were enormous puffs of steam pouring from the train so that it looked as if it were coming through a thick fog.

The whistle blew several more times, and the wheels screamed on the track as the brakes stopped the massive iron engine. The crowd stepped back to avoid the last blast of steam before readying to surge toward the doors. Men dressed in black uniforms with starched white shirts stepped off each car after the train came to a jerky stop. They took a stool from inside the doorway and placed it on the ground before checking tickets.

Erith, Annie, Sister Mary Joseph, and Sister Mary Clement stood in line to get on the third of the five cars. Most of the passengers let them go ahead when they saw the black robes and habits. Sister Mary Joseph very graciously accepted the attention as they neared the ticket master, while Sister Mary Clement kept her head bowed and face hidden. The man, in his mid-fifties, smiled and helped them navigate the step, and then they were inside.

The narrow interior was clean and bright with creamy walls off-setting the light blue benches and curtains. They watched the crowd finish boarding behind them. Erith anxiously waited at the window while the engine stirred to life and the floor beneath them made a few hearty jerks. They were off!

Annie chattered, and Erith listened and smiled, letting the little girl stand by the window, secured by both her knees and those of the nun who sat across from her. They were alone in the facing bench seats, though the car was mostly full. They watched St. John's pass before their eyes as they made their way toward Conception Bay. Houses were congested near the harbour, but a few miles into the countryside, there were mostly scattered farmhouses among the heavily wooded land. They made several stops, and passengers got off while others boarded. Before Erith knew it, the bright blue of Conception Bay came into view.

Soon they crossed the bridge over what Erith heard someone refer to as Manuels River, and the train slowed to a stop. Several people got up, and Sister Mary Joseph nodded for her to do the same. Erith picked up Annie and exited ahead of the nuns.

Wooden fences lined the trail. Footpaths led off behind and between vegetable gardens, barnyards, and hayfields. They walked amid chatting groups of passengers who gradually dispersed into the maze as the diminishing group continued toward the shore. Annie had tired on the train and quickly fell asleep in the morning heat on Erith's shoulder. Though the child wasn't very heavy, she felt relieved when a white Cross came into view above the sparsely treed vista. They walked out between two fences and onto a firmly packed road that fronted the grounds.

The huge white building resembled a church. As they neared, Erith could see there were four tall windows evenly spaced along the side with four equally tall windows above them. The upper windows sported fancy pointed tops ensconced in finely carved wood. The structure was partially hidden by a massive birch tree at one corner of a raggedly fenced plot. Several scrubby spruces at the other corner of the meadow blocked her view.

They trod along the road, and it became clear that the property owned by the Villa Nova Orphanage was simple in its majesty, unlike the adjacent property to the east. A white picket fence gleamed in the sun and seemed to run endlessly along the road and around a bend. Thick square posts sentried a perfectly trimmed laneway leading to the facade of the building. Above the door was a long, narrow window which matched the windows on either side of the entryway in height and shape.

At the side, and slightly to the rear, a two-storey building annexed from the church. Erith counted fourteen equally spaced windows on the top floor from one corner to the other. Underneath were three different doorways and nine windows aligning with those above. Nearest the church, a large windowed storefront showcased breads, cakes, and trays of cookies as well as a sign that said OPEN.

Sister Mary Joseph ushered her in. Erith wasn't prepared for the grandeur once she entered. What she thought was a church was actually a business. Inside the main doors, the building opened up completely, and she could see the large wooden beams high in the rafters. The back half of the room was split into two storeys, both visible from the main entrance, with an open staircase edged by a thin metal railing leading to the second floor.

There were rows of neatly piled paper on the first floor. Three young boys were attending some sort of machine while two others were sorting stacks of papers on a long table. On the second floor, several teenaged boys were cutting and sewing cloth. Several men's suits hung on display, while others were in various stages of completion. A man appeared to be in charge, as he had several measuring tapes draped around his neck and was helping one of the boys with a cutting.

Except for the floors, which had polished maple hardwood, all the inside walls, like the outside, were gleaming white. Erith recognized the wooden planks beneath her feet after having scrubbed and waxed similar ones a week before.

A lad not much younger than Erith stood behind a hardwood desk just inside the door. He wore a light blue shirt and a dark blue pants and vest. He saw Sister Mary Joseph, introduced himself as Simon, and asked how he could help her.

"I'm here to see Father Michael. Tell him Sister Mary Joseph from Belvedere is here."

The young man made a note and then looked to Erith.

"How may I help you?"

"Me? I'm with Sister."

The boy nodded. "Would you like to have a seat?" He directed them to a bench on the opposite side of the entrance, then looked beyond her. "Sir, how may I help you?"

Erith jumped when a man behind her spoke. She had been so caught up in her surroundings that she hadn't noticed others had followed them from the train. They moved to the bench, and the young lad quickly answered queries. Three others came and sat on the benches nearby. The boy called over one of the others who were working with the papers and whispered something. That boy left by way of a door behind the desk.

While they waited, several of the people on the benches were called back and given various packages or were escorted elsewhere.

"What is all this?" Erith asked in a hushed tone. She moved Annie from her shoulder to her lap.

Sister Mary Joseph explained that the buildings on the property had been the Belvedere Hotel and Tavern some years before. Father Michael Morris had acquired it for the orphanage after the owner, Mrs. Squires, died. He added the chapel but later converted it to a printing press and tailor shop. The hotel became the residence for the boys, and the tavern was used as a kitchen and bakeshop.

"How many boys are here?"

"Over one hundred and twenty, I believe," Sister Mary Joseph replied.

"One hundred and twenty-seven, to be exact." They were startled by the voice. Sister Mary Joseph stood and smiled. She extended her hand.

"Ah, Father Michael."

"Sister Mary Joseph. Nice to see you again," he said. "Sister Mary Clement." He nodded to the younger nun. "And who have we here?"

Erith placed Annie on her shoulder once again as she stood. The movement woke the child, and she burrowed into Erith's neck.

"Father Michael Morris, this is Erith Lock, and this is Annie Ryan."

Erith extended her hand to Father Michael, a tall, dark-haired man no more than ten years her senior, if he was that. He had a pleasant smile, and his grasp was warm and firm.

"Pleased to meet you, Father," Erith said as she blushed.

The priest smiled at her, then laid his hand on Annie's back and tried to peek at her.

"Such a pretty little girl you have here," he said as he tousled Annie's hair. Annie burrowed further into Erith's neck, and Father Michael chuckled. Erith liked him immediately.

"I was in the conservatory tending to the lilies when John came to fetch me. How can I help you?"

Sister Mary Joseph told him of Erith's situation and her relationship to George and Tommy, who were now housed there.

"Ah, yes, Tommy. The boy doesn't speak. Were you aware of that?" He turned to Erith as he asked the question.

"Yes, Father. Tommy hadn't spoken up to the last time that I saw him."

"I see. I've had a doctor check him out. I thought he might have been deaf, but the doctor says no. The older fellow, George, he looks out for his brother. They're the youngest two here. I wasn't sure if we would take them or not, but there was nowhere else for them to go." The young priest swept his arm around the room. "As you can see, many of the boys here are in their teenage years. The home is devised to give them skills to use when they are old enough to leave."

"I was telling Erith about the shoe shop, the tailoring, and the printing."

"Yes. We also have a flower shop, thanks to the conservatory, and we've recently added a bakeshop as well. Oh, and there's the farm on Kelly's Island."

Erith was dumbfounded. She didn't really know what to say. She thought it a shame that the boys would have to work. A sudden and unexpected anger caused her to blurt out, "How will George and Tommy work for their keep? They are so young." She almost covered her mouth for being so bold.

Father Michael laughed at the question before he realized she was serious. "You have it wrong, Miss Lock. There's a school in the dormitory. We make sure the boys can read and write, and then we teach them skills that will keep them off the street when they are old enough to leave. Some of the boys who have left here have become apprentices at businesses in St. John's. Two have gone on to own their own enterprises. That wouldn't have been possible if they hadn't been schooled here at Villa Nova."

Erith was intrigued. Father Michael went on to talk about how the children could try several trades until they found one that suited them. Many people looked for teenaged orphans to put them to work at hard labour, and the boys often ran away because of ill treatment and ended up on the streets. The orphanage didn't let that happen, and the boys were able to become good citizens instead of starving or relying on the benevolence of others to feed and clothe them.

Money earned was put back into the operations and programs. When they were ready, the boys could leave with a small allotment to get them started.

"Now, I could go on about this place all day, but that's not why you're here."

Annie wanted to get down. Father Michael took her from Erith and gently bounced her a few times before laying her on the floor. Annie giggled and took Erith's hand.

"The boys are in class right about now. They will soon get out for lunch. They're a bit young for school, but George knew many of his letters, and Tommy seems to be good with numbers, which is astonishing for children so young."

Erith's work with George had paid off. "Are they in a classroom with older boys?"

"We have sixteen children here who are under eight years old. Two boys who have been with us for about seven years want to return to the west coast as educators, so they are teaching the boys. It's working rather well." He stopped suddenly and turned to Erith. "What are your intentions for the boys, Miss Lock?"

Erith knew what she wanted, but she knew it would sound foolish. "I intend to reunite the three children under my care."

"How old are you?"

"Seventeen," she said rather forcefully.

"And how do you propose to care for them?"

"I'm working two jobs. I can get another. I'm hoping to have enough money by the time I'm eighteen to fulfill my obligation."

"And just what obligation is that?"

"I promised George," Erith stated simply.

"Well, Miss Lock, if we had more people as committed as you, we'd have no need for this orphanage. I admire your courage and determination. I wish you well, and I'll pray for you."

Father Michael ushered them through the doors behind the desk, where they entered a short corridor leading to the back of the kitchen. He asked the cooks to prepare lunch for Erith and the nuns before leading them out into the garden at the rear of the building.

Erith remarked on the size of the structure. Sister Mary Joseph told her most of the first floor held classrooms, laundry, supplies, and storage, while the top housed dormitories. There was also a basement full of wood to keep the boilers hot and the place heated.

Annie chased a butterfly, and Erith shifted several times on the bench. She was beginning to feel nervous. She hadn't seen the boys for a long time and wasn't sure that they would recognize her or that they would want her to claim them.

She didn't have long to wait. The two children burst from

a door, with George leading and tugging Tommy along by the hand. Both were crying, and George was almost screaming, "Erith, you came for us!" He looked back at Tommy and shouted, "She came for us! Look, Annie, too!"

Before Erith could stand, they launched themselves at her and knocked over the seat, sending them all sprawling backwards on the grass. Erith couldn't untangle herself from the legs of the chair because the two boys hugged into her, their cries muffled by her coat. Annie, who had fallen to the grass, picked herself up and plopped down on top of them all. She joined them in crying, too. Erith couldn't stop her tears, and she kissed the tops of each of their heads.

Sister Mary Joseph dried her eyes with a handkerchief as she stood and moved toward the group. Sister Mary Clement joined her. She picked up Annie, and Father Michael lifted Tommy, then George, from atop Erith. She got up on her elbows, and Father Michael helped her the rest of the way. The nuns brushed the brambles and dried grass from her back and her hair while she straightened the front of her clothes.

Erith was shocked by how much she had missed the two little ones. She knelt and opened her arms one more time to a hug. Both boys were eager to be in her embrace. She tenderly stroked their hair. Annie slammed into the back of them with her arms open wide.

"Look how much you've grown," she said as she stood each one away from her to get a good look. Her eyes could hardly see for tears as she looked them up and down. "Is that really you, George Ryan?"

George smiled between hiccups. "It's me, Erith."

"And look at you, Tommy Ryan. You've grown so tall!"

The little boy smiled and hugged her. He squeezed tightly

and kissed her face. Whatever doubts Erith had felt now disappeared. Her resolve was stronger than ever that she would make the boys and Annie her own. Maybe not right then, but certainly as soon as she could manage.

The clergyman and the nuns left her alone with the children. Simon brought a basket and blanket a short time later, and they had a picnic right there on the grass. Erith stretched out the red patterned cloth, and they all sat around in a circle. She put ham and cheese on warm, fresh bread slices. A flask of lemonade and four cups were poked in the bottom of the basket. Cinnamon raisin buns topped off the meal.

The picnic reminded her of Dog Cove Pond and Agnes and Maggie. Those happy times seemed so long ago. She didn't want to ruin the afternoon by telling the boys that they couldn't come with her that day. Erith waited for the nuns and the priest to return before she broached the subject. When Sister Mary Joseph nodded from the doorway, Erith gathered the three children back to the blanket.

"George and Tommy, I have to leave now, and it breaks my heart that you can't come with me today," she said. She tried not to let them see how upset it made her, but she was going to be strong for them.

George and Tommy looked around and saw Father Michael and the two nuns approach. "We're not going?" George cried. He scrambled to grab her. "Please, Erith! Please don't leave us!"

"I don't want to leave you, but I have no home yet to take you to."

"What about our home in Dog Cove? With Maggie," George argued.

"Honey, your home is not there anymore. Maggie's not

there. Everyone is gone," Erith said as she stroked the side of his face. Tommy snuggled into her on the other side and started to cry. "I need you to be really good boys now. I need you to be strong. George, I need you to look out for Tommy." The boys cried harder, and Annie joined them.

Father Michael knelt on the quilt beside Tommy. He pried the child away from Erith and tried to console him. Erith gently pushed George away from her and stood him on the quilt. "George, I made you a promise that I will keep. I just can't keep it now. But if you will let me, I will come back every Sunday with Annie for a visit until I can take you home. I will try really hard to make that soon."

After a little cajoling, George agreed, and Tommy nodded. Father Michael walked them to the train, and Erith's eyes were full when she watched the boys walk away holding his hand. They were trying to be brave and strong.

That was how the ritual began. Sister Mary Joseph and Sister Mary Clement accompanied her on rare occasions. Father Michael, when he was at the orphanage, or one of the caretakers always walked her to the train with the boys. Despite Erith's protests, Father Michael always paid for her ticket. Though her heart broke every time she left the boys, they seemed to accept their fate. Her resolve was strong, but her circumstance didn't get much better, no matter how much she worked and saved.

21

Now here she was, many years later, ready to dock in North Harbour with the three children. Her life had come full circle, it seemed. Two of the mates were ready to throw the lines to the dock when Erith heard her name being called, then, George's, Tommy's, and Annie's. She looked toward the shore, and there, nearly running toward them, was Maggie! She was shouting their names. Erith hadn't seen her since she left Dog Cove eight years before, but there was no mistaking Maggie Ryan.

Once they docked, Danol and Mary helped her onto the wharf. Mary had to warn Maggie of her injury, but it didn't keep the woman from hugging her. She shed a few tears at Erith's predicament—and when the children didn't recognize her right away.

"Erith, Erith, Erith! Not a day has gone by that I didn't think of you and those three little dears. I wish I could have done more."

"Oh, Maggie, I was so sad to hear of the accident. I'm so sorry that you lost John and Dinn."

"Thank you, Erith. I miss them terribly."

"And nobody can blame you for the children. What would you have done to survive?"

"It was a dreadful time." Erith could see the anguish in the woman's face. "Thank God for Patrick's children for keeping me occupied."

"Maggie, what are you doing here?"

"I came to help Agnes with the new baby," Maggie replied. "I missed you by a few days when you were back the time Kathleen died. God rest her miserable bones."

Erith had been so caught up in thoughts of Beatrice that she hadn't even gone to see Agnes. She had heard her friend was expecting any day, and Agnes wouldn't have been able to come to her. Erith would have to apologize to Agnes and catch up on all that had happened.

"Why are you here on this side of the harbour?" Erith pressed her further.

Mary ushered them all from the wharf to the house, where Maggie had already set the kettle to boil and had made supper. "I was waiting for you, no matter what time you arrived. I just had to see you and those little darlings. Not so little now, though," Maggie told Erith. "I put fresh clothes on the beds in preparation for the children. It saddens me to no end that they don't know me."

"They were so young."

"Now, what happened to your shoulder?" Maggie asked.

"It's a long story, Maggie," Erith said.

"I'll pour the tea," Maggie said with a tone that brooked no argument. Saying no to her was out of the question.

While Maggie kept her company and Erith told her the news, the men unloaded her cargo and the children picked out their rooms. When Maggie realized that Mary and Peter were coming back to spend the night with her, she wouldn't hear of it. She was staying with Erith until she heard from the courts. Agnes didn't need her any longer, but Erith did.

Erith was delighted to have her. However, Danol said he was concerned for their safety without a man in the house.

"The Nolans have a small child. There's no need for them to be traipsing back and forth here every night," Maggie said. "You have neither chick nor child and a big empty house for company. I'll make up a place for you in the room behind the shop."

"She has a point," Danol said to Mary and Peter. "It wouldn't hurt me to stay here for a few days. I'm sure you have things to do."

It was settled. Danol took Peter and Mary to John's Pond. The two boys wanted to go with him, and Annie wanted to stay. Erith protested, but Danol wouldn't hear of leaving George and Tommy behind. The six crewmen went along with him, while only the two who lived in North Harbour would return. He would drop two men off at their home in the Tickles and another two who belonged to John's Pond.

On their return, he showed George and Tommy his method of telling how much daylight was left. As they stood on the bow, Danol told the boys to hold out their hands ahead of them.

"Now make a fist," he said. Both boys did as he asked, and he pointed to the horizon. "The sun is going to go down there behind the church."

"How do you know that?" asked Tommy.

"Because it went down there yesterday."

"But you weren't here yesterday," George said.

"That's true," said Danol. "Okay, it went down there the last time I was here."

"Oh," they both said together.

"Now, look at your fist and pretend that you're laying it on the trees." He closed one eye and asked them to do the same. "Then put your other fist on top like this." He took George's hand first, laid it on the other, then did the same with Tommy's. "Now take the bottom hand and keep going until you reach the sun. For every fist you make, that's the number of hours until sunset. You both know how to tell time, right?" He was relieved when they nodded.

Danol paused and watched while the boys made fists and looked to him for approval. For a fleeting moment, he saw in their faces his own youth at their age when he was trying to impress his father. He smiled and adjusted their hands, tousled their hair, and gave them words of encouragement, feeling as proud now as he hoped his father had ever felt for him.

One of the crew called to him, and the boys tried to stay out of the way while Danol helped moor the boat. He collected the items he needed for his stay at Erith's, then helped Tommy and George climb into the dory. They waited for him on the beach while he tied up the little boat. The boys walked on either side of him the mile or so to their new home.

Danol couldn't cage his smile. He liked how it felt to be with them.

"Where is your mom, Danol?" Tommy asked.

"She died when I was very young," he replied.

"Do you know where she is?"

"I'm afraid I don't."

"Maybe she's with our first mom," said Tommy. "I don't remember her, but George does."

"Perhaps she is," said Danol. He hadn't thought of his mother in a very long time.

"Erith's become our new mom," said Tommy. "She came for us."

Danol wasn't sure what to say, so he said nothing.

"She's a good mom," George said.

Tommy agreed. "We call her Mom sometimes. She likes that."

The sea was calm as they continued toward the house. "Have either of you boys skipped rocks?" Danol asked as he tried to steer the conversation from a subject that made him uncomfortable.

George told Danol that they sometimes snuck down between the wharves at St. John's harbour, but it was difficult to skip rocks because of all the boats.

"Well, we have a big ocean ahead of us. Let's see who can skip one the farthest."

They spent some time picking out flat rocks and taking turns in what ended up being a contest. George came out the winner, with Tommy a close second. On the way home, George and Tommy talked about different things they were going to miss about St. John's, but for the most part they just wanted to be together. They were going to be fine young men under Erith's care, Danol thought.

It turned out that Maggie was just what they needed. She kept the house in order and the children in line while Erith convalesced. The men on both sides of the harbour were alert to boats that weren't customarily in port. Danol stood on the wharf each time the mail came to make sure nobody un-expected got off.

His crew took the *Angel Endeavours* on two separate freight runs while he stayed put. Erith wasn't too pleased, but he wouldn't leave the community while there was a threat to her well-being. Her wound healed, and she had gotten almost all movement back in her shoulder. Mary said that with a little bit more time it would be as good as new.

Erith made some outings to the south side to be with Agnes. While she was there, Danol would work on his house. Tommy and George often joined him, and he was surprised at just how capable both boys were with their hands. No doubt they had learned some carpentry skills during their time at the orphanage. Annie begged Erith to let her go with them, and sometimes she relented. She wanted to help as much as her brothers, so Danol showed her how to use some of the tools.

It was near the end of June when he heard from Constable Jeffries. Erith's day in court was scheduled for Wednesday, July 11, 1894. Mary and Peter were due to go back for Mary's last year of medical school. They planned to take another two-week medical trip in August, but they would have to cancel if the court date were much later. Erith, of course, would have been furious that she was causing so much upheaval, but it turned out Mary had to be in Boston by the end of August, so the July court date suited them fine.

Danol liked living at the Lock home. The children were great company. Little Annie had taken to him and followed him everywhere. Her curiosity for life was infectious. At nine years old, she was like a mother hen to Mary's baby, Petie. Maggie stayed on, and the children came to regard her as a grandmother. Maggie was wary of Danol at first. She even asked his intentions toward Erith, but he assured her they were honourable.

The next day, he checked the rigging on the *Angel Endeavours* for the St. John's trip. It was a perfect day for fishing—grey skies with no wind. All boats in the harbour had gone, and none were seen on the horizon. The tip of Colinet Island looked like it was pointing up out of the water. George and Tommy were on board with him, and he taught them how to make knots.

Tommy notice the mail boat first and mentioned it to Danol. A day early? The hairs on the back of his neck rose, and he hastily tied the sail on the jib.

"We should go in," he said. They headed starboard to where the dory was tied. George grabbed the line to haul the dory closer, and Tommy watched with the gaff, ready to hook it. He could swing the little boat around when it was close enough, making it easier to get off.

Danol felt a piercing pain in his back before he heard a hollow crack bounce off the land on both sides of the harbour. He was already falling when the other boat rammed the *Angel Endeavours*. Tommy and George were sent flying over the rear railing. Danol heard screams, and the dory slammed into the back of the boat. What had just happened? The pain was excruciating. He tried to crawl across the deck to get to the boys. The floor was slippery underneath him. Looking down, he saw that the boards were covered with blood.

Danol rolled from his belly and instantly recoiled. He knew he had been shot in the back below his ribs. Tilting to the left, he tried to move again. He had to get to the boys. He had to warn Erith. She would have heard the shot, but she might pay it no mind. He yelled as loud as he could while he continued to push to the stern.

"Erith, they're here! Hide! Hide Annie! Erith!" He heard a *whoosh*, and then another. He felt a stinging in his leg at the same time the railing shattered above his head.

"Erith!" he yelled one last time.

Erith and Maggie lowered their teacups to the table when they heard the loud report. Marie ran in from the shop.

"Miss Erith! Miss Erith! Something's wrong, come quick!"

"What's wrong, Marie?"

"I heard a shot. I looked out, and there's a strange boat out near Mr. Cooper's."

She headed to the front step with Maggie close on her heels. Then she heard Danol.

"Did he say to hide Annie?" She turned to Maggie and Marie. Marie nodded. "My God, where's Annie?"

"She's out back," Maggie said. "I'll get her." She disappeared around the side of the house, shouting Annie's name.

Erith looked on as an unfamiliar boat came toward the wharf. Two men stood on the deck, and one fired a shot, then a second, at Danol's boat. He reloaded and turned toward her house just as Maggie and Annie came around the corner. Erith pushed Maggie inside and to the floor and grabbed Annie at the same time. She heard a gunshot followed by another. The clapboard near the door cracked each time. She slammed the door shut and lay covering Annie while Marie ducked into the kitchen.

"Marie, take Annie and go out through the back!" Erith shouted. "Go into the woods to your mother's house! Don't let anyone see you, and don't come back until you hear from me!" Marie grabbed Annie as the girl latched onto Erith.

"Annie, I love you. Now you have to go."

Annie hugged her and started to shake and cry. Marie tried to pull her away, but Annie clung fiercely to Erith.

"Annie Ryan, you do what I tell you. Be quick and go," Erith commanded. "We're wasting time."

Marie took Annie under her arm and disappeared through the kitchen. Soon, Maggie recovered and sat up. "Do you have a gun?" she asked calmly.

"There should be a couple in the store," Erith said. "Why?"

"We can't let them think we're here alone. Even to fire a shot, no matter where it lands, might make them think twice."

"Maggie, you should hide."

"Hide? I'm not hiding. John taught me how to shoot a gun. A person can't be much more difficult than a caribou. I'm not leaving you, Erith."

Erith wasn't scared for herself. She was scared for Annie. Where was Danol? Where were the boys? The two women crawled into the store, and Erith knocked the shotgun and shells from the rack.

"You load it, Maggie, and I'll fire. I don't want you to have a dead person on your soul."

It was surreal. Her children were being threatened, and she wasn't having that. She popped her head up to see the boat had almost made it to the dock. One man was bent behind the wheelhouse, while the one with the gun was preparing to jump ashore. She heard a shot, and the men looked toward the beach. The stranger raised his gun toward whom she thought must be Danol. Danol would save them.

On impulse, Erith broke the window and stuck out the barrel of the shotgun. She pulled the trigger and was instantly driven back on her rear, almost landing on top of Maggie. She scrambled toward the window and gave Maggie the gun and another shell. The man was motioning for the other fellow on the boat to keep going. Quickly, Maggie reloaded and passed the gun to Erith, and she fired again. This time she was prepared for the jolt and stayed upright. She was surprised when the shot hit the water just below where the man stood on the boat. She heard another shot, and both men squatted down in the shelter behind the gunwales as the boat steamed toward the mouth of the harbour.

"They're leaving, Maggie," Erith breathed.

Maggie was sitting with her back to the wall. She clutched her chest and heaved a sigh.

"Maggie? Maggie, are you all right?"

She didn't answer immediately, and Erith dropped the gun and ran to her side.

"Of course I'm all right. I'm thanking God right now," Maggie said. All colour had drained from her face.

Erith was startled when she heard the back door burst open.

"Erith, where are you?" It was Peter Nolan.

"In here!" she shouted.

"Where are the children?" The urgency in his voice wasn't lost on her as he ran into the room.

"Marie took Annie, and the boys are with Danol." She looked at him and blinked twice. "Wait. I thought you were Danol. Where's Danol? Where are Tommy and George?"

She clambered to her feet, raced past Peter, and stared at Danol's boat. Peter came out behind her. "There's no one there," she whispered. Then they saw a head come up over the gunwale of the *Angel Endeavours*. It was Mary.

"She must have rowed from the point," said Peter.

He explained that they had heard the shot when they almost made it to the other shore on their way to Erith's place, and then they heard Danol yell for her to hide Annie. Peter had broken into Danol's house and grabbed a gun and shells while Mary had gone to Mrs. Whalen's to leave Petie.

"Mary must have grabbed a rowboat from one of the other neighbors and went for the boat."

His wife stood and waved frantically. "Peter! Peter!" she shouted. "I need help! It's Danol!"

Peter bolted up the beach. Erith ran behind him, but she couldn't keep up. He had put a small dory in the water by the time she caught up.

"Tommy and George," she gasped.

She was up to her knees in water when she launched herself over the side of the little boat and fell into the pound. Peter grabbed the oars and covered the distance as quickly as possible. Mary had disappeared out of sight, and Erith assumed she was tending to Danol . . . and possibly the children.

When they reached the *Angel Endeavours,* Peter pulled to the back, where the rope ladder hung. Their dory was partially sunk and sported a big hole in its side. It had taken a hit, and its yellow colour shimmered eerily beneath the surface. Peter scaled the ropes at the rear of the boat and reached back to pull Erith aboard before turning to help Mary.

Erith glimpsed several fishing boats in the distance making their way toward them. She saw Peter and Mary standing over Danol, who was lying in a pool of blood. Mary had ripped pieces of material from her dress to tie around Danol's leg and to press into a wound on his back.

"It's bad, Peter," Mary said. She was rattled. "I thought he was gone when I found him." Her lips trembled as she looked at her husband.

Erith disappeared below. "Boys, where are you?" she shouted. "Tommy! George! Please come out! It's Mommy! Everything will be fine."

Erith tried not to panic. She quickly and methodically went through the boat, checking under bunks and in the cupboards, and she checked in places she knew the boys couldn't fit. When she came back on deck, she was frantic.

"The boys are gone," she whispered.

Fishermen were piling into the boat. Art Power took control and brought the boat to the wharf in front of the store. Someone had been sent to John's Pond for Peter's surgical kit. Peter and Mary worked on Danol and then helped four men move him from the boat to the wharf and then on to her house. They carried him on two oars and a piece of canvas from the sail. Erith refused to leave the boat. Erith heard words like *He's in pretty bad shape, Don't think he'll make it, The boat was rammed, There's a hole above the waterline, There's damage from gunshots*, and *The dory's a loss*, but nobody said *The boys are gone*.

Maggie was waiting on the wharf after Danol was removed from the boat. She wasn't able to climb aboard, so she asked one of the men to get Erith. Mr. Art Power tapped her shoulder. "Miss Erith, are you all right?" The last time he had touched her was when he carried her home those many years ago.

"No, I'm not. Tommy and George are gone. They were on the boat with Danol."

"Are you sure?"

"As sure as I can be. They left with Danol to check the rigging, but they're not here."

"Don't worry, Miss Erith. You go on to the house now," he said. "We'll look for the boys."

Maggie met her on the wharf and helped her to the house. Peter and Mary were working on Danol on the kitchen table when Maggie and Erith rushed in. Peter followed them out to talk to them in the hall. He was covered in Danol's blood.

"Where were the boys?"

"They were with Danol," Erith said.

"But they couldn't be," he said. "We didn't see them." He paused for a moment. "Maggie, get Art Power for me, and then make Erith a cup of sweet tea and one for yourself."

"They're all on the harbour," Maggie said. "All the fishing boats are out."

Erith wouldn't drink at first, but Maggie forced her. After a few swallows of the sweet liquid, Erith began to hear the sounds around her. Maggie began saying the rosary aloud. Peter and Mary were talking about Danol in the next room. She didn't understand some of the things they were saying, but she knew it was serious. Somebody was fixing the window in the store. A fly buzzed somewhere behind her head. The sounds of the children were no more. Dear God, the children. It couldn't end like this.

"Maggie, I need Annie to come home."

"Are you sure? We don't know anything yet."

"She's probably scared. I need to hold her."

Maggie left, and the sounds of the man fixing the window stopped. A short while later, Annie ran in with Marie close behind. Annie was crying, and she threw her arms around Erith. Erith kissed her head and rocked the little one back and forth.

"I'm sorry, Annie. I'm so sorry this happened." Annie stayed buried in her dress and refused to let her go. "Thank you, Marie. I'm so sorry. You must have been scared."

The young girl nodded. "Annie was a good girl. She did as you asked."

Erith rubbed the child's hair. "I know. She's such a good girl."

She hugged Annie even tighter. The girl stopped crying but didn't raise her head. Her soft hiccups were muffled by Erith's dress. Marie left them, and soon Erith heard the straw broom pushing glass and the clink as Marie put the shards in the tin dustbin. She heard her rustling around putting things back in place.

Where were the boys? She asked Annie to sit with Maggie, and after some cajoling, the little girl complied. Erith went to the doorstep and saw that Art Power had come back to the dock. She could see a number of small boats moving back and forth at the bowl of the harbour. The broken dory was pulled up on the beach.

Mr. Power's eyes wouldn't meet hers. "Miss Erith, I'm sorry, we can't find them."

"Did you check the shore on either side? They're good swimmers."

He pointed across at the opposite shore, where people were walking the beach. "Yes, miss. We haven't found a trace."

She didn't want to allow the words to sink in. She wasn't giving up. "I'll look on this side. They may have run into the woods."

"Somebody is checking this side, too," Mr. Power said. She looked and saw townspeople in the distance toward the point.

A shout drew their attention to the harbour. "What's going on?" It was Patrick Ryan. They waited for him to dock.

"Danol's been shot, and the boys are gone," Erith said flatly.

"What?" Patrick looked to Art, who nodded. "Where's Mother? Is she all right?"

"Yes, she's in the house with Annie," Erith replied.

"Where were you?" Art asked Patrick.

"I broke an oar. Did you say the boys were missing?"

"Yes," Art said as he bowed his head.

"I knew I saw the boys," Patrick said.

"What do you mean? You saw them?" Erith grabbed him. "Where?"

"I saw a boat and two men. I didn't realize they came from here. I shouted a greeting to them. I was sure I saw two heads pop up over the gunwale, but one of the men threw something over them," Patrick said. "To tell the truth, I thought I was seeing things."

"Oh, Patrick, it was the boys! It had to be," Erith said with renewed hope. She ran back to the house as Art waved the boats in. Patrick followed.

Inside the kitchen, Erith closed the door. Mary and Peter were cleaning up, and Danol was lying on his side on the table. His shirt was gone, and most of his pants had been cut off. Erith's hand went to her mouth when she saw him. She stepped forward and tenderly touched his foot.

"The men took the boys," she said quickly. "Patrick saw them." She paused for a second. "How is he, Peter?"

"We don't know," Mary said. "He's strong." The sadness in her eyes was echoed in her voice. "Can we keep him here?"

"Of course," Erith said as she continued to stare at Danol. There was blood on the table and floor. He looked white against the crimson background. But Erith didn't have time for the feelings that were flooding her. She let go of his foot as if she had been scalded.

"I'll stay," Mary said. "First, I have to get Petie."

"Where is he? I can send Marie," Erith said.

"I'd appreciate that," Mary said. She kissed her fingers and laid her hand on Danol's face. Her voice cracked when she said, "Here we are again, Danol. You better come back one more time."

Peter put his hand on her shoulder. "He'll pull through. He wouldn't dare die on you." Mary gave him a pained smile and turned to embrace Peter. "He'll make it, Mary."

"Now, what's this about the boys?" Peter asked. Erith relayed what Patrick had told her, and Peter left to speak to him.

Erith was torn in two. She needed to go—her boys came first—but she was also drawn to Danol. What had happened on that boat?

"He would have tried to save Tommy and George," Mary said.

"I know," Erith replied. She glanced at Danol as she tried to swallow the lump in her throat. "I can't be here, Mary. I need to focus on the boys."

"I know that. Danol knows that, too. He would not want nor expect that. He's a good man, Erith."

"He's here because of me. I won't forgive myself."

"Don't say that," Mary said. "Danol does what he wants. He needed to be here."

Erith grabbed Mary's hand. "I have to go. Take good care of him, Mary."

She slowly released Mary's hand, and without looking back, she slipped out of the kitchen to join the conversation between Peter and Patrick.

"We have to assume they are heading to St. John's," Peter said.

"Why?" asked Erith.

"Because it's most likely where they came from. Did you recognize either of them?"

"No," she replied.

"Well, I think I did. I can't be sure, but I think the fellow shooting was one of the crew from the boat that we arrested Simmons on." He looked at her with eyebrows raised.

"I didn't see anyone that day," Erith said softly.

"I'm going to St. John's," said Peter. "I need to talk to that constable."

"I'm going, too," Erith said. When he looked like he was going to argue, she said, "Don't even try to talk me out of it. They're my boys."

"I have to talk to Mary," Peter said. "Get ready!" He instructed Patrick to ask one of the fishermen to land them in Colinet. Patrick's boat was loaded down with fish, but all the others who had been in earshot of the gunfire had dumped their catches and raced back. From Colinet they would get a wagon and go the fifteen miles overland to Whitbourne to catch the train. Peter figured they might arrive in St. John's ahead of the two men.

"Maggie," Erith said. "Will you stay here with Annie?"

"I'd like to meet the person who'd take me out of here."

"What if the men come back?" Patrick asked. "You should come home with me, Ma. Annie can come, too."

"Indeed I won't. Danol needs care," Maggie told her son. "They won't come back here now."

"Well, I'll stay," he said lamely.

"Nonsense. You go home with Agnes. She's probably worried to death over there."

Art Power volunteered to stay ashore. Nobody would get into the harbour without him knowing about it.

Erith grabbed a few items of clothing and money from the cash drawer and stuffed them in a small canvas bag. Moments later, she was waiting by the door for Peter.

Mary hugged him. "Be careful, love," she said. She held both sides of Peter's face.

"I will." He kissed her and whispered words of encouragement in her ear as Erith watched from the door. Soon, they got aboard the boat and began their search for answers.

22

Too late to catch the last train, they stayed in a boarding house overnight and wired the constabulary in St. John's. The next day they got off the train in Fort William and were greeted by Constable Jeffries, who escorted them to Fort Townshend.

"Are you certain, Peter?" the constable asked.

"Not for sure, no."

"We've been watching the *Vagabond*," said Jeffries. "Cooper said there was something odd. He said the captain gave up Simmons too quick."

"Danol said that? When?" Erith asked.

"The day you were stabbed, ma'am," he replied. "Cooper wasn't convinced that Simmons had the means to get anyone to supposedly try to save him."

"He did mention that," Peter agreed.

"How is he, by the way?"

"We don't know. I'd like to say he'll recover," Peter said. He looked at Erith and smiled. "What of the *Vagabond*?"

"They've hired out space at the Newman Wine Vaults in

the west end of the harbour. It's a bit secluded there and well-fortified. They've been coming and going every few weeks."

"Is that out of the ordinary?" Peter asked.

"Well, it wouldn't be if they were paying tariffs to the harbourmaster. All the ships that use the vaults come from Spain and have their cargo examined. All except the *Vagabond*."

"How does that help us?" Erith asked.

"We have a man down there. He's been watching the place. We believe they're storing rum from Saint Pierre."

"But how does that help my boys?"

"A fisherman from Petty Harbour was found in the water a week ago. His boat wasn't recovered. We think it's related to the attack. We think they used that boat and that they'll bring the boys back to the wine vaults. Since they didn't kill you, they'll use them to keep you from testifying. We have yet to determine why Simmon's is so important to them."

"So, what are you prepared to do?" asked Peter.

"The harbourmaster assures me that the boat hasn't come in yet. He'll keep watch and notify us immediately. If they should slip into port, the man we have posted near the vaults will let us know. I have six men ready to rescue the boys."

"Seven," said Peter. "I'll be going."

Jeffries warned them that the place was heavily fortified with thick rock walls leading into the bedrock. If the officers didn't get there before the boys were taken into the vaults, it would be difficult to get them out.

"It may not end well," said Constable Jeffries. "I'm sorry, Miss Lock. You must be prepared for the worst."

The constable told them they were welcome to wait there, but it could be days before there were any developments. They chose to wait, at least for the rest of the day. Peter was better at waiting than Erith. He sat patiently in the chair, but she kept pacing. Her mind was too preoccupied for conversation.

It was almost dark when a young lad burst into the station asking for Jeffries. Erith watch as the constable grabbed his coat and shouted the names of five other men. Peter stood and donned his coat, too.

"Erith, you are not going. No arguments," he said. "I'll look out for the interests of Tommy and George." His tone left no doubt that she was staying put.

Not wishing to put the boys in any more danger than they were already in, Erith didn't say a word. Instead, she nodded and took Peter's hands in hers. "Bring them back to me," she said.

"I'll do everything I can. I promise." Peter gave her hand a reassuring squeeze, then followed the constables as they rushed from the building.

Erith sat and prayed. Her thoughts raced. Perhaps she should have gone. The boys would be scared. What was she thinking? She was afraid they wouldn't be there. Then they would be gone from her. Like Beatrice. She didn't know if she would come back from that place in her heart—or if she could come back anymore. Erith shook her head. She wouldn't give up. They would be all right. Oh, why hadn't she gone? Her thoughts kept cycling through the same thing over and over, always beginning with a prayer.

She heard them before she saw them. The clock had long since struck midnight when the door of the station house opened and George ran in, followed by Tommy. Erith met them halfway across the room, and they fiercely embraced. They talked incessantly about their adventure.

They raved about a standoff and how Peter had jumped on the man who was holding them. The rest of the bad men gave up when the constables took out their guns. Erith locked eyes with Peter above their heads and mouthed her thanks.

"They're safe. That's all that matters," Peter said.

Erith hugged the two boys. She couldn't agree more.

"Where are all the constables?" she asked.

"Taking prisoners to the penitentiary. I came straight here with the boys." He told her that Jeffries had gone to speak to Judge D. W. Prowse.

Erith and Peter sat and listened as the two boys told her how they had been knocked off the boat and into the water. The dory had smashed, so they swam to the ladder at the rear. Before they could make it, the two men hauled them out of the water. Their clothes were stuck to them, making it hard to move, and they couldn't get away. One of the men stuffed something in their mouths and tied them up. He told them if they moved, the other man would shoot them. Then he fired shots to prove it before putting them under a piece of sail. Somebody else was shooting, too. George heard the man say, "Take them in case we don't get the woman," and the other one had agreed.

"The one without the gun said he didn't want to be killed," said George.

"His partner wanted to hurt us," Tommy cut in. "We got each other untied, and we were going to jump out of the boat."

"That's when we saw Patrick," said George. "The man who didn't have a gun told us to get down and keep quiet or the other fellow would shoot Patrick. So we did."

"You poor things," said Erith. "I bet you were scared."

"We weren't scared. We knew Danol would come for us," said George.

"By the way, where's Danol?" asked Tommy. "Why didn't he come?"

"Honey, Danol was hurt when those men came," Erith told him.

"Is he going to die, too?"

"Doctor Nolan is working really hard right now to make sure that doesn't happen," said Peter. "Now, let's all get out of here and go to a hotel and get something to eat."

Erith silently thanked Peter for changing the topic. "Yes, you must be starved," she said.

A helpful constable gave them the address of Mrs. Mullet, who owned a boarding house on Duckworth Street. Constable Jeffries found them there after they had just finished a meal of meat and potatoes and fresh bread. He looked bedraggled but still managed a smile. The policeman asked to speak to Peter and Erith out of earshot of the children. Mrs. Mullet, a grey-haired widow in her early fifties with a kind smile, brought the boys to the kitchen for a piece of chocolate cake.

"Miss Lock, I spoke to Judge Prowse and informed him of what had transpired. He was none too happy with these types of shenanigans going on and said that law and order must prevail."

Erith and Peter gave him their full attention when he explained that, though the courtroom wasn't ready at the Star of the Sea Hall premises on Henry Street, Judge Prowse was prepared to go ahead with trial the next day. He wanted to keep them safe and said a speedy trial was the only answer.

By order of Judge Prowse, Jeffries and another constable were to stay at the boarding house that night. Erith was happy with the news, as was Peter. Although Peter said he had no intentions of going back without her and the boys, and assured Erith that Mary was as capable as he in caring for Danol, he was glad the trial would be swift. Erith knew he was worried about Mary and how she would cope if Danol didn't make it.

The boys slept in the room with Erith, and Peter was in the room next door. The constables stayed in the hall. Despite feeling safe, Erith felt restless for the few hours left in the night. She would doze, and her dreams were filled with Simmons and Hand and the man shooting from the boat. Then she would wake and fall back to sleep only to dream that Danol, Tommy, and George were dead. They were all pointing at her and screaming that it was her fault. Finally, after waking in a cold sweat, she remained vigilant until dawn, pulling the boys closer as they slept.

As Erith watched the sun spill daylight over the steep hills that sheltered St. John's harbour, she heard Peter stir beyond the thin papered wall. He must have heard her, too, because he brought a pot of tea a short time later. They sat in silence at the little round table by the foot of the bed, each with thoughts of home. Erith thought it funny that North Harbour was home—her outlook had been changed by the two little people sprawled across the bed and their sweet baby sister.

When the boys awoke, they all went for breakfast in the large dining room at the foot of the stairs. Mrs. Mullet had pancakes and molasses for the children. She said she didn't often get to cook for boarders so young. Peter and Erith enjoyed eggs, ham, and toast while the boys filled up on the sweet treats.

They planned to spend the morning inside, although Erith knew that Tommy and George would want to go out and see friends. However, Peter kept them occupied. At mid-morning, they had a visitor.

When a man in his early sixties, with long, bushy sideburns beneath a black top hat and dressed flawlessly in a dark grey suit showed up asking for Erith, Peter didn't immediately recognize him. He told Tommy and George to go upstairs, but Constable Jeffries stopped them.

"Good morning, Your Honour," the constable said. "Peter Nolan, Miss Lock, this is Judge Prowse." He included Tommy and George in the introductions.

The judge shook their hands and asked if he could have a word with them. Mrs. Mullet showed them to the sitting room, where they would be alone.

"This is nasty business we're dealing with, Miss Lock," Judge Prowse said. "I wanted to speak to the two young lads and let them tell me what happened. With your permission, of course."

The judge explained that he wanted to keep the boys away from the trial, but he also wanted to have the full account. He asked Tommy and George several questions about their parents and who Erith was to them, and then he asked about what had happened just two days earlier. The boys were talkative, and the judge said he had what he needed. He asked if there was somebody who could keep the boys for the afternoon, and Erith told him about her friends at the Sisters of Mercy.

By mid-afternoon she was at the Star Hall on Henry Street. It was a huge wooden building, freshly painted a deep blue colour, with white trim around the doors and windows. The Henry Street entrance felt like it brought them below ground because of the cut of the hill. Peter and two constables accompanied Erith as she was escorted through a lobby and past two heavy wooden doors. The interior was lamplit and carried no natural light.

A few well-dressed men were seated near the front of the

room. A man in a constable's uniform came through a door at the rear, followed by Judge Prowse, who was sporting a long black robe.

Erith's heart raced. Her palms grew moist, and heat rose in her cheeks. She anxiously awaited her two assailants, but she wasn't scared—she was mad. The constable called the court to order and listened as Judge Prowse issued a few remarks. Another constable entered, went to the judge, and whispered something. There was a short silence, then the constables and the judge left.

Erith looked from Peter to Jeffries. Neither seemed to know what was happening. The makeshift courtroom resonated with soft mumblings while they waited. Soon, a constable came in, tapped Jeffries on the shoulder, and beckoned for him to go outside. He excused himself and said he would be right back.

Erith began to fidget in her seat. Peter laid his hand on her arm to give her comfort and strength.

"I will leave when you're called up, if you prefer," he said.

She hadn't really thought about it. With all these people here, how was she going to tell the judge what happened to her? Although she didn't really know Peter well, she believed that seeing a friendly face in the room might help her.

"You don't have to do that," she said. "I'll be fine."

"That you will, Erith. I admire your bravery."

She didn't think of herself as being brave but thanked him anyway. Her heart was still pounding when the judge returned. His scowl filled her with trepidation. The constable cleared the room, with the exception of Erith and Peter and the two finely dressed men. Constable Jeffries returned moments later.

Peter grabbed her hand. Jeffries stood behind them and leaned in.

"There's been a development. No need to worry, though."

The judge spoke a moment later. "Miss Lock, it seems as if we have a problem. Both accused, Simmons and Ralph, as well as Harmon, the man whom the boys identified as the shooter, have all been found murdered in their cells. A lad from the *Vagabond* named Dixon is believed to have killed the lot. He, as well as several other prisoners, escaped from the penitentiary during the noon meal."

Erith gasped and looked at Jeffries. "Who was Ralph?"

"He was Hand to you," the constable replied.

"Dead? They're all dead?" she asked, bewildered.

"It seems we no longer have need of your testimony. You are free to go home," said Judge Prowse.

Peter leaned forward. "Will she be in danger, Your Honour?"

"No. I've confirmed she will not," the judge said.

He told them that the *Vagabond* had been smuggling rum from Saint Pierre and storing it at the Newman Wine Vaults for later delivery to Toronto and Montreal. Simmons and Ralph had taken a shipment and claimed that they had been pirated. The captain found out that they had been stealing for years, even before employment with him and before they had wintered in North Harbour.

"The captain intended to confront the pair when he got them at sea in hopes of recovering the goods," Judge Prowse said. "But Mr. Cooper showed up and ruined that plan."

He went on to explain that if Erith had been unable to go to trial, the captain would have had the opportunity to find out where his bounty was hidden, recover his money, and then get rid of both men. That's why they had gone after her. According to the informant, who was the second man on the boat, they were supposed to take Erith, keep her hidden, and demand the release of the men. The captain only wanted his goods. He also wanted her to know that the second man had ensured that the boys were kept safe.

"It appears that Dixon, the shooter, was conspiring with Simmons and Ralph and had other plans for you," Judge Prowse said, giving Erith an uneasy look. "I won't tell you what those plans were, because I'm a gentleman, but they would have murdered you and probably Dixon in the end."

Erith gasped and sat back on the chair.

"I apologize for being so frank, but I want you to understand that the threat is over now that those men are dead. I don't want you to live in fear."

Erith nodded, her eyes wide as she stared at the judge. "I thank you for your candour," she said.

"The informant who was with Dixon spilled the tale to the captain. He ordered the men killed."

"They didn't put up much resistance at the vaults," said Jeffries. "They needed to go to prison to get to Simmons and Ralph."

"What of the *Vagabond*?" asked Peter.

"She left port this morning. She's gone," Jeffries replied.

Judge Prowse cleared his throat. "I asked to hold the last train for you. If you hurry, you can be in Whitbourne before dark."

23

Erith approached the house with foreboding while Peter carried Tommy and George walked beside her. Art Power, who had been standing in the shadows, walked out to greet them. He startled Erith at first, before she realized he must have been keeping watch.

"It's some good to see the boys," Art said. "The missus has been praying."

"Thanks," said Erith. She was afraid to ask about Danol— she didn't think he could have survived. And she couldn't be with the children when she found out. The longer she went without news of his well-being, she reasoned, the longer he lived.

"No need to keep watch any longer," said Peter. "Everything's settled." He shook Art's hand.

Erith thanked him again. Tommy raised his head for a second, then put it back on Peter's shoulder. George complained he was tired. She patted the top of his head and squeezed his hand.

"You can go to bed when we get in," Erith whispered.

Inside the house, Peter quickly took Tommy upstairs, and she followed. Both boys were asleep before they left the room. When Maggie met them in the hall, she wore a grave expression.

Erith felt panic begin to rise. She was sure that Danol was dead. Peter didn't say anything as he disappeared into the darkness of the downstairs, looking for Mary.

"Is he gone?" Erith asked in a voice no louder than a whisper.

"No," said Maggie. "I'm just happy to see you." She hugged Erith. "Little Petie is in with Annie. The other young fellow stayed in John's Pond with friends."

Erith wasn't sure if she wanted to see Danol. She didn't trust her emotions.

"He asked for you," said Maggie. "Go see him."

"It's too early."

"Then he'll be asleep. Mary stayed with him. She saved him with her care. I'll wait here for a spell to see if the youngsters are asleep."

Erith knocked lightly on the door before opening it. Moonlight splashed over the still form on the bed. On the edge of a cot set up against the opposite wall, Mary and Peter were holding hands. They both stood when she entered.

"We'd like to have a word in the kitchen," Mary said. "Would you stay here for a little bit?"

"Yes, of course." Erith took a seat in the wooden rocking chair near the head of the bed.

"We won't be long," Mary said softly. She clasped Erith's hand. "Peter told me that it's all over. I'm glad the boys are safe. And you, too."

The door closed, and Erith's eyes adjusted to the darkness. She grasped the arms of the rocker to quell the sudden rush of emotion she was feeling as she watched Danol's chest rise and fall. His breathing didn't sound laboured. She had gone on many calls with the nuns at Mercy Convent and learned to recognize the struggle. She hadn't gotten accustomed to the waiting. Waiting for life or waiting for death. Either one was just as painful for her. The nuns would spend their time in prayer at a bedside while she paced or tended to things. Things like cleaning or making food or anything that didn't involve prolonged sitting. But now it was different. She would sit, she would keep company, she would wait, and she would pray.

Had Danol been awake? Maggie said he had asked for her. Was he dying? Her stepmother had asked for her not too long before she died. His death would be her fault. She knew that as sure as she breathed. How could she learn to live with that?

He stirred, and she heard him say, "Mary."

Erith had seen how upset Mary had been over Danol. She knew the woman cared for Danol and that he felt the same. That touched a place in Erith where she had no right to go—a place she had no business having. She had three children, and that was enough.

He moved, and she heard him wince and take a sharp breath.

"Danol, be still. I'll get Mary."

"Mary."

Both doctors came in. Peter stayed back while Mary settled him and hummed softly, almost under her breath, then helped her turn Danol from his side to his stomach. Erith moved out of the way and didn't look, even when she heard him gasp in pain.

"Stop complaining," Mary muttered. "You make a bad patient."

Danol said something to her, but Erith couldn't make out his coarse whisper.

"Everything's all right," Mary said. "They're all in bed."

She wiped the hair back from his face and wet a cloth in the pan on the washstand, then washed around his hairline and neck before covering him again. Her hand lingered on his head before she tossed the cloth.

"He has to come out of this, Peter. He just has to."

Peter hugged his wife and said nothing.

Mary turned to Erith. "He was asking about the boys."

24

Danol was running behind two young boys. He had to catch them, but they were out of reach. Something seized onto his leg. He tried to pry it off, but the more he pushed and tugged, the more it pained. He couldn't see what held him in its grip, but he had to get free and save the boys. The tentacles grabbed him around his chest, squeezing and tightening. He couldn't breathe.

Then she gently laid her hand on him, and he grew calm. She said everything was all right. He closed his eyes. Where was she? Gone. She wasn't coming back. He had to save her. She needed help. He couldn't help her, because now he was adrift on the sea. He clung to a stick. Looking around, he couldn't see land. The waves were rolling over him. He gasped for air. Something hit him in the ribs. He was drowning. Opening his eyes, he saw her. She was sleeping. She was safe. He closed his eyes again.

He was adrift again, and the sea pounded over him. Unrelenting. He couldn't breathe. The stick was gone. He sank beneath the surface and gasped for breath, but there was none to have. He was dying. A hand reached out and pulled him to the surface. He sucked in air.

"Don't let go," he said.

"I won't," she said.

He closed his eyes and heard whispers. He must be dreaming. His hand clung to something warm. He squeezed, and it squeezed back.

"You have to go now. You can't be in here."

There were more whispers. He didn't know what they were saying.

"Just once."

He opened his eyes, and the little girl came into focus. She smiled. He smiled. She held his cheeks in the palms of her hands and kissed his nose. He closed his eyes.

There was a sound. He heard humming. It was familiar. He opened his eyes. It was Mary.

"This is going to hurt," she said. She was pushing him. Somebody was moving his legs. His hand clung to somebody out of his view. Pain engulfed him. He rolled over and held on tighter. His leg throbbed.

"You're right," he said. "It does hurt."

"Finally, a response," she said.

"Where am I?"

"North Harbour."

"Why?"

"You were shot."

"Shot?"

"Twice."

"Twice?"

"Peter has something for pain."

"Shot?"

"Yes, Danol. Shot twice. Now drink this."

Peter helped him sit, and he let go of the hand. He drank a dark liquid, and Peter eased him down.

"Where am I?"

"North Harbour, like Mary said."

"Yes, but where?"

"Lock's store."

"Where's Erith?"

"Right here, Danol," she said from somewhere behind him.

He closed his eyes.

Within a week Danol was sitting. A week later he was on his feet. Mary and Peter went home, but Mary returned each day to check on him. Maggie tended on him like he was a king. The children came and went, keeping him company, until Maggie shooed them away. Erith avoided him as much as possible. The only time she couldn't make excuses was at mealtime, so he pushed himself to make it to the table.

Danol had let her down. He knew it, and he knew she knew it. But even that couldn't keep him from wanting to see her.

After the third week he was able to get around much better. He moved to his own house and finished recuperating there. Despite Mary's advice to the contrary, he was soon back on the water. He only knew of one way to make up for letting Erith down.

25

Danol stepped aboard the train in Fort William. The evening before, he had visited the Cathedral of St. John the Baptist and spoken with Bishop Howley about the accident that caused Father Fleming's death. Bishop Howley was helpful when Danol told the man about Erith's baby and her need to know where the child was buried. The bishop was a little confused at first. He had thought that Father Fleming had met his death due to failing health, and he had not heard anything about a baby. He had been the bishop in Corner Brook on the west coast of Newfoundland at the time Father Fleming died, but he believed he would have taken notice of an accident, especially if a baby were involved.

Danol asked the clerk to check the records of Father Fleming's death. The clerk said a note on the records mentioned that he had died in Holyrood and was buried, as was custom, at Belvedere Cemetery. That was the extent of the information.

The freight he was waiting on from Boston wouldn't arrive for at least two more days. Armed with the lead he had gotten from the bishop, Danol was even more eager to find information about Beatrice. He had given himself time to start an investigation. Erith deserved answers—she had waited long enough. He wouldn't fail her again.

With a place to start, he would be in Holyrood before noon to start making inquiries. Surely the residents would have knowledge of the accident. During the train ride, he tried to focus on his business ventures and plans to finish his house, but his mind kept wandering back to Erith. She intrigued him. She beguiled him.

He thought back to when he had first encountered Mary Rourke and his fascination with her. However, it was nothing compared to the allure of Erith Lock. He was sure it would pass when the mystery of her daughter was resolved, but he didn't like how she was occupying his thoughts and distracting him.

At Foxtrap, the train followed the ocean along Conception Bay. He had heard that local residents were concerned about the railway crossing through their land and interfering with their farming operations and their livelihood. The farmers had toiled and slaved to clear the woods and barrens in order to survive outside the fishery when the catch was poor. There had been an uprising in Foxtrap in 1880 when the surveyors were going through, so the decision was made to build along the shore. Danol liked the view of the ocean from his window seat. He would have enjoyed it more if not for recurring thoughts of Erith Lock.

It was near midday when he stepped off the platform on the beach in Holyrood. His leg bothered him on occasion, but for the most part, full use had returned.

He spotted a nearby sign for Veitch Hostel and Restaurant. It was as good a place to start as any. He was welcomed by the proprietor, Mary Veitch, a woman in her late forties with greying hair tucked beneath a white cotton bonnet. With a brilliant smile, she showed him to a small wooden table over-looking the train station and harbour.

"You can see clear to Bell Island from here today," she said as she laid a place for him. "There's beef stew on the stove and fresh bread just out of the oven, if you're interested."

"That sounds perfect."

The smells from the kitchen were irresistible. He ate heartily, and when she offered seconds, though he was tempted to say yes, he declined. He had a cup of tea and a piece of dark fruitcake to finish the meal. Two couples came in and ate at nearby tables. They were waiting for the train to return them to St. John's.

"What brings you to Holyrood?" Mrs. Veitch asked as she cleared away his dishes.

He figured a little lie wouldn't hurt. "My name is Fleming. My uncle died somewhere near here. He was a priest."

"Father Fleming." The woman blessed herself. "God rest his soul. He was on his way here before going to celebrate Mass over on the point when he fell. They said it was his heart."

"Oh, I heard from my father that it was an accident of some sort."

"No. My husband, Joe, had gone to meet him at the train to bring him here for a rest and a bite to eat before Mass. They weren't ten steps from the train when Father grabbed his chest and fell. Joe got to him first and helped ease him down. Father blessed himself, and then he was gone."

"Was there anyone else with him?"

"No. Father was alone. He always found those trips long and hard. I guess the last one had been too much."

"Where was he coming from?" Danol asked.

"It was his spring visit to St. Mary's Bay. I believe he had to do twelve or fourteen Masses in different communities. He caught the train in Whitbourne. Joe knows more about it than I do." The woman stopped and looked out a window in the back. "Joe's out by the woodshed. I'll get him."

She disappeared into the kitchen before Danol had a chance to tell her that he would go outside. Within minutes a tall, lanky, grey-haired man in his early fifties came in, extended his hand to shake Danol's, and introduced himself.

"My wife tells me you're inquiring about your uncle."

"Yes, my father talks about him often. I met with Bishop Howley yesterday, and he mentioned that he died here in Holyrood, so I wanted to see the place for myself." That seemed to impress the man.

Joe Veitch talked for quite a while about Father Fleming. He had stayed with the Veitches every three or four weeks when he was coming and going to the bays for Mass. Danol was starting to think he would have to retrace the priest's steps back to Whitbourne on the next train to see if he could find out more.

Mrs. Veitch returned to serve a meal to a couple a few tables over and then came to stand by her husband. "Sorry we couldn't tell you more," she said.

"Yes, I'd have liked to learn more about his last trip. I might learn more in Whitbourne from people he may have spent time with there," Danol said.

"You could always speak to the MacDonalds," said Mr. Veitch.

"The MacDonalds?" his wife asked.

"Yes, John and Alice."

"Yes, of course! They got off the train the same time as Father Fleming."

Mr. Veitch nodded. "He must have known them, because

he was bringing them here for tea that day. They bought a place on the road just past George's Mountain."

"George's Mountain?" asked Danol.

"That big rocky hill there behind us," Mrs. Veitch said as she pointed. "There's a road not too far from here. They're about a mile in. Small white house. Nice people."

Danol thanked the couple, paid the bill, and left the restaurant. He gazed at the mountain behind him and walked in the direction the woman had indicated. His leg tired easily, forcing him to rest a couple of times. It was near mid-afternoon when he spotted the residence. Mrs. Veitch hadn't said it was the only house on the dirt track. He almost turned back, thinking he had gone the wrong way, when he spotted a man near the barn.

"Would you spare a drink of water?" he shouted.

The man beckoned for him to come in. As Danol neared, he saw the man smile. He was tall and stout, a man familiar with work, maybe a few years older than Danol. His dark hair was thinning near his temple.

"Are you lost?"

"I think I might be," Danol said. "I'm looking for a crew of surveyors who are supposed to be cutting a line for a road across to St. Mary's Bay."

"That's interesting. I haven't heard of such a thing."

"I'm Danol Cooper." He extended his hand.

"John MacDonald," the man said. "Now, about that water. There's a bucket in the house, just inside the door."

They walked together to the rear of the house. The man was about to open the door when it burst open. A blonde-haired girl about seven years old ran out.

"Daddy, Daddy, Mommy has buns for you!"

"Beatrice, they're supposed to be a surpr—"

A tall, thin, dark-haired woman was racing behind the child when she saw Danol. "Beatrice, honey, come to Mommy." She held out her hand to the little girl and gently led the child behind her skirts.

"Danol Cooper, this is my wife, Alice, and my daughter, Beatrice." Beatrice ran from behind her mother and jumped into her father's arms. She quickly gave him a hug and a kiss.

"Pleased to meet you, ma'am," Danol said and nodded at the woman.

"Mr. Cooper," she said and nodded back at him. "Beatrice, come with Mommy to check on the pan of buns."

The little girl with the wild strawberry blonde hair squirmed from her father's arms and ran in the house ahead of her mother. Danol watched her go and stared at the door long after it closed. Erith's child was alive and well, and she was the spitting image of her mother.

Mr. MacDonald spoke behind him. "You're not with a surveying company, are you?"

"No, I'm not."

"I hoped this day would never come, but I waited for it every day, just the same." The man lowered his head and leaned on the fence for support. His voice was full of emotion.

"I'd still like that glass of water. Then we can talk."

"First, I need to know if you're here to take our Beatrice."

"No, I don't believe I am," Danol said. "I'd still like to have some answers for her mother."

John MacDonald returned with a glass of water and a cookie. "Beatrice wants you to have this," he said with a half-hearted smile. They walked toward the barn. He leaned against the fence and sized Danol up. "Mr. Cooper."

"Danol, please."

"Danol, I dreaded this day and had plans to pack up my wife and child and flee if it should come. Now that it's here, I don't think I can do that. That would be no life for the child. It's a relief of sorts. I know that sounds strange."

"Please tell me how you came to have Beatrice."

"She was a gift from God. There's no other way to describe her. Me and Alice had three babies. Neither one lived more than a few days. After the last little boy, James, died, I almost lost Alice." Mr. MacDonald took a deep breath and swallowed hard. "There were complications, and the doctor said she wouldn't be able to carry another child. We were devastated. We wanted a big family and have the kids live around us in our old age.

"My Alice was a broken woman and wouldn't get out of bed after James. Finally, when she was well enough, I suggested that we move. I had to get her out of that house."

He told Danol how they had met the train in Whitbourne when Father Fleming was there. He was travelling with a baby, and the lady who was supposed to meet him in Whitbourne to take the child to St. John's hadn't shown up. Father Fleming didn't know what he was going to do.

"That's when the baby cried, and Alice picked her up. She was wet and hungry, and Alice saw to her needs." John Mac-Donald spoke with pride and love for his wife. "She saw her name sewn into her blanket, and Father Fleming said that the child's name was Beatrice. He didn't say where she came from. Alice still has that blanket."

Danol listened without interrupting. It was obvious the little girl was well cared for. He believed the man was genuine and telling the truth. However, he still had to see for himself so he could assure Erith that her baby was indeed in a good place. The decision would ultimately be hers. Danol didn't envy her.

"We thought about going to St. John's, but when the priest said he had to have Mass in Holyrood first, he asked if we'd be willing to stay with the child. Father said he'd put us up at the hostelry for the night and to keep the baby with us. We could continue in the morning. Alice was delighted. Father Fleming was pleased with the arrangement, since it would be difficult finding somebody else."

John MacDonald explained that he had just stepped down from the train and turned to help Alice with the baby when he heard a commotion. Father Fleming was being eased to the ground by another man, who turned out to be Mr. Veitch.

"I ran to his side, and he looked me in the eye and made the sign of the Cross before dying. We stayed at the hostelry for a few nights, waiting to see if somebody would come for the baby. Alice was flourishing. The child couldn't find a better mother. So, when nobody came, we said nothing about her. We rented this house and lived under a shadow of fear that somebody would find us." His voice trailed off. "Why is the mother looking now after all these years?"

"I'm not at liberty to say, Mr. MacDonald. John."

"We're not educated people, Mr. Cooper, but we want nothing but the best for Beatrice. As far as anyone in Holyrood is concerned, she's our child. She's happy."

"I can tell you that is what the mother is interested in for Beatrice," Danol said. "I'd like to spend a few minutes in your wife and daughter's company, though."

"Do I have your word that you won't say anything to Alice?"

"Of course," Danol replied. "You have my word."

"Mr. Cooper. Danol. I'll take you at your word. Please don't make me regret it."

They went inside. It was obvious that the MacDonalds

were not a family of means. The house was modest but clean. There was a smell of fresh baked cookies and bread in the air. Alice MacDonald apologized for the heat. Danol tried not to stare at the younger version of Erith.

"We're having toutons," Beatrice said. "Do you want some?"

Danol looked from her to the couple.

"We have lots of dough to fry," said Alice. "John, bring the molasses from the pantry." Her husband quickly drained the last of the cask into a small porcelain bowl.

"Well, maybe I'll have just one," Danol said. "Then I have to be going."

Danol ate with the family. Beatrice was well-mannered and clean. She seemed like a happy child. She had lots of questions for him, despite her mother and father's telling her it was rude. Danol didn't mind. He told her about his boat.

"You sound funny," Beatrice said.

"Beatrice," her mother and father said as one.

"That's not a very nice thing to say," said Alice, obviously embarrassed by the comment.

Danol grinned. "That's because I come from a far-away land."

"A far-away land?" Beatrice asked. Her eyes went as big as she could make them, and her mouth opened in wonder. Danol wasn't very good at it, but he tried to describe New York, where he was born, and Boston, where he served as a policeman, as magical places with lots of people who talked funny.

He ate two more toutons with the family before he said he had to leave. Beatrice was disappointed and asked if he could come and visit again. "You never know," he said.

He left the house with Mr. MacDonald.

"Don't judge us by what we have," John said.

"You have more than I had," Danol returned. "Much more. You have a beautiful family and a wonderful little girl. I'll be in touch in a few weeks. I have to talk to her mother."

"Tell me about her."

"She's a fine woman, sir. She has three beautiful children whom she rescued from an orphanage. Her parents died when she was very young, and she had a cruel upbringing. She wants to make sure that is not the case for her daughter. I can assure her of that. As for her intentions, I can't tell you, because I don't know. I'm not sure if she even knows. She believed her daughter to be dead."

"Is she your woman, Mr. Cooper?"

"No, sir, she's not."

"You talk about her like I talk about Alice," John said absently.

"I'll be in contact. Thank you for your kindness today."

John merely nodded and returned to the house.

Danol made his way back to the train station, where he learned he would have to wait until morning. He got a room at Veitch's and spent a restful night there.

Before leaving Holyrood, he visited Carroll's Dry Goods and asked if John MacDonald had a bill owing. He paid John's debt, just over $5, and asked to have some items delivered to the MacDonalds. Mrs. Carroll picked out a dress that would fit Beatrice, tobacco for John, and perfume for Alice, which was added to flour, sugar, molasses, raisins, pork, tea, lamp oil, and a few additional items for the pantry. Mrs. Carroll was happy to make the sale. When she asked Danol who he was, he said a friend of the family and left it at that. He had her assurance it would be delivered that day.

26

Two weeks later, Danol docked the boat in North Harbour. He went straight to Erith's, telling himself it was because he had news and not because he just wanted to see her face.

Annie ran down the lane and jumped in his arms. For a fleeting moment Danol thought of John MacDonald. He twirled her around and she laughed. The two boys came running when they heard Annie. He ruffled their hair, and they skipped along behind him.

"What did you bring us?" asked Annie.

"Why, nothing, of course," said Danol.

"Aww."

"Well, maybe something," he said and laid her on the step. He reached into an inside pocket of his coat and pulled out three multicoloured hard candy sticks. The three children took one each and thanked him before scooting off around the house when Danol told them he needed to speak to their mother.

He entered the store, guessing that was where he would find Erith. She was behind the counter with her back to him. His heart skipped a beat, and he felt the sudden urge to grab her and twirl her like he had done with Annie. Maybe steal a kiss. She turned when she heard the bell over the door. He watched her eyes and was sure, for an instant, she was glad to see him.

"Why, welcome back, Mr. Cooper."

"It's good to be back." Erith couldn't know just how much he meant that, and in that moment he had the strangest sensation of coming home.

"Where were you this trip?"

Danol told her he had gone as far as Trinity Bay. "I also took the train to Holyrood."

"Holyrood?"

"Yes, I spent a night there."

"Oh, is that unusual?"

"Yes. Can we talk in the house?"

Her pallor changed as recognition dawned on her face. "Danol!" She grabbed the counter to steady herself.

"It's good news, Erith. I promise."

"Where's Maggie?" Mrs. Ryan was like a permanent fixture in Erith's home now, helping out whenever she was needed.

"She went to visit Agnes and Patrick."

Erith straightened up, lifted her chin, and quickly walked to the kitchen with Danol close behind. Danol pulled a chair out for her at the end of the table, trying not to touch her. He didn't trust himself to touch her. She motioned for him to sit.

Danol chose the chair farthest from her. He didn't know what was wrong with him. His breathing quickened and his heart raced. For years he had delivered both good news and bad news to people. Once upon a time he had been able to put himself outside the situation, distance himself. But this was good news, and he felt like he was part of it. He shifted in the chair, trying to hide his discomfort. He didn't want to feel anything. Maybe after he intervened for Erith, things would go back to the way they were supposed to be. By getting too close he had let her down, and they both had the wounds to prove it. Danol was a loner, and liked it. He just needed to be reminded.

Erith looked at him expectantly. Her eyes were big and glassy. Tears were close to the surface.

"I found Beatrice. She is with a couple in Holyrood. They're taking good care of her."

The words seemed to do injustice to the fact that he was telling her that her child was alive. He couldn't begin to guess what was going on in her head. She didn't speak as she blinked away a tear, which trailed down her cheek and disappeared into her dress. Danol watched its progress, unable to look away.

Erith finally heard the words that she had longed for. Her baby girl, with the little wisp of strawberry blonde hair and eyes that had not yet come to colour, was alive!

All the silent, ageless anguish she had suffered stood poised for her command. But what would that be? How could she undo grieving? Did it unwind like a spool? Did it leave pitilessly and pare the hardened outward facade in its wake? Did it remove the barriers and let real emotions bloom? Could she allow her heart to beat as a whole again? Would it even know how?

Beatrice . . . alive!

The words seeped in and ran through her, surrounding her, changing her. She wanted to jump. And twirl. And dance. She wanted to shout and tell the world. She wanted to exorcise grief and give it a good thrashing for its constant torment. Erith wanted it to be seven years ago. She wanted to begin again. But where? Unfamiliar feelings assaulted her. She was giddy with joy yet restrained by deep-rooted binds of hurt and pain.

With her voice raw, she simply whispered, "What's her name?"

"Beatrice MacDonald. They found your stitching on her blanket."

"What colour are her eyes?"

"Blue. She looks like you."

Assaulted by anguish, Erith put her head in her hands and wept. What else was there to do? The sun had shone on her child. She had learned to walk. She had learned to talk. She had lived her whole life, the only life she would remember, with a stranger. A stranger to Erith but not to her baby. And Erith, who carried her, nursed her, loved her, and wept for her, was a stranger to her child.

She heard Danol close the distance between them. He gathered her to him and gently embraced her, and she didn't resist. She fiercely grabbed the lapel of his coat as if she were holding on for dear life and buried her head in his chest. He laid his face against the top of her head. It felt right.

When she stopped crying, she squirmed. What was she doing? He immediately released her.

"I'm sorry," she said.

"Don't be. It's a lot to take in."

She wiped her eyes and turned from him, moving to the window, sidling gracelessly to avoid his gaze. "Where are the children?"

"I gave them a candy stick, and they went out back."

"Did Annie hurt you? You shouldn't let her tackle you like that."

She had been watching, he noted.

Erith tried to compose herself. She had only the words of this man to bring Beatrice back alive in her heart. She swallowed the pain so as not to distract her from any detail. "Please tell me about her. Tell me how you found her."

Erith didn't look at him. She sat once again and stared out the window, taking a few deep breaths before he began. Danol told her about his visit to the bishop and how he eventually ended up at the MacDonalds'. He described their home and what their life was like. More important to Erith, he told her about Beatrice.

He reminded Erith that he was only there for a short time, but he really believed the child was well cared for. "If she wasn't, I'd have interceded."

Erith stood and went to the stove. "Did they know why you were there?" she asked.

"The husband knew. He guessed and had been expecting someone. He didn't know when, but he knew someone would eventually come."

Her eyes fixed on the steam from the kettle. Fire crackled in the stove. The occasional trill of laughter broke through from outside. She turned suddenly, her words rushed.

"Danol, I didn't thank you."

"No thanks necessary," he replied.

"I know I have no right to ask a favour. I can commission you, if you like."

"Commission me? Erith, I will do what you ask."

"You've already done so much. I don't want to owe you," she said.

"Owe me? I don't even know what that means. You have it wrong. How could you owe me? I can never do enough to repay you."

"I didn't want nor expect you to become vested in our lives. I don't have room for that," Erith said.

"If it will make you feel better, you can pay me a token dollar."

"A dollar? You mock me."

"Tell me what you want. I won't be taking money." His voice sounded harsh. He shoved his fingers through his hair and moved toward the door. "You asked me to find your daughter. I've done that. I told you I wasn't in that business, so it's not a business transaction. I'll be back tomorrow. Or is that too early?"

"Tomorrow's fine."

Danol turned on his heel and left. She followed him to the door and watched him stride out the lane and slam the gate. He didn't look back. Erith fell back against the wall, and her legs gave out beneath her. She held her knees and rocked back and forth as she wept once again.

27

The next day, Erith heard Annie's high-pitched laughter and peeked out to see what the commotion was about. She should have guessed. Annie was in Danol's arms, hugging him. The little girl was drawn to Danol. He smiled at her and said something that made Annie laugh again. He laid her down and gave her something, and she raced off in search of George and Tommy. Danol smiled as he watched her go. He straightened his jacket and headed for the steps. When he glanced toward the shop window, Erith quickly looked away.

She heard the bell and rushed around the counter to meet him by the door. "I'm sorry, Danol. Yesterday was hard. That's no excuse, so I'm sorry. You've done so much for me already, and I felt I didn't have the right to ask you to do more."

Danol had been about to say something before she cut him off. He cleared his throat. "I wanted to apologize, too. I shouldn't have gotten mad. I don't know what I was even angry about," he said and smiled at her. "Now, I only consider the job half-finished. Tell me what you want to do."

Erith hesitated. "I can do it by letter, Danol."

"It's none of my business, but can I ask what you plan to do? I gave my word to John MacDonald that I'd deliver news personally. I know I shouldn't have done that, but my word is my bond."

She told him she had a letter for her barrister. In it she instructed him to set up a monthly payment for the MacDonalds. Erith wanted to take any financial burden from Beatrice's family.

Danol agreed. "That makes sense. I believe they could use the support."

"I'm going to send a letter to the MacDonalds. I need to send a private letter to Beatrice, too, to be opened when and if her parents want her to open it."

"So, you've made a decision about Beatrice?"

"There is no decision to make. Beatrice is happy," Erith said. She held his gaze and continued. "I know how hard it is to lose parents. I've seen many children go through the orphanages. When they come in, they are overwhelmed, and some don't get over it. Taking Beatrice from her home would devastate her, as well as the MacDonalds, who have nothing but the best intentions for my girl.

"You must think me a terrible person," she concluded.

Danol stepped forward and pulled her into his arms. She was shocked by his actions but welcomed the warmth and embraced him. He released her abruptly.

"I'm sorry, Erith. I shouldn't have done that."

She was supposed to be afraid, but she wasn't. It could have been the turmoil from her sleepless night, but whatever it was, she wasn't fearful of his touch. That brought another dilemma for which she was not prepared.

"Yes, you shouldn't have done that."

She turned and grabbed the kettle to push it off the damper. The water sloshed from the bib, and she had to jump back as the droplets hissed at her from the hot stove.

"Careful, you'll scald yourself." Danol took her hands and turned her wrist toward him.

"It didn't get me," Erith replied as he gently inspected her skin before releasing her.

"Tell me what you want for Beatrice. I'll take your mail to the MacDonalds—that's not open for discussion." He looked as if he wanted to say something else. He paused a moment before saying, "They deserve to have it hand-delivered."

"I know, Danol, but I can't go. If I see her and can't take her with me, it will be like she's died all over again. I don't want to ask you to go."

"You're not asking. I'm offering."

"You have so much work. Why are you doing this?" she pleaded.

"I told you, I need to finish what I start. I won't consider this finished until I speak to the MacDonalds again. Besides, I'll be in St. John's, anyway, so it's not really out of my way."

Erith left it at that. "I haven't started the letters. Well, except to my solicitor."

"I don't leave until tomorrow. Is that all right?"

"Yes."

"Good," said Danol. "I'm going to an auction to get some furniture for the house."

"That's where I got mine for Devon Row. I'm just happy that my father's stuff is here."

"I'm looking forward to purchasing some items to fill my house," he said.

"My lawyer bought the pieces for me and had them delivered before I got there." Erith paused for a moment. "That sounds very entitled, but it was nothing like that," she said with a rueful grin.

"Erith, again, this is none of my business, but how did you go from leaving with nothing to amassing wealth in St. John's?"

"It's a long story," she said as she gazed out the window at the calm sea. She didn't mean to be dismissive when she replied. "I have some letter-writing to do."

"Of course. See you tomorrow," Danol said.

Erith watched his back as he walked down the lane until he was out of view. She thought about his question. It truly had been a long road.

28

Five years earlier . . .

Her hands were raw, but Erith continued to apply the wax with a fervour borne of frustration. She didn't know how she was going to get the children under one roof. She had saved every penny she could spare working two jobs during the week and another one on Saturdays, yet there wasn't enough to give her independence. If she were to get the children, she wouldn't see them, because she would have to continue to work—possibly even more—just to make ends meet.

Annie had an opportunity to be adopted. But for Erith's friendship with Sister Mary Joseph, she would be gone. Was she being fair to the child to keep her in an institution? Annie was being well cared for, and Erith got to tuck her in every night, but was she being selfish? It was no life for a little girl. Erith didn't know what was right. The line was getting greyer with each passing day. Determination didn't pay debts nor make one self-sufficient.

Erith shoved the yellowed cloth back into the can and looked up to the heavens. "God help me find an answer!" she whispered, before gouging out another chunk of wax and fiercely rubbing it on the maple floorboards.

T *HE PROMISE*

The nuns had been praying for her. Their continued support kept her going most days. Even when she was in the depths of despair, they had a way of pulling her out. Her journey seemed to have no end, her possibilities no chance of becoming reality. Erith would have herself worked to the bone before she saw results. Maybe it was time to give up, as some girls at the dormitory had suggested.

"Miss Lock. Miss Lock? Erith, do you hear me?" asked Elizabeth Harvey. Her impatience couldn't be hidden behind the forced smile pasted on her face. She was a tall, thin, dark-haired woman in her early forties. "Have you gone deaf, girl?"

"Now, Betty, no harm done. Can't you see she's engrossed in her work?" remarked Augustus Harvey.

Erith turned and saw the couple staring at her. Mr. Harvey was a stout, balding man in his mid-forties with light brown eyes and long, thick, mostly grey and brown sideburns. He was kind to his five boys and his daughter, Gertrude. Erith wasn't wary of him. Thankfully, in this job she didn't have to avoid the male family members. She had reluctantly quit four jobs because of advances from either the patriarch or one of his children. That behaviour made her afraid—more than she cared to admit. She avoided situations where she would be alone with a man, but because that wasn't always possible, fear was her constant companion. The convent was the only place where she felt at ease.

Behind Mr. Harvey stood an older, bearded gentleman. His face bore the signs of a weather-beaten existence. However, he was finely dressed in a beige tweed suit and sported a blue tie. The man's eyes were trained on her. It was a look unlike anything she had seen before, yet not one that made her uncomfortable.

Mr. Harvey served on the Legislative Council of Newfoundland, so Erith was accustomed to many government officials meeting at the home on Circular Road. That was one of the reasons why Mrs. Harvey demanded that the study be immaculately cleaned and the floor always luminous. She had a fashion of pulling the toe of her shoe across the polished floor before it had a chance to dry. Erith believed it was to ensure the "help" was busy all the time—she often made them redo the entire room even when she was the one who smudged the wax.

Erith suspected the guest was there on fisheries issues. He had a look of the sea about him. Mr. Harvey was a strong advocate for the local fishermen and often lobbied on their behalf to the government of Robert Thorburn and even to England. Mrs. Harvey wasn't too keen on local issues, but she wasn't opposed to sailing to England with her husband when the time was right.

"Mr. Harvey and Captain Bartlett would like the room to discuss business," said Mrs. Harvey.

Erith apologized and quickly gathered the rags and wax. She smiled and cast her eyes downward as she passed the trio.

The man named Bartlett quickly blocked her exit, and Erith stopped abruptly. Startled, she dropped the can cover, which rattled and clanged on the wooden floor. She bent to retrieve it and pulled back as the man laid his hand on her forearm. Instantly, he let go of her.

"Sorry, miss. Is your name Erith Lock?" he asked softly.

Erith stammered out, "Yes."

"Pardon our maid, Captain. I don't know what's gotten into her today," said Mrs. Harvey. She stood aside for Erith to retrieve the can cover. "Erith," she said flatly.

"I'm sorry, Mrs. Harvey." Erith attempted to recover the item, but the man blocked her way once more.

"Captain Bartlett, are you all right?" Mrs. Harvey asked. "Erith, prepare some tea for the men, please."

"No tea, Betty. We'll have the Scotch," replied Mr. Harvey.

"Pardon me," said Captain Bartlett. "I know this girl. I met her once. I knew her father."

Erith felt heat rise in her cheeks. "You knew my father?" she asked. Her hand went to her mouth. Tasting wax, she quickly wiped her lips with the hem of her apron. Realizing what she had done made her turn a deeper shade of red.

"Begging your pardon, sir," she said. She tried to fix her clothing and stand straighter.

"Isaac, are you coming?" Mr. Harvey called from the other room.

"Just a minute, Gus. I need to speak to Miss Lock." Captain Bartlett looked at Mrs. Harvey. "Could we have a moment to talk?"

"Of course," Mrs. Harvey said. "I'll be in with Gus." She entered the parlour and grabbed the sparkling glass knob. Her eyes were on Erith. "Now, Captain Bartlett, don't you try to steal our best maid." She laughed as she closed the door. Erith could hear muffled voices behind the curtained glass.

She stood, rather awkwardly, in front of the man. "You knew my father, Ben Lock?" she asked tentatively.

"Yes. He was the engineer on my boat when we had that horrible mishap. I was with him when he died. I brought him home to be buried. That's where I met you. He was a good man. He spoke of his beloved Erith. I was shocked when I heard your name. You look like him, you know."

Erith hadn't known that. She had always believed she looked like her mother.

The seaman pointed toward the settee near the foot of the stairs and offered her a seat. Erith almost tripped over her own feet, and he took her arm to steady her. She flinched, but she didn't think he noticed. She smelled of wax, her knees hurt, and her hands hurt, but she wanted to hear news of her father. Mrs. Harvey surely wouldn't mind if she sat for a moment.

"Why are you here?" Captain Bartlett asked.

Erith wasn't sure what he meant. She didn't answer right away, so he continued.

"You're a wealthy woman, Miss Lock. Why are you a parlour maid to the Harveys?"

"Pardon me?" She almost laughed aloud.

"You're a wealthy woman." He paused, and when he saw no sign that she understood what he was saying, he said, "I take it that you didn't know that."

Erith slowly shook her head.

"Your father's estate paid a monthly stipend to your stepmother, and you were to get the balance when you turned eighteen."

"My father's what?"

"His estate. He trusted me with the details before he died. I set up the specifics at the bank. Did your stepmother not tell you?"

"No, Mr. Bartlett, she did not."

"He left a letter for you. I wrote it out for him myself, but he signed it. I put it in safe keeping with the bank."

"A letter?" Erith asked. She was baffled.

"This is a lot for you to take in, my dear. I have some urgent business to discuss with Gus—Mr. Harvey. Where are you staying?"

"St. Clair's Boarding School."

"Can I come there tomorrow for you?"

Erith didn't know what to say. She still had to work for the Harveys until after tea, then race to the Rosses and help with supper for the ten kids, then go back to the orphanage to play with Annie before putting her to bed.

"I have to work. I'll be here," she stammered.

"Miss Lock, you don't understand. You don't have to work."

"I don't?"

"No, you don't. Not ever again, if you don't want to."

That was the last thing she remembered before opening her eyes. Mrs. Harvey was bent over her, tapping her hand, and Mr. Harvey had brought a glass of Scotch from the parlour. She must have passed out from the wax fumes.

"Erith! Erith. Are you all right? Here, drink this."

Mrs. Harvey lifted her head and held the glass to her lips. The smell of the liquor was enough to bring her back to her senses. She shook her head and didn't take any. Mrs. Harvey laid her head back on the rug.

"Let me help her up, Betty," Mr. Harvey said as he pushed past his wife and extended his hand. She hesitated, then grasped it, and he pulled her up with ease.

"I'm sorry. It must have been the wax."

"Or the news of your good fortune," said Mrs. Harvey. "Carmelita? Carmelita! Where is that girl?" A dark-haired girl around Erith's age scurried from the kitchen and stood before Mrs. Harvey. "Help me take Erith to the kitchen for a cup of tea."

Captain Bartlett came out of the parlour. "I have urgent business, but I'll be by to see you tomorrow, Miss Lock."

He was real. This was real. She had to take a second look to be sure.

"Yes, I'll see you tomorrow," Erith said.

"I have some business to attend to at the bank. I'll be at the boarding school by ten."

Mrs. Harvey ushered her into the enormous kitchen. Carmelita grabbed a tea towel and hoisted the heavy kettle from the hook in the massive stone fireplace. Steam rose from the bib, and a few droplets spilled and sizzled on the fiery logs. Mrs. Harvey fussed over her as she helped her to a bench at the side of the large wooden table. She then pushed herself in beside Erith.

Erith thought the woman had gone mad. She was smiling at Erith and smoothing Erith's tangled mass of hair, which had escaped from the bun, all the while stroking her other hand.

"You poor child. Is there anything I can do for you?" Mrs. Harvey asked, her eyes expectant, her eyebrows raised.

"Uh, no. I'll be fine," Erith said hesitantly. This woman, who had been very direct and dismissive toward her since coming into their employ, was suddenly being nice to her. She didn't know how to deal with this new version of Mrs. Harvey.

"Take all the time you need. Rest here and drink your tea. I'll stay with you."

Carmelita exchanged glances with Erith, her wide eyes asking what was going on. She poured tea for both the women at the table. The look on Erith's face told Carmelita that the strange behaviour was bewildering to her as well.

"Carmelita, finish waxing the floor in the parlour when the men conclude their business."

"Yes, ma'am."

"Oh, and if you know another young woman looking for work, bring her here. We need a new girl to replace our Erith here. Oh, and tell Hector, or whatever his name is, to go to the Rosses and let Mrs. Ross know that Erith won't be coming back."

"Yes, ma'am."

By the time she left the Harveys, Erith still wasn't convinced she hadn't been overcome by the wax fumes. Mrs. Harvey had even invited her over for a game of cards!

29

After leaving the Harveys, she went directly to the convent to give the nuns her news. She would have to wait until the next day to confirm, but it seemed like their prayers had been answered. She could claim the three Ryan children as her own!

When Erith found them, the convent was in a state of flux. Sister Mary Joseph was packing a bag with the meagre medical supplies she had on hand. She was giving orders to Sister Mary Clement, who was rushing to help the older nun with her task.

"Erith!" Sister Mary Clement said with surprise. "What are you doing here?" She glanced nervously at the older nun.

"I have some news," Erith said, her grin wide.

"I don't have time for your news, Erith! I have to catch the train," said Sister Mary Joseph.

"The train? Are you going to the Villa Nova Orphanage?"

The two nuns looked at each other and then at Erith. Both looked panicked and frantic, but Erith had been too caught up in her own notions of suddenly living with financial security to have seen it.

"Where are you going?" Erith asked. Her smile faded as she took in the demeanour of the two nuns. "What's going on?"

"Erith, you need to sit down," Sister Mary Clement said. She gently pushed Erith toward a nearby chair.

"I'll not be sitting. Tell me what's going on."

Sister Mary Joseph put her hand on Erith's shoulder and guided her toward the chair. Reluctantly, she sat. The older nun took her hand. "Erith, there is something you need to know."

Erith didn't know how to prepare herself. She felt that secret place that had almost consumed her all those years ago beckoning once more. She took a fleeting glimpse at Beatrice's precious baby face, in that room in her heart, to remind her of the pain she had felt.

"Some boys have come down with typhoid fever. Many of them are not doing well. I can't tell you whether George or Tommy have it, but I have to go and will send word."

"I'm going, too," Erith said immediately.

"You can't. It's too dangerous. I'm not taking Sister Mary Clement for that reason."

Erith realized the gravity of the situation. The nuns didn't travel alone. "I'm going. I am finally able to claim the boys, and I'll not lose them without a fight."

"It's not up for discussion," Sister Mary Joseph said.

"You're right. It's not up for discussion. I'm going."

"What of Annie?"

"What of George and Tommy? They may need me more now than ever. It's not a choice."

Erith asked Sister Mary Clement for a piece of paper and a pencil. She scribbled a note saying that if she should die, all her worldly belongings were to go to Annie Ryan at the Belvedere Orphanage, and if they were to survive, the money would also be equally shared with Tommy and George Ryan at the Villa Nova Orphanage. She asked Sister Mary Clement to deliver that note at ten o'clock the next day to a Captain Isaac Bartlett, who would be at the boarding school looking for her.

She didn't take time to go for a change of clothes, opting instead to take a robe from the nuns. Sister Mary Joseph tried to dissuade her once more, but Erith wouldn't listen. She quickly took one last look at Annie before racing for the train.

On the journey, she felt compelled to tell her friend and confidante, Sister Mary Joseph, about Beatrice and the shame she had felt at her conception. She talked about her father, her stepmother, and the brief discussion with Captain Bartlett. The older nun listened, her head bowed. When Erith finished, Sister Mary Joseph shed a single tear that made its way down her face and splashed onto her joined hands.

"Erith, you've moved me to tears." She paused and gave Erith a long, soulful regard. "Maybe its the thought of an early death that has me reminiscing. My aunt, Sister Mary Baptiste Tarahan, was the reason I entered the convent. She was very young when she gave herself to God. Unheard of here in Newfoundland for a local girl to join the Mercy Order, yet she did it. She had determination. I was only eighteen when she passed at thirty-five. She died because of service to others."

Sister Mary Joseph looked out the window. When she turned back to Erith, she said, "You remind me of her. She told me there would be someone who would strengthen my resolve for following in her footsteps. She said that I reminded her, every single day, of how whole she felt when she went about her ministry." She held Erith's hand. "I understand why you have given yourself to the three Ryan children. I'm humbled by that revelation. You do for me what I did for my aunt. You remind me of all that is good in this world, and I thank God for that gift."

They sat awhile, holding hands in silence. Erith was drained. Finally, Sister Mary Joseph said, "Erith, I can't give you the forgiveness you think you need. That has to come from within. The shame is not yours to carry. You will come to learn that you are not meant to do everything alone. You have a loving heart to share with more than just those children."

"I don't understand."

"I know you don't. But someday, when you're ready, you will."

They prayed in silence for the rest of the journey. When they arrived in Manuels, a young man got off the train and followed them to the orphanage. He was tall, with short dark hair, and spoke with a distinctive Irish accent. He introduced himself as Doctor Lawrence Keegan. He was in his early twenties and had studied in Ireland before moving to Newfoundland. He had heard of the difficulty in the Dominion and was determined to help.

Erith was devastated to learn that over one third of the boys—more than forty—were sick. Included in that number were Tommy and George. Anyone who wasn't sick had been moved to Father Michael's residence at Woodstock in Topsail to ensure their continued good health. This foresight had surely saved many lives, according to Doctor Keegan.

Sister Mary Joseph was an unrelenting strength while she ministered to the children. Father Michael worked tirelessly, day and night, and passed his thirty-seventh birthday caring for the bedridden.

Erith stayed with George and Tommy. They were roomed with six more boys under Erith's care. Tommy held her hand and didn't make a sound while George and the others screamed in pain and suffered delusions. She was glad she had followed the two nuns when they tended to the poor and sick in St. John's. It helped her get through the next week. Although the boys had severe stomach pain and muscle aches, the high fever was the worst of it.

One day, Erith overheard Sister Mary Joseph speaking to Father Michael before he came into the room.

"Father, with all due respect, you've got to eat, and you've got to rest."

"I'm all right, Sister. The boys are not. I'll rest when they're better."

"I'm afraid you'll be in the room next to them if you don't get some sleep."

"God will take care of me."

"Yes, He will, but He expects you to put in some effort, too," Sister Mary Joseph admonished.

"I'm aware of your concerns. I really must tend to the children. The staff, you, Miss Lock, and Doctor Lawrence all need the help. We have to save the children."

"Father, you're burning up," the nun said.

"It's warm in here, that's all."

"Your sister has been sent to your brother's place to recover. Perhaps you should consider going."

"I heard she's doing better, thank God. But I'll not leave here," Father Michael replied. "Now, I have to see how Miss Lock's room is managing. Don't worry about me, Sister."

He brought fresh water to the room and helped Erith place cold cloths on the boys. He told her to get something to eat, and she quickly complied. The printing press, tailor shop, flower shop, and bakery had all been shut down, and many of the workers stayed away from the premises. However, people left food for the sick at the gate. Erith found soups and stews in the kitchen, thanks to the charitable community. When she returned, Father Michael was sitting with his head resting on the wall. His eyes were closed, and Erith thought he was sleeping, but he heard her and got up.

"Father, where did this disease come from?" Erith asked as she helped him put fresh cloths on the boys.

"Near as we can tell, some of the boys drank water from a bog hole two weeks ago while on the island tending cattle. There must have been something in the water."

"All this from drinking water? It sounds like it couldn't be possible," she said.

"I know. Doctor Herbert Rendell came here early on. He passed the diagnosis of typhoid and believes the bog to be its origin."

George cried out for Erith, and she returned to his side while Father Michael moved to the next room to provide relief. There were ten more rooms like this one, five of them serving as infirmaries. Fifty-six boys were sick, along with several staff.

Two days later, Father Michael collapsed. Sister Mary Joseph sent word to Bishop Power, who notified the family. His brother, Edward Morris, commissioned a private train car and had Father Michael transported to his residence on Military Road.

Two staff members, Mary Ann Power and James Corbett, battled the fever as long as they could before Doctor Keegan bedded them down with the other sick boys. Both died during the night. The following evening, three orphans—Patrick Maher, Matthew Kenny, and Richard Byrne—were gone. They were buried behind the building. Sister Mary Joseph said a rosary, and the caretakers circled the graves with rocks. That same day, they got word that Father Michael had succumbed to the illness.

Erith and Sister Mary Joseph worked alongside eight other caring souls. Doctor Keegan insisted they rest at intervals and wash their hands often. He didn't want more getting sick. Ten days later, the last of the boys made a full recovery.

Erith and Sister Mary Joseph stayed on for two more days to wash the bedding and scrub the rooms. The sick boys who had recovered were bathed in a saltwater pond out behind the site, given new outfits which had been donated, and then taken to Bishop Power's summer residence in Power's Court. Another group of caregivers was housed there as well. Once everything was clean, the orphans would return.

Reverend Colley, a minister with the Church of England and a good friend of Father Michael's, collected funds to keep the orphanage up and running. When he was done, Bishop Power would send Father James McGrath from St. John's to take over.

Erith refused to leave the place without Tommy and George, who were now at Power's Court. She didn't know what had become of Captain Isaac Bartlett, and she didn't care—she was taking the boys with her, no matter what she had to do to keep them. Sister Mary Joseph intervened for her with the Reverend Colley, who agreed to let them go. The nun gave her word that the boys would not be left homeless. They stayed in a small room at the convent with Erith and Annie for a week while Erith endured a whirlwind of meetings with lawyers and accountants who were all vying for her business.

Doctor Keegan and his wife, Minnie, helped her find a house since they had just recently bought theirs and were acquainted with the market. She moved into the modest three-bedroom home on Devon Row more than a week after taking the children from the orphanages.

She had kept her promise. It was over three hard years in coming, but she had kept it nonetheless. The children were hers at last.

All of St. John's was in mourning over the loss of Father Michael, especially at such a young age, and the deaths at the orphanage. Window blinds were closed out of respect for all he had done for orphans. The church struck a committee to commemorate his life, and Erith contributed to the memorial. Donations poured in from the United States, where Father Michael had travelled and spoken about the plight of the orphans in order to raise money for his cause. An engraved pillar and marble bust were commissioned in his honour a few short months after he died. It was later erected at Bannerman Park.

30

Captain Isaac Bartlett came to see Erith soon after she moved into her house. Over a cup of tea, he told her about the accident that had claimed her father's life.

"Ben Lock was a hero," he said. "He knew the boiler was going to burst on the *Tigress* and put himself in the steam between me and several others. The loss of life would have been much greater if not for him." He paused and took a few sips of tea to allow Erith time to process what he was saying.

"Your father was a wise man. He had savings, and he also had an insurance policy, which he entrusted to me, along with instructions about your well-being." Captain Bartlett told her about the letter that her father had dictated. It was to be given to her at the bank when she turned eighteen.

"I didn't get a letter," Erith said.

"I know. I'm named on the account by way of correspondence from your father," he said. "I wanted to deliver it personally. I wanted you to know that you were the last person he thought about before he died." He took a yellowed envelope from the inside pocket of his charcoal suit coat. For a moment he held it in his hand and cast his gaze downwards as a look of sadness crossed his face.

"I have let you down, Miss Lock. I promised your father that I'd see to your comfort, and I thought I had done that when I set up the monthly payment to your stepmother. I spoke to her at the funeral and told her of the arrangements. When I heard the name Erith Lock uttered from the lips of Mrs. Harvey and saw your station, I knew I had done a grievous injury to your father's memory." He closed his eyes.

Erith watched the play of emotions on the old man's face. She wanted to say something but didn't know what she could add. Part of her wanted to reach out to show some comfort, but didn't know how to do that, either, so, she just sat there with her back straight and her hands clasped and waited for him to continue.

"When I received your note at the boarding school, the young nun told me you had gone to the orphanage. When she told me about your wishes to keep the children together, I recognized the traits of your father," Captain Bartlett went on. "Before I give you this letter and leave you to read it, I want you to know that I set up a trust for the three Ryan children from my personal savings. If you had not returned, the children would have been united and cared for, regardless of your father's money.

"I'm a man of few words, Miss Lock, but you, like your father, have set me to thinking. I can never make up for what you've had to endure because of my actions or inactions, so I want you to know that I'll not let you down again. My wife and I, God rest her soul, were not blessed with children. I've made you and your children heir to my possessions. They are quite substantial, and I have paid outright for this house. Your title is kept with my solicitor, W. H. Horwood, barrister at law, at the Home Industries Society Hall on Duckworth Street. It's not too far from here. He has agreed to represent you in all your dealings as well."

Erith stared at him, already feeling uncomfortable with her new wealth, and now there would be even more. He could see she was overwhelmed by his offer.

"Don't worry about a thing. Mr. Horwood, William, is a good friend of mine. He will do right by you."

"I don't know what to say, Captain Bartlett."

"Please call me Isaac."

"Isaac," she said, then paused. "I still don't know what to say."

"Please accept my offer. I don't want distant relatives to be fighting over my estate when I'm gone. This way, it'll only be bones they'll have to fight over." He grinned. "The deed is done, and there'll be no trouble for you. If for no other reason, think of the children."

Captain Bartlett was right. Erith had three children to think about now. She nodded.

"Good," he said. "I must be on my way. I'll leave you to your letter. If you need to contact me for any reason, please see Mr. Horwood, and he'll know what to do."

Erith was in a daze when he left. She sat at the end of the table and stared at the yellowed envelope. Her father's words were inside. She caressed the envelope and held it to her heart, suddenly afraid to open it. So much had happened in the last few weeks, and so much had changed. She was having trouble keeping up.

She drew the envelope into the light from the window and cautiously broke the seal before pulling the letter free.

Carefully unfolding the paper, she stared at the words—the way they formed on the paper, the curves of the letters, the way the ink blots signalled where the pen had been dipped—but she didn't read the words at first. She wasn't sure she was ready. Gently refolding the paper, she held it to her heart again. This was as close as she would ever get to her father again, and she wanted to savour it.

Finally, she delicately opened the paper one more time.

> *My darling Erith,*
> *I have so much to say. I don't know where to begin. The day you were born was the happiest day of my life and only compares to the day I met your mother. In your smile I saw her. She stole my heart, as did you, and she lives on in you. Your mother came from a wealthy family in Erith, England. She ran away with me to the colonies rather than accept an arranged marriage. We married on the ship, and when you came along, she wanted to name you for her beloved birthplace. She said you were her piece of home.*
> *When she died, she took a part of me with her. I couldn't cope with her death, nor the loss of my son, and foolishly went to sea to ease the pain. Now, here I am, dying. I won't get to see your beautiful face again, won't get to sing you songs from my knee. So many things lost.*
> *I'm sorry I can't be there to see you grow into a beautiful young woman, to see you become a wife, a mother, but it's not to be. The best I can do now is to leave you an inheritance so*

you can make your own choices. Follow your heart as your mother did when she chose me.

Kathleen knows not of your riches. I hope you will do right by her to allow her to live out her days in comfort. She was kind enough to marry me before I left so that you would be cared for. I'd like to show her that continued kindness.

Your beautiful face is the last thing I will think about before I leave this world, and I pray your mother's is the first I see on the other side. Her family doesn't know where she went, nor do they know about you. I hope someday you can change that.

I'll be in the warm breeze caressing your hair, in the sunshine kissing your face, and in the smell of the salt sea air. Live your life, my child.

Until we meet again.

Forever in love,

Your papa

Erith saw the ink spread out across the paper and one word bleed into the other before she realized she was crying. Her tears had soaked the page. She quickly moved the letter from where it had settled on her lap. The last line was written in a different hand—he had signed it himself while in pain.

Her father loved her! At one time she had been angry at him for leaving her with her stepmother. Now she realized he had been chasing demons of his own. He had loved her mother, and he had loved Erith. She thought he had thrown her away and forsaken her. She had to make amends for not believing in him.

At first when she learned of the monthly payment to Kathleen Lock, she had planned to cut it out. But now she changed her mind. She would allow it to continue for her father's sake. It was her way to honour him and had nothing to do with any feelings she had toward the woman.

Erith contacted her barrister and asked him to draw up papers for the legal adoption of George, Thomas, and Annie Ryan. They would be hers. She chose to leave them with their familial name to honour Dinn Ryan, a man who had wanted to help her in her time of need.

31

Present day

Danol approached the house with unease. He knocked on the weathered wooden door but heard no sound from inside. He checked the barn. Both the front and back doors had the top half opened. That might not mean much, just that there was hay in the loft. It might be a fool's errand, but he was going to wait. He sat on the grass in the shade with his back to the peeling clapboard on the red barn. He could hear a bee work on a flower somewhere close. He grabbed a straw of hay from the long grass and chewed while he rested.

Feeling hot breath on his face, he opened his eyes and almost jumped out of his skin. A black-faced mare was sniffing his shirt—no, it was eating the straw of hay that had dropped when he dozed. Danol gently pushed the horse away and stood up. Well, at least now he didn't think they were gone. He didn't think John MacDonald would have left the horse.

It was mid-afternoon before he heard laughter. On the far side of the meadow he spotted three heads coming toward the house. The string of trout on the stick told the tale of where they had been. Danol kept out of sight until they went into the house. He listened to the playfulness of family life, and it gave him a weird sensation in the pit of his stomach. He thought about himself and Erith taking Annie and the boys on an outing. This was how it would be. He shook his head as if to clear away the want he felt.

Danol waited for a time, intent on knocking, but then he heard the door open. John MacDonald was coming to the barn. Danol didn't want to give the man a start, so he stepped out and gave a nod.

"I thought you'd gone," Danol said.

"Don't think I didn't consider it," John replied. "Because I did. Then I talked to Alice. She said that she'd lost babies and she couldn't imagine what Beatrice's mother must be going through. So, we waited. We've tried to pack as many good memories into the last few weeks as possible. Hoping for the best but preparing for the worst."

"Beatrice's mother doesn't want to take her from you."

Danol watched the play of emotions on John MacDonald's face, culminating with the glassy eyes of a man who had been given his life back. He grabbed for the stall as he tried to control what he must be feeling. Then he reached for Danol's hand. "Thank you for coming to tell us."

Danol clasped his hand in a strong and hearty shake. His own emotions were raw. "It was a very hard decision for her, but she was thinking of Beatrice's welfare before her own wishes."

"I understand. Can't say as I'm not glad, though," John said.

"You're great parents," Danol said. "I have something to ask, though." Danol went on to tell him about the monthly payment and the letters. He also had a special request.

When Danol was finished, John took both letters. "I'll talk to Alice about the one for Beatrice. We'll decide when it's the right time," he said. His face reddened. "Can you read, Danol?"

"Yes."

"Neither me nor the missus can. Would you read the letter for me? I can tell Alice what's in it."

"Of course," said Danol. He took the envelope and hesitantly opened it.

> *Dear Alice and John,*
>
> *Since we all love Beatrice, I think I can call you by your first names. My name is Erith, and I had no choice when it came to Beatrice staying with me. I still have no choice, but this time it's for her sake.*
>
> *I want to thank you for finding Beatrice and loving her for me like I do. You know the pain of losing a child as do I when I thought I'd lost her. I am very sorry for your loss. I felt that every day until Danol found her for me. Now that I know she is safe and loved, I have peace in my heart. Although I'd wish for nothing more than to have raised her, I'm very grateful that she had somebody like you. I know you can love another's child like your own, because I have the privilege of doing just that.*
>
> *I have written a letter to Beatrice to tell her that I love her. As her parents, it is your choice whether she gets it or not. I'm hoping she will, in your own time.*
>
> *I won't contact you again. That wouldn't be*

fair to Beatrice. But I want you to know that I have tried to make your life a little easier so that neither you nor Beatrice will want for anything. Please accept it as a gift and nothing more.

Contact me if you should ever need anything for yourselves or Beatrice. Again, thank you for loving my little girl. My mind can rest now that I know she is part of your family. Hug her a little bit harder today and every day for me.

Erith Lock

Danol folded the paper, put it back in the envelope, and handed it to John. His insides were churning. He felt like an intruder.

"She sounds like a real nice woman," John said.

"She is indeed," Danol said. "She is indeed."

Danol reached inside his jacket and pulled out another piece of paper. He offered it to John.

"What's this?"

"This is the deed to your house and land. It's yours now, free and clear."

The man's hand was shaking when he grasped the paper. "How?"

"Don't ask how. Accept it for what it is. You know, John, it's not too late to build a new house for your family," Danol said.

"We talked about that, but we couldn't because of Beatrice. Now that we know we can keep her, we'll have to talk about it again." This time John hugged Danol and clapped him on the back. "Thank you for coming."

"I wouldn't have done anything else."

"Thanks for your gifts to us. Beatrice was very happy with the dress."

"I didn't do anything," Danol said as he smiled. He gave John the contact information for Erith and her lawyer.

"Do you want to come in for a mug-up?"

"I have to get going," Danol replied. "Take care of yourself, and take care of that little girl."

John MacDonald was beaming. "You have no worries about that," he said. "Will you be back?"

"I don't believe I will."

John shook his hand one more time, and Danol went on his way. Erith's business was done. He should have been relieved now that things would go back to normal. He just didn't know if he liked the new normal.

32

Christmas had arrived. Except for that one year he had spent with Mary Rourke's family in Boston a few years before, Danol couldn't recall celebrating another Christmas. As a boy, his father always worked on Christmas Day, and he was either alone or spent it with a neighbour. As a man, he had always worked the Christmas Day shift at the Boston Police Department. He hadn't bothered with Christmas the last two years in his own house.

Danol had cut his first Christmas tree a few days ago. He had been on the north side delivering a bottle of rum to every household. Men had given up several days of fishing to watch Erith's place and fix his boat and dory while he was laid up. He had offered to pay, but not one person would take his money. The bottle wasn't much, but he knew that everyone appreciated his gesture.

He hadn't been the only one with that idea. It seemed like Erith had somehow overstocked raisins, dates, dried fruits, and molasses before Christmas and was afraid they would go bad. She had to share it out equitably between every household. The bigger the family, the more they got. She even included flour for Christmas bread and cakes. Danol heard that peppermint candy sticks were included, too.

Danol had been offered sweetbread in almost every house. He had two loaves with him when he reached the store. There he found the boys and Annie getting ready to hunt for a tree.

"Please, please," said Annie. "Please come with us!"

"I'm not sure if I'd know what a Christmas tree looks like," Danol said.

"You mean you haven't cut a Christmas tree before?" asked Erith.

Danol liked the fact that she seemed more at ease. "Can't say as I have."

"What about when you were young?"

"Not even then."

"Well, today's your lucky day," she said.

"I'm afraid I've got to get back."

"You tell me one thing that can't wait, and we'll go alone," Erith said. "All morning the children have been asking if you would come with us."

Danol couldn't think of anything. He wasn't sure he wanted to. "You're going, too?"

"Of course. We're a family, and this is a family thing."

"Well, I don't want to intrude."

"Nonsense, Danol! We'll make sure you bring it out." Erith's grin lit her face.

"I don't know."

"You're family, Danol," Annie argued. She ran to him with outstretched arms, grabbed him around the legs, and hugged him. She asked him to help with her mittens.

"Annie, what did I tell you about bothering Danol?" Erith asked. The reproach in her voice didn't reach her eyes.

"Sorry," Annie said.

Danol ruffled her hair and smiled, then bent to help with her mittens while she kissed the top of his head.

"Come on, Danol," said Tommy. "You can help us get the biggest tree!"

"Yes," said George. "We won't need to tackle the horse if you're with us."

They all looked at him expectantly.

"So, it's me or the horse! All right, all right, I'll go," he said.

And that was it. His first hunt for a Christmas tree. The children each took a sled. Once he assured Erith that he was perfectly capable, he pulled the large one that was meant for the tree. His had runners on it, while the children's sleds were made from three barrel staves with a piece of board on each end, one for sitting and one for the feet. In the middle was a small strap to keep them together. George had made them. It was one of the many skills he had learned at the Villa Nova Orphanage.

The snow was ankle deep on the path and over his knees and higher in drifts where it hadn't been beaten down. They walked up the hill and into the woods. The boughs on the trees were laden with fresh snow. George and Tommy led the group, followed by Annie, and then it was Danol, with Erith behind him on the trail. They listened to the children talking among themselves. George and Tommy each had an axe fastened to their sleds. Danol couldn't help but grin all the way.

They took their time on the easy uphill slope framed by the snow-burdened trees. The air was crisp, and the sun was shining. There was no wind, so it was a perfect day for tree hunting. At least, he guessed it was. The children were laughing at their breath misting in the air. At one point, Annie fell and landed on her side in a bank of snow. George pulled her up, and Tommy brushed her off. Behind Danol, Erith was trudging along with her gaze fixed on the path. The hem of her beige woollen coat was swinging from side to side, her hair was trying its best to escape from beneath her woollen cap, and her mittened hands helped her keep her balance on any icy spot beneath the snow. She glanced up when she noticed he had stopped. She smiled, her breath obscuring her face in a fog, and her cheeks and nose were crimson.

"Are you cold?" Danol asked. She sure was a pretty picture.

"Not at all," she said. "Are you?"

"No, no." He turned and continued on his way.

"We're almost there!" cried Tommy.

"How do you know?" Danol asked.

"We looked before the snow came," said George.

"Oh, I see," Danol replied. He didn't realize there was such planning to obtaining a tree.

A short time later, the boys stopped and lifted their packs, made with rope and flour sack, and untied the axes. "We're here," they said in unison.

Annie squealed in delight. "Which one is it?" she asked, her eyes wide.

The boys looked all around. "They all look alike," said Tommy.

"We should have marked it," George said, disappointed.

"We'll find it," said Erith. "Let's set up first."

"Set up?" asked Danol.

"Yes, we're going to light a fire and have tea," she said. "I have some bread and jam packed. The kids will slide on that hill for a little while. Then we'll cut the tree and head back home."

"Oh. Well, tell me what I have to do."

She helped him dig a place in the snow to make the fire

while Tommy and George cut some boughs for them to sit on. From his pack George brought out dry splits to start the fire, and Annie gathered some Old Man's Beard from beneath the limbs of a big spruce tree. The dry, webbed material made it easy to get the flame started. In no time at all the fire was going well.

George cut a long branch to extend over the burning wood. Once it was securely anchored, he hung the tin can which was fashioned with a wire handle over the fire. They filled it with snow and set it to boil. Erith unpacked the tea, milk, sugar, bread, and jam. She laid it out on a tea towel near the fire and unwrapped the cups.

"I brought one for you," Erith said. "I saw you coming in the lane and figured the kids would convince you to join us."

"And did you want me to join you?" Danol teased.

Her face turned redder. She picked up a handful of snow and threw it at him. He laughed. Before long, they all turned on Danol and knocked him down before covering him with snow. He grabbed Annie's leg and pulled her down on top of him. She howled in pretend fear and scooted away. He reached out once more, and this time it was Erith who fell on him. She shrieked and rolled away, dousing him with snow in the process.

The children pulled their sleds to the nearby slope and traipsed to the top. For their first few attempts, they pushed each other until the track was beaten down. Then they sailed down the hill, over and over, sometimes crashing in a pile at the bottom if either one wasn't fast enough getting out of the way.

"We should join them," Danol said. He didn't know where that had come from, but it was something he really wanted to do. He stood and reached for Erith's hand.

"You're sure you're well enough?"

"Erith, I keep telling you I am."

Erith hesitated for just a moment before allowing him to pull her up from the nest she had made in the boughs. "Why not!" she exclaimed. She piled more snow in the can for the tea, and the two of them raced each other to the top of the hill.

George gave Danol his sled, and he got on with Tommy. Danol's legs were too long to fit, so he lay down on it and pushed himself off the hill. Tommy and George followed behind, hooting and hollering as if they were giving chase. Erith lay on Annie's sled, and Annie sat on her back. Erith screamed the whole way down while Annie laughed. The sled dug in a few times and sent spits of snow in her face, which made Annie laugh harder. When they reached the bottom, they stopped abruptly, and Annie flew off. Danol grabbed her and planted her in the snow. He helped Erith up, and she brushed herself off before heading back up the hill.

At the end of the last trip down, they all lay on their backs with their heads in the centre and their frosty breaths shrouding them. There wasn't a cloud to be seen, and every now and again a dust of snow would shift on a bough above them and they could feel the cold pecks on their faces. They lay there and enjoyed the stillness.

Danol hadn't felt as free in all his life. His smile reached his heart. Before he could contemplate what was happening to him, Annie walloped him with a mittenful of snow as her laughter filled the air. After a few minutes of play, they went to the fire. When Erith removed the makeshift kettle, they hung their snow-encrusted mittens on the stick to dry. The sizzle of water and fire was immediate as the snow fell into the flames.

Erith put tea in the can and let it steep. Annie used snow to cool hers. Danol pushed a stick through his slice of bread and held it over the fire. Annie wanted hers like that, too. Erith handed him her own slice as well. Tommy and George got a stick each and mimicked Danol. They ate in a flurry of stories about their escapades on the hill. Danol was awed by how little it took to make them happy. To make *him* happy. It felt odd to admit it to himself.

When lunch was over, they donned their mittens once more and went in search of the tree. Erith was particular about what they cut. She sized up each potential tree from all sides and then checked its height before they finally picked the perfect one.

"I'm sure that's the one we said was the best," Tommy piped in, and George agreed.

The boys took turns chopping before they asked Danol to finish it off. They pulled it to the sled, where George strapped a rope on it to keep it steady. Erith and Danol made sure the fire was out while the three children took one more run on the hill. They packed up all their belongings and left their packs on the bigger sled. Danol was in charge of the tree. The children wanted to use their sleds the whole way home.

Danol and Erith let them lead the way. Erith walked beside the tree to keep it on the pathway, and Danol kept it from racing away down the hill.

"This is harder than it looks," he said while trying to keep control of the sled. On the steepest part of the ridge, the tree stump tripped him, and he lost his balance. He dropped the towing rope, and it tangled around his foot as the sled picked up speed. The next thing he knew, both he and Erith were in the snowbank, and the tree was gone.

He was on his back, and Erith was sprawled on top of him, her back to his front. The more they moved, the further they burrowed into the snow. She was startled first and thought he might be hurt. He assured her that he was intact, except for his pride. She started to giggle nervously. With each movement, the snow groaned and pulled them down farther.

Danol didn't think he had ever heard her laugh. He liked it. The effort he put into getting them on their feet was in vain. They kept sinking, but he didn't mind at all.

"Should we shout for help?" he asked.

"We must be able to get out," Erith said. "Perhaps if you pushed me." Danol tried to push her up, but he just kept sinking, and the snow started to fill in on top of them.

"I think you have to turn over," he said. She stopped wriggling. "Or we can stay here all night."

"Help me turn," she said.

He pushed on one side and pulled on the other until she was facing him. Her long coat had twisted around her legs, and she kicked to free herself. She had her two arms on his chest to keep her distance. They both stopped moving when their eyes met.

Silence cradled them in her frosty cocoon. Their breaths mixed and crystallized into tiny flakes floating between them. Danol didn't know if it was him or the snow that groaned as they dropped a little deeper into the wintry den. Erith's hand slipped, and she plopped down on him, her arm jammed between his body and his own arm.

The white blanket beneath them gave way, and suddenly they whooshed down the embankment. Danol threw his arms around Erith and held her tight as their downward travel picked up speed. She buried her head into the crook of his arm to keep the snow out of her face, and she couldn't help but shriek until they stopped. They were a tangle of arms and legs, laughing as the snow filled in around them.

They were nose to nose when he said, "Erith." He desperately wanted to pull her to him and kiss her. For him, she was like . . . happiness. He hardly even knew what that meant, but he knew it was something warmer than he had ever experienced.

The sound of George's voice penetrated the heat between them. "Where are you? Danol? Mom?"

Danol pulled his head away and into the snow. He sputtered, welcoming the cold on his face and the shattered spell. "It's George," he said. "We're over here! We need help!"

Erith, red and confused, squirmed to get her arms loose. She could see George and Tommy's heads bobbing toward them through the trees.

"Over here!" she called. "Danol, help me get untangled before they see us."

"Hold on," he said as he grabbed her around the waist and plopped her on her back in the snow next to him. "That's the best I can do."

Danol turned on his side and pushed his hand into the snow until he met solid ground. He managed to get himself into a sitting position, then stood in the place where they had landed. He grabbed her hand and helped her up. Pushing their way through a couple of low, snow-laden trees, they finally made it back to the path.

"We had an accident," Danol said. "The Christmas tree took off on the sled and then we ended up over there." He quickly brushed the snow from his pants and jacket. Erith followed suit.

"We saw the tree coming when we got to the clearing. We came back to look for you," Tommy said. They heard Annie calling to them and saw her in the distance. Tommy turned and waved to her.

"Well, thank you, boys," Erith said.

"Come on, then, let's get this evergreen home," Danol said.

"Wish we had brought our sleds back," said George. "That looks like a nice place for sliding. Maybe we can go another day.

"Maybe," said Danol as he straightened the boy's cap.

"Hear that, Tommy? Danol will go again!" George chased off toward home behind his brother.

Danol looked at Erith. He wasn't sure what to say, so he grabbed a handful of loose snow and threw it at the three of them. Erith yelped and raced ahead of him, laughing and shrieking for the boys to help her. They looked back and shouted for her to duck as Danol pretended to try and hit her with a snowball.

At the rear of the house, George retrieved the bucksaw, and with Tommy's help, he squared the base of the tree.

"What's next?" asked Danol.

"We have to stand it for a day in the shed to let the snow dry off the branches," Erith said. "Tomorrow we need to put it up."

"I thought people didn't put up the tree until Christmas Day." Danol wasn't sure where he had heard that. He was also sure that the children didn't participate but woke up to a decorated tree on Christmas morning.

"Yes, that's true for most families," Erith said. "However, we've missed Christmases together and decided that we would get every bit of joy out of it as possible. Together. What better way to do it than to do it as a family?"

"Are you going to help us, Danol?" asked Annie.

"Oh, I don't know. I have a lot of things to do tomorrow."

"Please, please, please," Annie begged.

"Annie, don't pester," Erith said.

"But we need somebody tall to trim the top of the tree," Annie countered.

"I don't want to intrude," Danol said quietly to Erith. "This is your first Christmas here."

"It's really not an intrusion. We've had Christmases together for a few years now. You're welcome to come help," she said. "Don't feel obliged, of course."

"I'll think about it."

The next day, Danol showed up and made paper snowflakes with Annie while Erith took out garland and beautiful multicoloured glass bulbs from a small wooden crate.

"Are they from your childhood?" Danol asked.

"No, I bought these the first year we were together. The children had been through so much that I wanted to make it memorable. I may have been too lavish, but they're worth it." She paused. "I may have had a tree when I was very young, but not after my father died. I hadn't thought about that. I could check the attic."

She showed Danol the hatch leading into the rafters of her parents' house. Danol pulled out a little dust-covered embossed silver box. Inside were seven delicate and intricately designed glass ornaments. Six seemed to be from a red and gold set, and the seventh was rose-coloured. It had BEATRICE painted on it in ornate white lettering.

Erith gasped and pulled it close to her heart. These must have been her mother's ornaments. "My mother's name was Beatrice, too," she said.

Danol saw the play of emotions on her face as she held the delicate glass. It must have been bittersweet for her to have the bulb hung on her tree to honour both her mother and her child.

33

On Christmas Day, Danol was again invited to Erith's house. He packed up gifts in a sack and made his way across the ice. The wind was howling from the north, and it started to snow. By the time he got down the harbour, it was difficult to see. If not for the scant daylight, he surely would have missed the house in the oncoming blizzard.

Danol was spending a lot of time with Erith and the children. He couldn't help himself, although he knew he shouldn't be allowing them to become attached to him. His conviction was no longer as strong as it used to be, but he was sure that when he got back on the water in the spring, that would change. Just for today, he would forget about the future and enjoy Christmas.

Annie ran into the porch when she heard the door. "Danol's here!" she shouted.

"Were you expecting anyone else?" he teased.

"We're waiting for you so we can open our presents," she said excitedly.

"Whose idea was that?"

"Mine," she said. Sweet little Annie had thought of him.

"What about if I hadn't come?"

"I knew you'd come," Annie said as she grabbed for his hand. His smile came honestly.

"Well now, I'd better hurry," he said. He gave her his hat and mittens to place by the stove, then shed his coat and opened the door, giving his coat a swift flick to take the excess snow off before hanging it on the spare hook. Danol had worn two pairs of pants. He discarded the outer pair and swept up the snow from under his boots before laying them aside. Annie came back and grabbed his boots to place by the stove.

"Where is everybody?"

"Mom's upstairs, Maggie's in the sitting room, and my brothers are by the tree waiting for you," Annie replied.

He heard Erith on the stairs before he saw her. She was a vision in a red dress and white apron and her hair in a loose bun at the back of her head.

"Merry Christmas, Danol."

"Merry Christmas to you, too."

"What's you got there, Danol?" Annie queried.

"It's a surprise. You're going to have to wait," he said with a wink.

"Aww," she said as she trudged off into the front room. Danol and Erith both laughed. Tommy and George peeked out and grinned.

"Come in, Danol! We're waiting for you," said George.

"I'm coming."

"Let Danol warm himself first."

"I'm fine, Erith. I can't believe they waited for me."

"Annie wouldn't let anyone touch a thing. Can I bring you a cup of tea? It's already steeped."

"Sure, that'd be good. There's an awful storm brewing outside."

Danol followed the children into the front room while Erith went to the kitchen. He was sure she could hear the giggles from the children and then the pleas for her to hurry. She brought tea and a tray of gingerbread cookies. Maggie was in the chair, so Erith sat on the sofa next to Danol.

The kids gathered closer to the tree. There were shouts of merriment as the children opened their gifts. Annie got a doll, a new dress, and shoes. George got a ball, a slingshot, and a tin whistle. Tommy got a wooden train, a book, and a set of pencils. Paper was strewn everywhere by the time they were done.

Annie scrambled under the tree. "Danol, we have a present for you."

She brought him a brown paper package tied with white line. He carefully unwrapped it. Annie stared at him. Inside was a pocket knife and case. He couldn't contain the feelings that overtook him. He oohed and awed over the present and thanked her, much to Annie's delight.

"Now I have something for you."

"You didn't need to bring presents, Danol," Erith said.

"I know," he said and shrugged.

He took the sack and carefully removed some of the contents. He had a pair of snowshoes for each of the boys, specially made by Danol's neighbour, Ron Whalen. The boys yipped and hooted at their gifts.

Annie moved next to Danol's knees. Her eyes were big and expectant as he put his hand back in the bag. He pulled out a set of toy dishes. There were cups and saucers, a teapot, and a serving tray. The dishes could have been fine china, as far as the child was concerned. She looked at the delicate red roses painted on the white ceramic setting. Annie threw her arms around his neck and kissed his cheek.

"Thank you, thank you, thank you!" she cried.

"Do you always talk in threes?" Danol asked as he gave her a hug and kissed the top of her head three times.

Annie took the toys to a chair in the corner of the room and began to set a place for the doll and herself to have a tea party. The boys were busy with their snowshoes, and Erith had to warn them to stay in the house. The snow was really picking up, and the wind whistled in the chimney and the windows.

Danol pulled out a package for Maggie. To her delight, she held up a golden chain that held a delicate white locket with a light-blue edging. She gasped at the exquisite gift. "I've never had something so elegant to call my own. Danol, thank you!" she exclaimed.

"There will never be enough to repay you for all the attention you've given me."

"Seeing you get well was my repayment," Maggie said. "Everyone here has lost so much." She put her hand to her heart. "It's about time for something good to happen."

"Let me put that on you," Erith said.

Maggie gently touched her neck. "If my John could see me now, he'd think I was something."

"He always said you were something," Erith said as she kissed Maggie's cheek. "He was right."

Erith began to pick up paper, and Danol looked around. This is what a family looked like. He swallowed hard. Dormant feelings were clawing to the surface, making him uncomfortable. He shifted in the chair. He still had one gift to give, but he would wait until he got her alone.

"I'll check the fire," he said, heading for the kitchen. A short time later, Erith followed with an armful of paper to throw in the woodbox.

"I have something for you."

"Danol, you didn't need to get me anything."

"I know, but you have to be alone when you open it," he said. He handed her a small package wrapped in a delicate lace. "You go upstairs, and I'll keep Maggie and the children company. Take as long as you need." He turned quickly and went back to the front room.

Erith watched him go and then stared at the parcel in her hand. She began to unwrap it, but heeding his words, she stopped and went upstairs. Sitting on her bed, she placed the gift on her lap and untied the thin red ribbon. She was both nervous and excited. As she peeled back the lace, she found a small silver frame and an old knitted baby blanket. Her hands went to her mouth, and she gasped. Her fingers lovingly caressed the raised stitches that spelled out BEATRICE. When she turned the frame over, there, looking back at her from inside the glass, was a seven-year-old girl with long, light wiry hair. She was smiling. She was beautiful. She was perfect.

Erith toppled back on the bed, taking the items with her. The wind left her, and she struggled for breath. She clutched the picture and blanket to her heart and quietly sobbed, staring at her baby girl through tears. It was just her and Beatrice in that moment. "Happy Christmas, my baby," she said as she gently kissed the glass and laid the picture on the little table by the bed. "Mommy misses you."

She wiped tears from her eyes and face with a cloth from the washstand, and when she felt calmer, she knew she was ready to go back to her family. Maggie was in the kitchen checking on the meal. She could hear the children in the front room. Danol met her in the hall. She didn't speak as she ran into his arms and fiercely hugged him.

"Thank you for the greatest gift of all," she said. Her voice was muffled in his shirt.

"You are most welcome," Danol said. Erith pulled away from him. Her face was red, and her eyes were puffy. She was beautiful. "Are you sure you're all right?"

"I'm more than all right," she replied. "I needed to see her. How did you know? How did you get it?"

He held her shoulders and stared into her eyes. "I just knew," he said, almost in a whisper. "John MacDonald is also a man of his word." He reluctantly let her go.

The children came looking for Danol, and Erith stayed in the kitchen busying herself with the meal and quietly remembering her precious three months with her baby. She told Maggie what had happened. A short time later, she called them all to the table for a feast of roasted hen with potatoes, parsnip, carrots, turnips, dumplings, and gravy. She had a dark fruitcake and tea to finish.

Danol had intended to head for home in the early afternoon, but the storm had picked up and Erith wouldn't let him leave. They sat around and played cards. Nightfall came early and there was no sign of the storm letting up, so he made plans to stay.

They lit candles on the tree and sang songs while George played the tin whistle. He was pretty good at it. He had an ear for music, like his father, so Maggie said.

The children went to bed early, and Danol and Erith sat in the front room. Maggie said she wanted to have some time to herself by the fire. Erith asked Danol to tell her again about Beatrice. She closed her eyes and listened to every word as it was inscribed in her mind and on her heart.

"Danol, I don't know how to thank you," she said. She stared at the tree for a long time and listened to the fury of the squall. "Danol, what's happening between us?" she asked softly.

"I don't know, Erith. I honestly don't know." He paused for a moment. "Go to bed, Erith," he said. "Please."

With that, she blew out the candles on the tree, leaving the lamp burning for him. She brought him a pillow and two quilts before retiring for the night. The storeroom where he had stayed just a few months before was full of winter supplies, so she made a bed for him on the chesterfield.

Erith went to bed and pulled the patchwork quilts over herself. She stared at the picture on the stand until her eyes blurred. She doused the lamp. The howling wind outside matched the tumultuous feelings inside her. Sleep was a long time coming.

The storm blew itself out by morning. Danol had put in the fire and boiled the kettle before Erith came downstairs. Tommy and George were close on her heels and anxious to try out their snowshoes. Annie gave Danol a big hug before scurrying off to find her doll. Maggie was last. The house was loud and chaotic. They ate a light breakfast together before Danol dressed and set out to shovel out the doorways.

George and Tommy were excited to help Danol clear a path to the well and the woodshed. The drifts were two and sometimes three times taller than Danol in places. He didn't come back in to eat before heading home, and the boys were disappointed to see him go. Erith wouldn't admit to herself that she was sorry as well. He told them he had to check on some of the other houses along the shore on his way home.

He came back to Erith's side of the harbour again and welcomed New Year's Day, 1895, with her and the children.

34

Mid-January, ice began to break on the river, prohibiting travel between the sandy points. It seemed to herald an early spring and, with that, the arrival of the schooner *Samuel V Colby*. A young man named Hayes had broken his leg. It would have been splinted aboard ship, but the bone was protruding through the skin. That had sent the crew in search of a doctor. The schooner rerouted to John's Pond, but the ice was extremely heavy, especially with the early river shedding into the bay, and the captain believed they might have damaged the ship's keel when they attempted to get through.

They moored next to the *Angel Endeavours*. Danol explained that the doctors were gone from John's Pond until April and the nearest was in Colinet. Rocky River cut a wide swath between the two communities and would not be passable due to the thaw. They would have to go by sea. Six of the crewmen carried the injured man two miles to John's Pond, where they borrowed a dory and left for Colinet. Danol made the arrangements for the little boat, including a guide who knew the shoreline.

On his return, he offered the slipway to the captain, along

with lodging, until they were ready to leave. The crew didn't come back that night, so Danol and Captain John Vibert sat alone in front of the fire. The captain had thick black and grey hair and a kindly round face that had seen a lot of sun and wind. On his third glass of rum, the skipper told Danol about his life on the sea.

"I'm fifty years old, Danol. An old man by many accounts, and sometimes I wonder how I got here," he said. "When I was a young man, I couldn't be tied down. Much like these lads that I've with me now. The two McLeans, McDougall, and McIntosh, neither of them has seen the companionship of a good woman.

"I was like them," he continued. "Foolhardy. Then, I met my wife ten years ago, and now I have three little children. They change so much each time I go home. I wish I'd spared the time to find her sooner. Hamilton, he's almost my age. He has a wife and five youngsters. He'd like to be home. Hayes will be ashore for a spell, but he has the draw of the sea in him. And young Ambrose Bennett, seventeen years old and straight off the wharf in St. John's, is still wet behind the ears. He thinks he'll make a life on the sea."

"Where are you headed?" Danol asked him.

"Fortune Bay for a load of herring. Then on to Boston and home," Captain Vibert said. "We'll have to pick up another mate with young Hayes gone. You interested?"

"No," Danol replied. "One time I would have." He told the captain how he had been shot and still wasn't able to do a good day's work. Regardless, he had his own enterprise to look out for.

"You get yourself shot over a woman?" Vibert asked.

"Something like that." Danol gave the man a condensed version of what had happened with the smugglers, the men who stole from them, and the kidnapping.

"She sounds like a good woman."

"You could say that."

"Is she spoken for?"

"No," Danol said.

"Well, what are you waiting for?"

"Like you said. I'm still foolhardy," Danol replied. He abruptly changed the subject and asked if the local men could catch some of the herring while the ship was in port. The captain agreed if the local fishermen were willing. The trip was already late, and he expected to be out in Fortune Bay to fill the hold within a fortnight before more river ice and sea pans trapped them in St. Mary's Bay.

The crew returned by mid-morning the next day. Danol had passed the word along about the herring, and many fishermen had launched their skiffs to make some early money. The schooner was pulled up, inspected, and back in the water by late evening. Fishermen were waiting to off-load their catch, receive their cash, and help ice the hold.

Two days later, Danol anxiously gathered his crew for an early trip to St. John's. He knew that he couldn't work on the boat like he had in the past and would have to depend on the crew to do most of the heavy work. At one time he would have done it alongside them. Not every trip had heavy lifting, though, and he believed he would be stronger in a month or so.

He had heard that iron mines would be starting on Bell Island sometime during the summer, and he wanted to purchase another schooner to be ready for the first ore shipments. The *Angel Endeavours* had more work than she could handle. His enterprise was taking off, and he had to see about hiring a bookkeeper while in the city. When he got back, he made plans to contract logs and lumber from mills in Colinet to begin building a schooner late in the fall.

Danol thought to have two trips in before he went to Boston to get the Nolans. Mary and Peter repeatedly told him that they would book passage on a liner to save him the trouble, but this was Mary's last trip for school. She would be a full-fledged doctor after this, and he planned to bring her home like he had done every other year.

It was going to be busy. That was the plan. He was sure that once he got the smell of the ocean in his veins, whatever feelings he had for Erith Lock would be long gone by the time he rounded Trepassey Bay and headed north for St. John's. He was anxious to get out of North Harbour to make that happen.

He successfully purchased another schooner, but he and the crew were delayed in St. John's with lawyers and bankers. Danol gave his men first pick where they wanted to sail, and all chose to stay on the *Angel*. He arranged to leave the new boat in St. John's and hire a crew when he returned from Boston. With the *Angel* loaded with freight, they headed back toward Trepassey and St. Shott's and then north for home. The sea was calm, and they made good time with deliveries along the southern shore coast. Danol felt stronger already.

As they crossed the mouth of St. Mary's Bay, the sky suddenly darkened to the south. There was little warning before the wind whisked the ocean into a frenzy all around them. Danol shouted orders to lash down anything that moved. They wouldn't have the time nor the right winds to seek shelter behind Colinet Island, so they turned the sails to try and make it to a cove on the other shore of the bay. They were at the mercy of the sudden vicious storm.

Balls of hail, some the size of fists, whipped across the bow. The hull whitened with thick crusted ice, and it became dangerous to stand. Icy ropes snapped, and the mizzen-mast groaned under the weight of the frozen, rigid sail. The men tied on to each other in pairs and anchored themselves to the wheelhouse. They had to cut the sails free or risk losing the ship. Danol fought the wheel to keep the boat into the waves, which were now three and four storeys high. He had never before witnessed such ferocity. If one wave hit side-on, they would surely capsize.

Two men hauled their woollen mittens on over the toes of their rubber boots to gain traction on the treacherous deck. With bare hands in the elements, they struggled to the third mast and chopped the labouring rope. The sail ripped the yard and the top of the mizzen-mast, and all landed somewhere out in the murky, churning waters of St. Mary's Bay. The top yard on the mainmast broke under the assault of the freezing rain and hail, and the sail came crashing down, taking the second yard and spar with it. Two men were trapped. Danol couldn't let go the wheel and was barely managing to stand upright. The remaining crewmen grabbed hold of the rigid cloth and tried to bundle and peel it port, keeping it low to the gunwale under a sodden weight. They freed the two men just as the foremast broke a few feet above the deck and took yards, spars, and sails with it over the side. Luckily, it sheared right off and the sail took it clear of the boat.

The four men crawled back to the wheelhouse with nothing more than a few bruises to show for the effort. The wind howled as they took turns battling the savage sea with all they had left— the wheel. Danol's thoughts went to Erith and the children. Their smiling faces comforted him and drowned out the violent storm. He couldn't give up. He had to fight to get back to them.

The gale showed some compassion and let up long enough

for them to see land. A dark strand scarred the whiteness—a beach! The bow struck something and sent them into a tailspin and nearly turned them over. They were righted when the aft struck and a huge wave grabbed the boat and sent it forward. Danol had the wheel and tried to keep the beleaguered vessel straight, but the rudder was stuck or simply gone from the second hit. They were at the mercy of the ocean as wave after wave hurled them forward and the bow dug in. They were tossed like pebbles onto the deck. Suddenly, the boat hove on her side and two of the crew slipped into the frigid water.

Danol didn't stop to think. He got his footing, cut their tether and his own from the wheelhouse, and jumped in after them. The shoreline was near, but the surf was pounding and the frigid, turbulent water took his breath. He quickly regained his wind and grabbed the ropes that kept the men together. He pulled them within the shelter of the boat and onto the sandy beach, away from the icy clutches of the greedy undertow.

He didn't notice the lanterns until someone threw a blanket around him.

"Where are we?" he gasped.

"Point Lance, sir."

Several people surrounded them. Some had ladders. They had fought the wind, snow, and surf to get the other four from the boat. Their rescuers had brought them to a home, where a family named Careen clothed, fed, and warmed them. Later that evening, a man washed ashore. They confirmed he wasn't from the *Angel Endeavours*, as all hands were accounted for, so people from the community ventured out once more to check the beach for another wreck. All were out searching most of the night, but nothing else turned up. Without an identity, the man was buried, nameless, a few days later.

The next day, the wind died out and the weather turned cold. Elders in Point Lance said they hadn't seen such a violent storm as the one that hit the day before. With all the debris on the beach, Danol was sure the boat would be irreparable. However, to his surprise, when they beat the ice off her and got aboard, she was tight. She would float. The sandy shore had saved her.

That day, men from the surrounding communities of Branch, Gull Cove, and Golden Bay also came to their aid. They were all eager to get the *Angel Endeavours* in the water so she could go back into service in the months ahead. Great logs were hauled by horse and sled from several miles away and chopped and fashioned and set into place. The mainsail and most of its ropes had been saved because they had been frozen to the deck. The rudder was repaired, and the keel had sustained no damage.

Two weeks later, with one of three sails, the *Angel Endeavours* managed to make her way to home port without incident. His crew were all greeted by families who missed them while Danol went to his big yellow house alone. He kept telling himself that was what he wanted. He couldn't face Erith and the children. It would be his undoing. He could no longer discern why it was a bad thing to be part of something bigger, to feel something, to need something. His years of living alone and wanting to be alone were threatened by a wild-haired woman and three precious children. But he didn't know how to give in.

It was like trying to hold back dawn. He couldn't stay away. He missed Annie's hugs, the boys' questions, and Erith's smile. When the mail boat came in the next day, he went to the store to check on his supplies.

Annie asked why he hadn't come sooner. He didn't know how to answer, so Erith told her he'd been getting ready for his next trip. It was partly true. George told him about the big wind that had been there. Tommy told him that a lot of trees fell on the path right behind the house. Erith smiled and asked him what he needed.

You, he almost said. "Rope."

He sent a message to St. John's to have the sails from his new boat shipped to him. After a week ashore, he would head for Boston.

"Thanks for sending word about your wreck," Erith said. "I was worried." She lowered her eyes.

He wanted to tell her that he was thinking about her every day, but he couldn't. "I knew the men's families would be worried."

Erith went behind the counter to take his order, and he gave her his list. When she had finished, she picked up the newspaper.

"Danol, was it the *Samuel V Colby* that took the herring here several weeks ago?"

"Yes," he said slowly.

"Did you hear the news?"

"No, I'm afraid not."

"The boat and crew were all lost in the storm they're calling the February Gale," she said. "The *Mildred V. Lee* is gone, too. A King boy from St. Mary's was on her."

"Are you sure?" Danol asked. Had it been only weeks before that he was speaking with the captain?

"Yes, Mr. Johnson with the mail told me. He brought the newspaper," Erith said.

35

Danol was in Boston waiting for Mary and Peter. Mary was anxious to see him and how he had recovered.

"So, that's it, you're Doctor Mary Nolan now," he said to her.

"It's not official until I have the paper, but my schooling's finished."

"We're going home," Peter said.

Danol and Peter stood back while Mary said her good-byes to her sisters. She promised them she would be back sometime.

"The kids are certainly growing, and the new little one, Catherine," Danol said. "I almost didn't recognize Eddy."

"Time is nothing," said Peter.

That reminded Danol of what Captain Vibert had said about becoming an old man before he knew it. He left to prepare the boat for departure. Mary caught up with him later.

"You're awful quiet. Are you sure everything is healed?"

"Mary, stop playing doctor with me."

"I'll play friend, then," she said. "I see you haven't asked Erith Lock to marry you yet."

"What?"

"You heard me."

"I have no intention of asking anyone to marry me, especially Erith Lock."

"Why? Has she found someone else? I was sure she was sweet on you. Especially when you were near death in the storeroom. She held on to you for dear life."

"I thought that was you."

"No, Erith stayed by your side for days before you came back to us."

"Well, that doesn't prove anything. Besides, as you know, I have no intention of marrying."

"And why is that?"

"Mary, stop asking questions. I'm meant to be alone."

"Why?"

"I do better alone. I've always been alone."

"How do you know you do better alone if you don't try the other?" Mary pressed.

"I just know."

"That's not an answer, Danol."

"Please stop asking me questions."

Over the next few days, Mary brought up Erith's name every chance she had. Danol was lost in thought about Erith when Peter spoke behind him.

"I came to give you some help."

"I've got the rope almost coiled," Danol said.

"I'm not talking about the rope."

"Mary sent you, didn't she?"

"She did and she didn't," Peter replied.

"Is that some kind of riddle?"

"No. It's not meant to be. She didn't ask me to talk to you, if that's what you mean. But I'm here because of Mary."

Danol stopped what he was doing. "Is she all right?"

"She's worried about you."

"There's no need. I've told her that. I healed nicely, thanks to her."

"That's not why she's worried."

"Not you too, Peter," Danol said. He went back to coiling the rope. Peter put his hand on Danol's arm to stop him. Danol hesitated, then dropped the rope. "Let me have it."

"Danol, I nearly lost Mary because of my stupid pride. I somehow thought honour and duty had to be separate from any feelings I could have for a woman. I thought I had lost her to you for a little while, but then I realized that you were more self-consumed than I was."

"What's that supposed to mean?"

"You're not that dense. I'm sure you can figure it out," Peter said. "Pride makes a lonely bedfellow, Danol. I had nobody for a long time, and it was my own fault. Trying to fix things for everybody else, I nearly lost the opportunity to spend the rest of my life with Mary. Mary had the sense not to give up. Look how that turned out for me." Peter smiled and clapped him on the shoulder. "I'm not sure Erith knows how to be like Mary, so you'll have to take charge. Go after her, Danol. You won't regret it. There's no reason not to be happy."

"I'm happy enough," said Danol. He was a little put out and uncomfortable with the conversation.

"If you have to keep reminding yourself of that, then that should tell you something." Peter turned and smiled when he saw Mary coming toward them.

"I'm a happy man, Danol," Peter said as he kissed his wife's cheek.

"What was that for?" Mary asked.

"Just for being Mary Ro," Peter said, laughing as she took a playful swat at him.

"It's your turn to see to our daughter," Mary said.

They both turned and walked away, hand in hand. He heard their laughter as they disappeared below deck. Danol pondered Peter's words. Maybe he didn't have to be alone. When he was lost in the storm, he wanted to live for Erith and Annie and the boys, yet when he got home, he didn't know how to go to them. He didn't know how to take that first step. Or was he afraid to take it? He thought of Erith, and all she had been through, and how hard it would be for her in comparison. And then he thought himself a coward.

Would he be like Captain Vibert and live with regrets in twenty years? Would he wait to find out, or take a chance on being something other than alone? Not just alone, he realized—he was lonely. The call of the sea hadn't made a difference. Not this time. Not since he'd met Erith Lock.

36

Erith thought about her life. The children were happy here, and the community had opened its arms to her. She was at peace with her decision about Beatrice. Her choice was hard, but it was best for her daughter. The room where Beatrice dwelled in her heart was opened and aired. The hurt seemed to ease.

She dusted the wooden shelves, laid the shiny oil lamps back in place, and moved her attention to the cups and saucers. The place was spotless, and she didn't know why she was bothering. She caught the muffled sounds of laughter and giggles in the garden—the neighbourhood gathering spot since the children were treated to a hard barrel-shaped candy after their dinner every Sunday.

Living here was like a balm. Erith wasn't afraid like she used to be. The people, the peace and quiet, the support, and so many good things for the children combined to allow her to let down her guard. Her terrible dreams and the suffocating dark times were shorter and came less often now that her attackers where gone. She was happy. Wasn't she?

Even George, at the awkward stage between boy and man,

took time to play on Sunday. Every other day he was chasing Danol Cooper, either in person or in stories. Danol had taken George with him on a few short freight runs in the fall. George had one story knocking down another when he returned.

She knew the soon-to-be young man wouldn't be hers for much longer. But that was life. She only had them on loan, and then they would be gone. At least she had been given the chance to make their lives better. She had kept her promise to the three orphans.

Erith smiled once more. Danol continued to come to mind for one reason or another. She missed his company. It was hard to believe she could even feel that way. He had spent less time with them of late. She knew he was a busy man and a man of the sea, but she couldn't help but notice how her heart raced each time she looked at him.

The bell over the door startled her. "I'll be right with you." The porcelain cups clinked together as she hastily, yet carefully, laid them back. She pulled off her apron and strung it across several sacks of beans and turned to go to the counter. She almost tripped over Danol, who was on his knee on the floor in front of her.

"Oh my God, Danol." Erith's hands instinctively grabbed for him. "Is it your leg? Are you hurt?" There was a long silence as she waited for an answer. "Or did you lose something?"

"I hope not," Danol replied.

"Haven't what? Here, let me help you."

But he didn't move. Instead, he clutched her hand in his and reached for the other one. Erith was confused.

"Danol, what are you doing? Are you all right?"

He was silent for so long she thought he had lost his voice, or something worse had happened. Her heart pounded.

"Erith Lock, would you do me the honour of being my wife?" Danol gazed up at her, his blue eyes sparkling.

She stared at him. When the words sank in, she burst out crying. Embarrassed, she tried to cover her face, but he wouldn't let her go. "Danol, I can't," she said.

He squeezed her hands. "Why can't you?" Her answer didn't seem to bother him. He let her cry.

"You know."

"I know what?"

"Danol, please don't make me say it." She felt a swell of panic rise in her belly.

"There's nothing to say, Erith. Nothing except yes."

"But Danol, my past." He just stared at her, his eyes big and blue and entrancing. "How could you even consider wanting me as a wife?"

"How could I not? Your past is behind you. A past is something you learn from, not something you live in. Bad men did a terrible thing to you. You had nobody to protect you. I'm truly sorry for that. But I am interested in your future. The road you think was laid out for you all those years ago is not the one you must walk alone. Keep your past where it belongs. I want to go forward with you, not back. Let it be us from here on in."

Erith felt the warmth of his hands covering hers. She could feel his strength.

"You don't have to be alone for the rest of your life." These were strange words coming from him.

"I have the children," she blurted out. "I'm not alone."

"That's what makes you the woman I want to spend the rest of my life with. I wouldn't have it any other way." Danol stood up and put his arms around her. She didn't pull away.

"Having the children doesn't mean you're not alone. I was never alone until I met you."

Erith considered his words and then remembered the words of her dear friend, Sister Mary Joseph, about doing everything herself. She gazed into his eyes and breathed in the scent of him, wanting to say yes, but . . . she only knew cruelty from men. Then again, she saw Mary and Peter, and they were happy. But she also saw other women who had harsh lives with their men. Could she bear more of the same? Would it be like that with Danol? He had been distant, yet he had always been tender.

"Erith Lock, a few years ago—hell, a few weeks ago—I wasn't ready for you. My head wasn't ready for anyone, but my heart has been yours for a long time. I didn't know what it meant to need somebody and to want somebody to need me. Then, I had to start saving your life." He grinned, and she saw something in his face and kindness in his eyes. "Truth is, you saved me. It's a long journey to travel alone, and I know that now. You've touched a place in me that I didn't know was there. I'll never be the same without you, nor will I be the same with you. It would be a lonesome journey without you, though. Be my wife and I will always show you just how much you've changed me, just how much I love you."

He loved her, and she loved him . . . she loved him! But there was more than her in all this. She had made a promise to three little children many years ago that she would not break.

"Danol, I grew up in a house without any affection. It's important that the children be loved. I'll not settle for anything else. Will being your wife somehow keep me from loving the children like I do now?"

"That's nonsense, and you know it. It will mean that the children have twice the love they have now. I love them, too."

"But Danol . . ."

Erith was running out of arguments. The children were no more blood to her then they were to Danol. She had chosen to leave Beatrice with her adoptive parents because they loved her and because she loved her enough. Danol supported her when it was hard. What a snarled-up life she had lived. Danol knew all the tangles, yet still he wanted her. Would she let her past determine her future? Would she let herself be brave?

She didn't recognize the new sensation. Beneath all the hurt and hardship she had endured beat the heart of a woman. Awakened, it fluttered for the first time and sent out a heat from the top of her head to the tips of her toes. She wasn't afraid—well, maybe just a little. It wasn't the kind of fear that made her cower, but the kind that was wary of a different kind of brokenness.

Erith raised her head. Her eyes fixed on his. She knew he was searching for an answer, as was she. Sometimes risk and recklessness accompanied hope.

"Yes," she said softly. She felt like she had just jumped off Cape Dog Head. Danol strained to hear it, and she almost couldn't believe she had said it. She couldn't take it back. Erith had leaped the precipice and survived. She was holding her breath, waiting for some unknown force to pull her back. She suddenly realized she was the owner of that force.

Danol was holding his breath. "Did you say what I think you said?"

"Yes," Erith said, louder and with conviction. "Yes! God help me, I'll marry you, Danol Cooper."

"I don't know if I should be afraid or elated," he said with a grin as he embraced her, spun her around, and kissed her. "Let's go tell the children."

"Yes, we should tell them."

"Oh, they already know I was going to ask you. I sought their permission. They were ready to convince you if you refused."

"Danol Cooper, what are you like at all?"

"I'm a determined man. Oh, by the way, the priest will be in North Harbour in a month."

"What?" Erith gasped.

He laughed. "I'm not a patient man, Erith. I've waited all my life for you, and the next few weeks will be as long again."

She almost panicked. Four weeks! She would have to talk to Mary about what it was like to be married. She would need a witness, too. Her thoughts raced.

Danol stared at her and kissed her tenderly. "You won't be sorry, Erith. I can promise you that much."

He turned the knob, and the door pushed in under the weight of Annie and Tommy, who rolled in a pile at their feet. Behind them, George quickly gazed toward the window and began to whistle innocently. Annie grinned from the floor, pushed Tommy away from her, and asked, "Well, what did she say?"

Erith and Danol both said yes in unison before being swarmed.

Four weeks later . . .

Erith stared hypnotized by her own reflection. Her eyes followed her hand in the mirror as she absently reached to wipe away the tears. The salty imprints seemed to dance on her cheeks to the tune being played by the breeze in the leaves of the lilac bush on the other side of the windowpane. Her glassy eyes spilled once more and blurred the image as sunlight flashed on the blade. She almost flinched when the cool edge of the knife glanced off the skin just below her ear. She knew what she had to do.

Today was supposed to be her wedding day. Danol's promises to build her ships, to bring her to England and find her mother's people, to raise a big family, and to love her forever were overshadowed by his recent news. She took a deep breath, and her body trembled. Her past hadn't quieted, nor her future taken shape, as the previous weeks had forecast.

Today was about Beatrice. The day she'd thought might never come had come unexpectedly.

She heard the commotion outside. She was running out of time. With a shaky hand, yet with strength of purpose, she gulped for air once more, closed her eyes, and thrust the knife.

She heard Maggie gasp behind her.

"Oh, Erith, what have you done?"

Maggie rushed to her and met her eyes in the mirror. She closed her hand over Erith's on the handle of the knife. Tears welled in the old woman's eyes.

"Help me, Maggie!"

First and foremost, Ida Linehan Young is a grandmother to the most extraordinary little boys, Parker and Samuel, a mother to three adult children, Sharon, Stacey, and Shawna, and a wife to Thomas. By day she works in the information technology sector in the federal government and has recently forayed into learning the French language in the hopes of becoming bilingual. She started writing several years ago and published her memoir, *No Turning Back: Surviving the Linehan Family Tragedy*, in 2014, followed by a novel, *Being Mary Ro*, in 2018. Influenced by her love of local history and the familial art of storytelling passed down by her father and her maternal grandfather, she escapes to writing any chance she can get. She enjoys writing historical fiction to keep the past alive for generations to come.

Facebook, Twitter: @idalinehanyoung